William Archer, Robert William Lowe, Leigh Hunt

Dramatic Essays

William Archer, Robert William Lowe, Leigh Hunt

Dramatic Essays

ISBN/EAN: 9783337389741

Printed in Europe, USA, Canada, Australia, Japan

Cover: Foto ©Andreas Hilbeck / pixelio.de

More available books at **www.hansebooks.com**

LEIGH HUNT

Dramatic Essays

LEIGH HUNT

SELECTED AND EDITED,
WITH NOTES AND AN
INTRODUCTION, BY
WILLIAM ARCHER AND
ROBERT W. LOWE

WALTER SCOTT, LTD.
24 WARWICK LANE, LONDON
1894

CONTENTS.

INTRODUCTION.

LEIGH HUNT may be reckoned the first English dramatic critic, in our present acceptation of that curiously inaccurate term. He was the first writer of any note who made it his business to see and report upon all the principal theatrical events of the day. No doubt he had predecessors and contemporaries in the craft; but oblivion has swallowed up not only their writings, but their very names. Leigh Hunt, in other words, was the first critical journalist who succeeded in emerging from the mists of anonymity. Probably he was the first who deserved to emerge. If his own account of the venality and incompetence of newspaper "critics" during the first decade of the century is to be accepted as anything like the truth, we certainly cannot wonder that the world has willingly let die the works of such perfunctory paragraph-mongers. To determine whether Hunt was actually the first journalist who brought real talent and sincerity to the task of theatrical chronicling would involve a wading through old newspaper-files which we cannot at present undertake. Certain it is that in his day no one conceived the possibility of really authoritative and influential newspaper criticism.

A theatrical antiquary, with plenty of time on his hands, would find in the growth of newspaper criticism an interesting subject of study. What were the "Opinions of the Press" on *She Stoops to Conquer* or *The School for Scandal?* How large a bundle of "notices" could a Press-Cutting Agency of the period have sent to Mrs. Siddons or Mrs. Jordan after her first appearance? By what degrees did the lawgivers of the pit, who delivered their judgments orally at the coffee-houses after the play, give place to the professional paragraphist and puff-dealer, the theatrical reporter, the newspaper critic? What printed criticism has come down to us from the seventeenth and eighteenth centuries is not only very scanty and fragmentary, but differs from the great mass of nineteenth century criticism in the fact that almost the whole of it consists, not of impressions served hot-and-hot, so to speak, but of *reminiscences.* The records of the seventeenth century, however, present one very important exception to the rule just stated. The invaluable and inimitable Pepys gives us his impressions hot-and-hot, if ever man did. He goes "to Deptford by water, reading *Othello, Moore of Venice,* which I ever heretofore esteemed a good play, but having so lately read *The Adventures of Five Houres,* it seems a mean thing." At the King's house he sees *The Humorous Lieutenant* of Beaumont and Fletcher, "a silly play, I think"; but "Knipp took us all in and brought us to Nelly [Nell Gwynne], a most pretty woman, who acted the great part of Celia to-day very fine, and did it pretty well : I kissed her, and so did my wife ; and a mighty pretty soul she is." At the same house he goes to see Dryden's *Maiden Queen* soon after its production, and records that "there is a comical part done by Nell, which is Florimell, that I never can hope ever to see the like done again by man or woman. . . . It makes me, I confess, admire her." Some time later, however, he goes "with my Lord Brouncker and his mistress to the King's playhouse, and there saw *The Indian Emperour*, where I found Nell come again, which I am glad of; but was most infinitely displeased with her being put to act the Emperour's daughter, which is a great and serious part, which she does most basely." Here is "snap-shot" criticism in very truth, the impression of the moment fixed for all time; but, alas! all Mr. Pepys's theatrical notes and criticisms could be collected into a very few pages of the present volume. How one wishes that he had more frequently broken his periodical self-denying ordinances, or had been more assiduous in the fulfilment of his marital duty of taking his wife to the play. Pepys apart, our extant notices of the actors of the Restoration are entirely *reminiscent*, most of them dating, indeed, not even from the seventeenth, but from the first half of the eighteenth, century. Wright's "Historia Histrionica," it is true, was published in 1699, but Downes's "Roscius Anglicanus" not till 1708, Cibber's "Apology" in 1740, and Antony Aston's "Brief Supplement" so late as 1747 or thereabouts. Steele, in *The Tatler*, gives us a noble eulogy of Betterton on the occasion of his burial, and the Queen Anne essayists in general afford some curious glimpses of theatrical manners and customs. But though Steele and Addison must often enough have been hard up for "copy," it unfortunately did not occur to them to go to the theatre and take critical notes of what they saw there. When we come to think of it, is it not surprising that these men should not have invented

theatrical criticism as we now understand it? Both were
intimately concerned with the theatre ; both had written
for the stage, though Addison's plays were as yet un-
acted ; theatrical advertisements appeared regularly in
The Spectator ;[1] yet in the whole 635 numbers of that
paper there is nothing that we should call a dramatic
criticism. There are some entertaining essays, by both
Steele and Addison, on the license of comedy, and two
or three delightfully humorous papers, by Addison, on
the barbarisms of romantic tragedy and tragi-comedy ;
but they are illustrated by general rather than particular
examples, and never by reference to any individual production or performance. *The Distrest Mother*, Ambrose
Philips's " namby-pamby " adaptation of *Andromaque*, is
industriously puffed, Sir Roger de Coverley being taken
to see it, and the propriety of the comic epilogue (attributed to Addison) being canvassed in a, no doubt ficti-
tious, correspondence ; but there is no attempt at serious
criticism of the play, and but for the statement that Mrs.
Oldfield, who spoke the epilogue, was the Andromache,
we should not even learn the name of a single performer.[2]
Steele in one or two cases gives a comedian or a dancer a
kindly paragraph to call attention to his or her benefit,

[1] Genest, writing of the Drury Lane season 1711-12, says, " All the
bills for this season (except four or five) are from the original numbers
of *The Spectator* in my possession." These advertisements were probably regarded as items of news, and published gratis.

[2] It is true that some six weeks before the production there appeared
a letter purporting to be written by George Powell, and opening as
follows : " MR. SPECTATOR, I am appointed to act a Part in the new
Tragedy called *The Distressed Mother*: it is the celebrated Grief of
Orestes which I am to personate ; but I shall not act it as I ought,
for I shall feel it too intimately to be able to utter it." It appears
that the worthy Augustans could teach even us Victorians a thing or
two in the way of the " puff preliminary."

but the actual performance passes unnoticed. At the end of the paper for Monday, April 7, 1712, it is stated that "this Day the haughty *George Powell* hopes all the good-natur'd part of the Town will favour him, whom they Applauded in *Alexander*, *Timon*, *Lear*, and *Orestes*, with their Company this Night, when he hazards all his heroick Glory for their Approbation in the humbler Condition of honest *Jack Falstaffe* "; but as to the result of the experiment no hint is given. One cannot help fancying that an account of Powell's Falstaff, and a comparison between it and Betterton's, would have made " good copy." But no ; in the next number Budgell holds forth on the Mohocks, and in the next again Steele gossips upon scandal ; of the new Falstaff we hear never a word. In the revived *Spectator* of 1714 (*Cato* had been produced in the interval between the two series) there is a curious paper by Addison which seems almost to imply the existence of a regular school of dramatic criticism, not at all unlike the so-called New Criticism of to-day— or yesterday. Here is a brief extract :—

" I do not indeed wonder that the Actors should be such professed Enemies to those among our Nation who are commonly known by the Name of Criticks, since it is a Rule among these gentlemen to fall upon a Play, not because it is ill written, but because it takes. Several of them lay it down as a Maxim, That whatever Dramatick Performance has a long Run, must of Necessity be good for nothing ; as though the first Precept in Poetry were *not to please*. . . . Most of the Smatterers in Criticism who appear among us, make it their Business to villifie and depreciate every new Production that gains Applause, to descry imaginary Blemishes, and to prove by far-fetch'd Arguments, that what pass for Beauties in any celebrated Piece are Faults and Errors. In short, the Writings of these Criticks compared with those of the Ancients, are like the Works of the Sophists compared with those of the old Philosophers."

This might quite well be the complaint of a successful playwright of to-day, whose works failed to command the esteem of the would-be "literary" critics. But we must not conclude from the indefiniteness of Addison's terms that he had really a school of professional critics in his eye. No doubt there may have been several pamphleteers to whom his sarcasms were more or less applicable ; but it can scarcely be rash to conjecture that the cap was intended to fit one writer in particular, to wit, Mr. John Dennis, author of "Remarks upon Cato, a Tragedy." The "Writings" referred to, in any case, must have been occasional pamphlets, not regular theatrical chronicles. It will be observed that the allusion to the actors does not imply that they were criticised along with the plays and subjected to the same rough usage. It is simply as parties interested in the success of the plays that they appear on the record.[1]

What we know of the actors of the eighteenth century, then, is mostly gleaned from memoirs and anecdotes. For example, the anecdotes of the feud between Quin and Macklin throw light upon the style and methods of the two actors. There is also a good deal of what may be called comparative criticism, very valuable in its way, of which Gentleman's *Dramatic Censor* and Davies' *Dramatic Miscellanies* are the best examples. The *Dramatic Censor* was a periodical publication, in each number of which some well-known play of the current repertory was gravely and somewhat stolidly analysed, while in a paragraph or two at the end, the actors who had played the leading parts within the writer's memory

---

[1] Steele's periodical, *The Theatre*, which ran to twenty-eight numbers in the year 1720, was devoted, not to criticism, but mainly to ventilating his grievances in the matter of the Drury Lane patent.

were compared and briefly criticised. No attempt was made, however, to follow the events of the day, to criticise new productions, or to describe any particular performance of a given part. Of direct, contemporary, non-reminiscent criticism, the best examples are probably to be found in the Garrick Correspondence, in which are preserved some very interesting letters of suggestion and remonstrance addressed to the great little man by acquaintances or even by anonymous strangers. Churchill's *Rosciad*, moreover, is in more senses than one a "hot-and-hot" record of impressions. There can be no doubt that the truculent and very unclerical cleric turned his contemptuous or eulogistic couplets under the immediate impression of the performances he dealt with, if he did not actually weave them in his place in the pit. These exceptions, however, do not invalidate the rule that the great mass of criticism which has come down to us from that period was written by men looking back, at some distance of time, upon performances which had pleased and impressed them. Perhaps the most memorable, certainly the most emphatic, utterance of direct and, as we should say, "impressionist" criticism is Kitty Clive's exclamation as she stood watching Garrick's Lear from the side-scenes. She was at the height of one of her many quarrels with her manager, and therefore indisposed to appreciate his acting. Nevertheless, she stood there weeping and cursing alternately, until at last her mingled chagrin and admiration found vent in the cry—"Damn him, he could act a gridiron!"

It is only fair to modern actors—or in other words to the actors of the age of journalism which set in with the present century—that we should bear in mind this distinction between contemporary and reminiscent criticism.

Had Garrick's performances been subjected to the close and constant critical scrutiny which followed (let us say) Macready throughout his career, his fame, indeed, might not have suffered, but he would have been more real and less legendary in the eyes of posterity. As it is, the man is more real to us than the actor. The man lives with the extraordinary vividness which he and others of his set owe in great measure to Mr. James Boswell ; but in the accounts of the actor we feel that there is a certain element of the miraculous. It is true that the closest sifting of evidence leaves unaltered the general impression that Garrick was in all probability the most marvellous histrionic genius that ever lived. We may even say that such a legend as that which grew up around his name, not in England alone but in France and Germany, affords evidence of his unexampled power of enthralling the minds of men. But we feel, none the less, that there is a certain lack of detail and definition in his artistic portraiture. We hear of the marvellous effects which he produced on this person and that ; those who admired him more calmly, or not at all, have for that very reason left no record of their impressions. Had criticism, as we now know it, existed in those days, Horace Walpole would assuredly not have appeared alone in the character of Devil's Advocate. Suppose, for instance, that we possessed a notice by Leigh Hunt or George Henry Lewes of the very performance which extorted from Mrs. Clive the above-quoted tribute, we might find that there was nothing miraculous about it after all, that this scene was good, that bad, and the other indifferent, just as in any performance by Macready or Charles Kean. No doubt many of the audience were carried away as Kitty Clive was ; but there must have been many others who remained comparatively unmoved, and among these, we may be sure, were the very people who would in our day have been called upon to record their impressions in the newspapers. It may be said that the balance is redressed in favour of the modern actor by the amount of indiscriminating adulation that falls to his lot. But this, I suspect, is a deceptive solace. Criticism, as a general rule, bears the stamp of its sincerity and competence on its face, and I greatly doubt whether any actor ever has profited, or ever will profit, in the eyes of posterity, from venal or merely mechanical and inept panegyric. Of John Philip Kemble, for example, it would no doubt be possible to collect reams of adulatory criticisms, but they are all to-day as though they had never been ; while Leigh Hunt's boyish essays, in right of their evident sincerity and thoughtfulness, survive to influence profoundly our estimate of the tragedian's art.

Leigh Hunt's two "campaigns" as a dramatic critic were separated by an interval of nearly twenty years. He was the theatrical critic of *The News* from its commencement in May 1805 until the end of 1807 ; from January 1808 until he went to prison in February 1813, he filled the same office, though with somewhat less assiduity and vehemence, on the staff of his own paper, *The Examiner ;* [1] and he was in his single person the

---

[1] Before leaving prison he announced his intention of "resuming the theatrical criticism" of the paper, and even wrote and published, during the last six weeks of his durance, a series of "Sketches of the Performers," male and female, tragic and comic. Very soon after his release he went to see Kean, the new star, as Richard III., and published (February 26, 1815) a criticism in which he confessed himself "on the whole disappointed," not finding the actor so natural as Hazlitt's eulogies had led him to expect. After this one paper he

whole staff of *The Tatler* (a daily paper) from September 4, 1830, till February 13, 1832. The present volume contains, it is believed, all that is of permanent interest in his theatrical lucubrations of these two periods. It is true that of the "Critical Essays" of 1807 only those in the Appendix had actually appeared in *The News*; but the main body of the book gives the writer's direct impressions of the actors of the day, and sums up the results of his evidently very close study of the contemporary stage; while nothing could possibly come fresher from the mint than the impressions recorded in his *Tatler* criticisms.

"The first time I ever saw a play," he writes "was in March 1800; it was the *Egyptian Festival* of one Mr. Franklin." This statement is no doubt accurate, for the opera in question was produced on March 11, 1800, with Charles Kemble, Suett, Bannister, Miss De Camp and Miss Stephens in the cast. Thus Leigh Hunt's theatre-going began when he was in his sixteenth year, very soon after he had left Christ's Hospital; and as he was pretty much his own master from that time forward, we may assume that even before he began to write for *The News*, he followed attentively the movement of things theatrical. Let us give a brief glance at the state of the stage during these early years of the century.

When Leigh Hunt commenced playgoing the Clan Kemble was at its zenith. Mrs. Siddons was forty-five and had twelve years of her career still before her. John Kemble was forty-three and had seventeen years yet to hold the stage. The youngest of the family, Charles

did no more for nearly two years, leaving the theatrical criticism to Hazlitt and others. Towards the end of 1816 his signature re-appears once or twice; but he seems to have lost his taste for theatre-going, and his criticisms are few and far between.

Kemble, now five-and-twenty, had joined his brother and sister six years earlier, and was beginning to take the place which he held for so long, as the handsomest and most charming of romantic actors. Dora Jordan, probably about thirty-eight years old, had been fifteen years on the London stage, and was at the height of her popularity. Of the male comedians, Lewis, who had only nine years of his stage career before him, had been twenty-seven years at Covent Garden. Suett and Munden were both about forty-two, and the one had been twenty and the other ten years on the London stage. John Bannister, the pupil of Garrick, was forty, and had been before the public ever since 1772. Leigh Hunt missed by a single year the chance of seeing Mrs. Abington, the original Lady Teazle ; but he no doubt saw Thomas King, the original Sir Peter Teazle and Lord Ogleby (incomparable, too, as Touchstone), who did not retire until May 1802. He may also have seen Quick, the original Tony Lumpkin and Bob Acres, who made a few scattered appearances during the early years of the century. Dowton, whose Falstaff Hunt was to criticise in *The Tatler* thirty years later, had already been four years on the London stage. Emery had been two years in London, but had as yet scarcely made his mark. Charles Mathews did not appear in London until 1803, and the same season witnessed Elliston's first real settlement in town, though he had made a few successful appearances in 1796–97. George Frederick Cooke made what was practically his first appearance in London on October 31, 1800, while Hunt was still very new to the delights of the theatre. On the other hand, he was proudly wielding his critical pen when John Liston " from Newcastle " made his first ap-

pearance in 1805, and Charles Mayne Young in 1807.
During the seasons 1800-1801, and 1801-1802, the
Kembles and Mrs. Jordan were at Drury Lane, while the
Covent Garden Company consisted of Holman, Lewis,
Emery, Fawcett, Munden, Pope, Mrs. Pope, H. Johnson,
Miss Betterton (Mrs. Glover) and G. F. Cooke; but at
the beginning of the season 1803-1804, John Kemble
became part proprietor of Covent Garden, where
he and his sister and brother thenceforward acted.
With Mrs. Siddons, John and Charles Kemble and
Cooke at the head of its tragic forces, the Covent
Garden company was now for several seasons an exceed-
ingly strong one. Here, for instance, are some of the
parts the trio played together :—

J. P. KEMBLE.	G. F. COOKE.	MRS. SIDDONS.
Young Norval	Glenalvon	Lady Randolph
Rolla	Pizarro	Elvira
Beverley	Stukely	Mrs. Beverley
Horatio	Sciolto	Calista
Jaffier	Pierre	Belvidera
Antonio	Shylock	Portia
Duke	Angelo	Isabella
Macbeth	Macduff	Lady Macbeth
Othello	Iago	Desdemona
King John	Hubert	Constance
Richmond	Richard III.	
Henry IV. (Pt. 2)	Falstaff	
Ford	Falstaff	
Hamlet	Ghost.	

Truly the playgoer of those days could not complain
that he was placed on starvation diet as regards the
poetic repertory.

In the matter of new plays, on the other hand, he had

to make the best of meagre fare. One or two of the latest and least successful comedies of Cumberland and Mrs. Inchbald were produced during the first five years of the century ; and one or two tragedies by Joanna Baillie, and "Monk" Lewis saw the light, along with several adaptations from the German of Kotzebue. The only plays of the period, however, of which even the names are now remembered, are the younger Colman's *Poor Gentleman* and *John Bull*, and Morton's *Speed the Plough* and *School of Reform*. Holcroft produced a few unsuccessful plays, and for the rest the stage was almost entirely given over to the careless improvisation of Frederick Reynolds, and the wretched hack work of Thomas Dibdin and Andrew Cherry, of whom we shall hear so much from Leigh Hunt. Whatever else they may have beeen, these were certainly not the palmy days of English dramatic authorship.

On December 1, 1804, Master William Henry West Betty made his first appearance in London, at Covent Garden, in the character of Achmet in *Barbarossa*. He at once become the rage, and continued so throughout the season, appearing at both patent theatres in turn, (at Drury Lane he figured on the play-bill as " The Young Roscius ") and attracting immense audiences. Among his principal parts were Hamlet, Romeo, and Richard III. ! His vogue was still at its height when the first number of *The News* was published, May 19, 1805, and Leigh Hunt, still five months short of his majority, made his *début* as the infant prodigy of dramatic criticism, his first article being heralded by the following paragraph, enclosed in square brackets :—

One novelty at least, it is trusted, will always gratify

our readers in their perusal of The News : *an impartiality of Theatrical Criticism. On this entertaining
subject we shall usually bestow a considerable portion of
our time and of our Paper, and shall embrace in our
strictures not only the merits of the Actors and Dramatic
Writers, but the management also of the Stage itself, and
all those little local proprieties, so requisite to a finished
Actor, which go under the general denomination of the
business of the Stage. By these means we presume that
while we are entertaining our Readers, we may offer some
useful hints to those who have so often entertained us,
and who form one of the most delightful enjoyments of a
great city.*

The new critic lost no time in proclaiming his dissent
from the idolatry of the hour. His very first article concludes with an " Accurate list of all the Infant Prodigies
of the dramatic art, as they appear *at present* before the
public :" the catalogue consisting of the Infant Billington,
the Infant Billington and Roscius, the Infant Columbine,
the Young Roscius, the Younger Roscius, the Ormskirk
Roscius, the Young Orpheus, the Infant Vestris, and the
Comic Roscius. Again and again he returns to the
attack, and at the end of the year (December 29) he has
the satisfaction of announcing that "Everything pro-
claims the decline of baby theatricals." It is time, however, that we should quote the account of this first critical
campaign given by Leigh Hunt himself in his " Auto-
biography" (1850). It would be unfair both to the critic
and to the actors and authors whom he criticises, not to
reproduce this passage in full ; for not only does it place
the essays in their true perspective, but it corrects and
humanises their crudities of judgment :—

" My brother John, at the beginning of the year 1805, set up a paper, called *The News*, and I went to live with him in Brydges Street, and write the theatricals in it.

" It was the custom at that time for editors of papers to be intimate with actors and dramatists. They were often proprietors as well as editors ; and, in that case, it was not expected that they should escape the usual intercourse, or wish to do so. It was thought a feather in the cap of all parties ; and with their feathers they tickled one another. The newspaper man had consequence in the green-room, and plenty of tickets for his friends ; and he dined at amusing tables. The dramatist secured a good-natured critique in his journal, sometimes got it written himself, or, according to Mr. Reynolds, was even himself the author of it. The actor, if he was of any evidence, stood upon the same ground of reciprocity ; and not to know a pretty actress would have been a want of the knowing in general. Upon new performers, and upon writers not yet introduced, a journalist was more impartial ; and some-times, where the proprietor was in one interest more than another, or for some personal reason grew offended with an actor, or set of actors, a criticism would occasionally be hostile, and even severe. An editor, too, would now and then suggest to his employer the policy of exercis-ing a freer authority, and obtain influence enough with him to show symptoms of it. I believe Bell's editor, who was more clever, was also more impartial than most critics ; though the publisher of the *British Theatre*, and patron of the *Della Cruscans*, must have been hampered with literary intimacies. The best chance for an editor, who wished to have anything like an opinion of his own, was the appearance of a rival newspaper with a strong theatrical connection. Influence was here threatened with diminution. It was to be held up on other grounds ; and the critic was permitted to find out that a bad play was not good, or an actress's petticoat of the lawful dimensions.

" Puffing and plenty of tickets were, however, the system of the day. It was an interchange of amenities over the dinner table ; a flattery of power on the one side, and puns on the other ; and what the public took for a criticism on a play was a draft upon the box-office, or remini-scences of last Thursday's salmon and lobster-sauce. The custom was to write as short and as favourable a paragraph on the new piece as could be ; to say that Bannister was 'excellent' and Mrs. Jordan 'charming ; ' to notice the 'crowded house,' or invent it, if necessary ; and to conclude by observing that 'the whole went off with *éclat*.' For xxiiINTRODUCTION.

the rest, it was a critical religion in those times to admire Mr. Kemble; and at the period in question Master Betty had appeared, and been hugged to the hearts of the town as the young Roscius.

" We saw that independence in theatrical criticism would be a great novelty. We announced it, and nobody believed us; we stuck to it, and the town believed everything we said. The proprietors of *The News*, of whom I knew so little that I cannot recollect with certainty any one of them, very handsomely left me to myself. My retired and scholastic habits kept me so; and the pride of success confirmed my independence with regard to others. I was then in my twentieth year, an early age at that time for a writer. The usual exaggeration of report made me younger than I was: and after being a 'young Roscius' political, I was now looked upon as one critical. To know an actor personally appeared to me a vice not to be thought of; and I would as lief have taken poison as accepted a ticket from the theatres.

"Good God! To think of the grand opinion I had of myself in those days, and what little reason I had for it! Not to accept the tickets was very proper, considering that I bestowed more blame than praise. There was also more good-nature than I supposed in not allowing myself to know any actors; but the vanity of my position had greater weight with me than anything else, and I must have proved it to discerning eyes by the small quantity of information I brought to my task, and the ostentation with which I produced it. I knew almost as little of the drama as young Roscius himself. Luckily, I had the advantage of him in knowing how unfit *he* was for his office; and, probably, he thought me as much so, though he could not have argued upon it; for I was in the minority respecting his merits, and the balance was then trembling on the beam; *The News*, I believe, hastened the settlement of the question. I wish with all my heart we had let him alone, and he had got a little more money. However, he obtained enough to create him a provision for life. His position, which appeared so brilliant at first, had a remarkable cruelty in it. Most men begin life with struggles, and have their vanity sufficiently knocked about the head and shoulders to make their kinder fortunes the more welcome. Mr. Betty had his sugar first and his physic afterwards. He began life with a double childhood, with a new and extraordinary felicity added to the natural enjoyments of his age; and he lived to see it speedily come to nothing, and to be taken for an ordinary person. I am told that he acquiesces in his fate, and agrees that the town were mistaken. If so, he is no ordinary person still, and has as much right to our respect for his good sense, as he is declared on all hands to deserve it for his amiableness. I have an anecdote of him to both purposes, which exhibits him in a very agreeable light. Hazlitt happened to be at a party where Mr. Betty was present; and in coming away, when they were all putting on their great-coats, the critic thought fit to compliment the dethroned favourite of the town by telling him that he recollected him in old times, and had been 'much pleased with him.' Betty looked at his memorialist, as much as to say, ' You don't tell me so !' and then starting into a tragical attitude, exclaimed, 'Oh, memory ! memory !'

"I was right about Master Betty, and I am sorry for it ; though the town was in fault, not he. I think I was right also about Kemble; but I have no regret upon that score. He flourished long enough after my attack on his majestic dryness and deliberate nothings ; and Kean would have taken the public by storm whether they had been prepared for him or not :—

One touch of nature makes the whole world kin.

Kemble faded before him like a tragedy ghost. I never denied the merits which that actor possessed. He had the look of a Roman ; made a very good ideal, though not a very real, Coriolanus, for his pride was not sufficiently blunt and unaffected ; and in parts that suited his natural deficiency, such as Penruddock and the Abbé de l'Epée, would have been altogether admirable and interesting if you could have forgotten that their sensibility, in his hands, was not so much repressed, as wanting. He was no more to be compared to his sister than stone is to flesh and blood. There was much of the pedagogue in him. He made a fuss about trifles ; was inflexible on a pedantic reading ; in short, was rather a teacher of elocution than an actor, and not a good teacher on that account. There was a merit in his idealism as far as it went. He had, at least, faith in something classical and scholastic, and he made the town partake of it ; but it was all on the surface—a hollow trophy ; and I am persuaded that he had no idea in his head but of a stage Roman, and the dignity he added to his profession.

"But if I was right about Kemble, whose admirers I plagued enough, I was not equally so about the living dramatists, whom I plagued more. I laid all the deficiences of the modern drama to their account, and treated them like a parcel of mischievous boys, of whom I was the schoolmaster and whipper-in. I forgot that it was I who was the boy,

and that they knew twenty times more of the world than I did. Not
that I mean to say their comedies were excellent, or that my common-
places about the superior merits of Congreve and Sheridan were not
well founded ; but there was more talent in their ' five-act farce' than
I supposed; and I mistook, in a great measure, the defect of the age—
its dearth of dramatic character—for that of the writers who were to
draw upon it. It is true a great wit, by a laborious process, and the
help of his acquirements, might extract a play or two from it, as was
Sheridan's own case ; but there was a great deal of imitation even in
Sheridan, and he was fain to help himself to a little originality out of
the characters of his less formalised countrymen, his own included.

"It is remarkable that the three most amusing dramatists of the last
age, Sheridan, Goldsmith, and O'Keefe, were all Irishmen, and all had
characters of their own. Sheridan, after all, was Swift's Sheridan come
to life again in the person of his grandson, with the oratory of Thomas
Sheridan, the father, superadded and brought to bear. Goldsmith, at
a disadvantage in his breeding, but full of address with his pen, drew
upon his own absurdities and mistakes, and filled his dramas with
ludicrous perplexity. O'Keefe was all for whim and impulse, but not
without a good deal of conscience ; and, accordingly, in his plays we
have a sort of young and pastoral taste of life in the very midst of its
sophistications. Animal spirits, quips and cranks, credulity, and good
intention, are triumphant throughout, and make a delicious mixture.
It is a great credit to O'Keefe that he ran sometimes close upon the
borders of the sentimental drama, and did it not only with impunity
but advantage ; but sprightliness and sincerity enable a man to do
everything with advantage.

"It was a pity that as much could not be said of Mr. Colman, who,
after taking more license in his writings than anybody, became a licenser
ex officio, and seemed inclined to license nothing but cant. When this
writer got into the sentimental, he made a sad business of it, for he had
no faith in sentiment. He mouthed and overdid it, as a man does when
he is telling a lie. At a farce he was admirable ; and he remained so
to the last, whether writing or licensing.

"Morton seemed to take a colour from the writers all round him,
especially from O'Keefe and the sentimentalists. His sentiment was
more in earnest than Colman's, yet, somehow, not happy either. There
was a gloom in it, and a smack of the Old Bailey. It was best when
he put it in the shape of humour, as in the paternal and inextinguishable

tailorism of Old Rapid, in a *Cure for the Heart-Ache*. Young Rapid, who complains that his father ' sleeps so slow,' is also a pleasant fellow, and worthy of O'Keefe. He is one of the numerous crop that sprang up from *Wild Oats*, but not in so natural a soil.

" The character of the modern drama at that time was singularly commercial; nothing but gentlemen in distress, and hard landlords, and generous interferers, and fathers who got a great deal of money, and sons who spent it.   I remember one play in particular, in which the whole wit ran upon prices, bonds, and post-obits. You might know what the pit thought of their pound-notes by the ostentatious indifference with which the heroes of the pieces gave them away, and the admiration and pretended approval with which the spectators observed it.   To make a present of a hundred pounds was as if a man had uprooted and given away an Egyptian pyramid.

" Mr. Reynolds was not behindhand with his brother dramatists in drawing upon the taste of the day for gains and distresses.   It appears by his Memoirs that he had too much reason for so doing. He was, perhaps, the least ambitious, and the least vain (whatever charges to the contrary his animal spirits might have brought on him) of all the writers of that period.   In complexional vivacity he certainly did not yield to any of them ; his comedies, if they were fugitive, were genuine representa tions of fugitive manners, and went merrily to their death ; and there is one of them, the *Dramatist*, founded upon something more lasting, which promises to remain in the collections, and deserves it ; which is not a little to say of any writer. I never wish for a heartier laugh than I have enjoyed, since I grew wiser, not only in seeing, but in reading the vagaries of his dramatic hero, and his mystifications of ' Old Scratch.' When I read the good-humoured Memoirs of this writer the other day, I felt quite ashamed of the ignorant and boyish way in which I used to sit in judgment upon his faults, without being aware of what was good in him ; and my repentance was increased by the very proper manner in which he speaks of his critics, neither denying the truth of their charges in letter, nor admitting them altogether in spirit ; in fact, showing that he knew very well what he was about, and that they, whatsoever they fancied to the contrary, did not.

" Mr. Reynolds, agreeably to his sense and good-humour, never said a word to his critics at the time. Mr. Thomas Dibdin, not quite so wise, wrote me a letter, which Incledon, I am told, remonstrated with him for sending, saying, it would do him no good with the ' d——d boy.'

And he was right. I published it, with an answer, and only thought that I made dramatists 'come bow to me.' Mr. Colman attacked me in a prologue, which, by a curious chance, Fawcett spoke right in my teeth, the box I sat in happening to be directly opposite him. I laughed at the prologue, and only looked upon Mr. Colman as a great monkey pelting me with nuts, which I ate. Attacks of this kind were little calculated to obtain their end with a youth who persuaded himself that he wrote for nothing but the public good ; who mistook the impression which anybody of moderate talents can make with a newspaper, for the result of something peculiarly his own ; and who had just enough scholarship to despise the want of it in others. I do not pretend to think that the criticisms in *The News* had no merit at all. They showed an acquaintance with the style of Voltaire, Johnson, and others ; were not unagreeably sprinkled with quotation ; and, above all, were written with more care and attention than was customary with newspapers at that time. The pains I took to round a period with nothing in it, or to invent a simile that should appear offhand, would have done honour to better stuff.

" A portion of these criticisms subsequently formed the appendix of an original volume on the same subject, entitled 'Critical Essays on the Performers of the London Theatres' [1807]. I have the book now before me, and if I thought it had a chance of survival I should regret and qualify a good deal of uninformed judgment in it respecting the art of acting, which, with much inconsistent recommendation to the contrary, is too often confounded with a literal instead of a liberal imitation of nature. I particularly erred with respect to comedians like Munden, whose superabundance of humour and expression I confounded with farce and buffoonery. Charles Lamb taught me better.

" There was a good deal of truth, however, mixed up with these mistakes. One of the things on which I was always harping was Kemble's vicious pronunciation. Kemble had a smattering of learning, and a great deal of obstinacy. He was a reader of old books, and having discovered that pronunciation had not always been what it was, and that in one or two instances the older was metrically better than the new (as in the case of the word *aches*, which was originally a dissyllable —*aitches*), he took upon him to reform it in a variety of cases, where propriety was as much against him as custom."

He then closes the chapter and the subject by giving

the same instances of Kemble's " vicious orthoepy," which the reader will find upon p. 113.

It must be admitted that there was more than a touch of the cruelty of youth in Leigh Hunt's treatment of Reynolds, Dibdin, and Cherry. Except, perhaps, in the case of Reynolds, he does not seem to have underrated their merits—" seem," I say, for I do not pretend to have studied the *Théâtre* of Dibdin, Cherry, and Cobb—but there was doubtless something a trifle inhuman in the persistency and virulence of his attacks. He even found prose inadequate to the full expression of his scorn, and on March 29, 1807, he plunged, either in person or by proxy, into poetry. *The News* of that date contains a long copy of verses entitled, " La Ciriegia : an Austere Imitation of Milton's L'Allegro," and signed thus :—

—. —.

B. F.

There can surely be little doubt that the two blanks stand for L. H. ; and in the B. F. we may perhaps recognise Barron Field, the friend of Hunt and Lamb. The verses seem scarcely brilliant enough to have required the co-operation of two intellects. They begin as follows :—

> Hence loathed SHERIDAN
> Of envious Wit and stupid Humour born.
>
> .   .   .   .   .
>
> But come thou sing-song poet CHERRY,
> In Drury Lane yclep'd the Merry,
> And by critics MERRY-ANDREW,
> Whom Impudence, with prophet hand, drew
> With two giggling brothers more
> From shivering at the prompter's door.

To the phrase " giggling brothers " is appended a foot-note : "Everybody must perceive that this *par nobile fratrum* can be no other than Messrs. Reynolds and Dibdin "—an explanation which the constant readers of *The News* must certainly have found quite superfluous. Not very dignified fooling this, but it was fair enough after its fashion. The same can scarcely be said, unfortunately, for Leigh Hunt's treatment of Tom Dibdin in the case of the letter above alluded to. Hunt's remembrance of the matter must surely have been imperfect, or he would have expressed his regret less equivocally. The facts were these : In criticising (April 19, 1807) the pantomime of *Ogre and Little Thumb*, Leigh Hunt wrote :—

". . . This grave author we should conceive, from the internal evidence of the piece, to be no other than the famous Mr. Thomas Dibdin, for in the very short songs introduced into the piece he has contrived to write very bad English. . . . It requires some degree of condescension in a critic to enter into a disquisition on the comedies of Mr. Dibdin, but to notice his pantomimes would have been an intolerable task, had we not thought it necessary to caution parents how they introduce their children to spectacles in which both the human mind and the human body are rendered disgustingly monstrous, and which may excite a prematurity of imagination without exalting, refining, or moralising it."

In reply to this diatribe Dibdin writes a short and very temperately worded letter, saying that the article seems to show "something more than a fair critical hostility against him," and assuring the writer that he had nothing to do with the pantomime so confidently ascribed to him. Here, obviously, was an occasion for a handsome apology; but nothing of the sort is forthcoming. On the contrary, Leigh Hunt returns to the attack in a still more violent article, in which he argues as follows :—

" Suppose a watchmaker has imposed so many bad watches on the town that a person on seeing a bad watch were to exclaim, ' This must certainly be the manufacture of that fellow X., whose works are good for nothing '; ought the watchmaker, on hearing this speech, to think himself ill-used, even though the work in question were not his own? . . . Mr. Dibdin, with the usual importance of endured scribblers, talks of the frequent indulgence shown him by the public ; that is, he has assisted to deprave the taste of the town, and then he is tolerated by it. . . . After all, where is this fancied indulgence shown to Mr. Dibdin, or Mr. Reynolds, or Mr. Cherry, or Mr. Cobb, or to any other disgrace of the stage?"

This heaping of insult on injury was no less unreasonable than ungenerous. However grave a man's sins may be, he has clearly a right to demand that those of others be not laid at his door, and Leigh Hunt's retort cannot be acquitted of sheer truculence.

Throughout the year 1807 there are frequent allusions in *The News* to the forthcoming volume of " Critical Essays," quotations from it, and apologies for its non-appearance. At last, on December 13, Leigh Hunt bids farewell to the readers of *The News*, and at the same time avers that the " Critical Essays " " will appear, most certainly, before the expiration of the month." This manifesto is signed with the hand (☞), which was afterwards the writer's private mark both in *The Examiner* and *The Tatler*. When at last the " Critical Essays " did appear (probably very early in 1808, though the title-page is dated 1807) it contained, as an appendix, the prospectus of *The Examiner*, with a foot-note stating that " The first number of this paper appeared on the 3rd of January, 1808." " The gentleman who has hitherto conducted the theatrical department in *The News*," says the prospectus, " will criticise the theatre in *The Examiner ;* and as the public have allowed the possibility of impartiality in that department, we do not see why the same possi-

bility may not be obtained in politics." A little further
on we read :—

> "With respect to the theatre criticism, the proprietors merely observe
> that it will be in the same spirit of opinion and manner with the *present*
> theatrical observations in *The News*. The critic trusts he has already
> proved in that paper that he has no respect for error, however long
> established, or for vanity, however long endured. He will still admire
> Mr. Kemble when dignified, but by no means when pedantic ; he still
> hopes to be satisfied with Mr. Dibdin in a Christmas pantomime, but
> is afraid he shall differ with him as to his powers for comedy. Yet the
> town may be assured that if either Mr. Dibdin or Mr. Reynolds should
> suddenly become a man of wit, the critic will be as eager to announce
> the metamorphosis as if it were the discovery of transmuting lead into
> gold."

In *The Examiner*, however, Leigh Hunt was not nearly
so savage as he had been in *The News*, and as time went
on he seems rather to have wearied of theatre-going. For
example, he does not go to see Mrs. Siddons's farewell
appearance, but contents himself with writing a somewhat
frigid and perfunctory appreciation of her genius. On
the whole, *The Examiner* criticisms fulfil the promise of
reproducing "the same spirit of opinion and manner"
which characterises the "theatrical observations" of *The
News*. The chief difference is that the enthusiasm and
assiduity of youth are declining.[1] The critic is no longer

[1] As a proof of the interest excited by Leigh Hunt's criticisms
among "the profession" we may quote the following passage from
the "Memoirs of Charles Mathews, Comedian," by his wife (1838-39) :
"At the Haymarket this year (1808) Mr. Mathews first played Sir
Fretful Plagiary before a London audience ; and the success of his
performance was recorded by the greatest dramatic critic of that day,
Mr. Leigh Hunt, whose judgment was universally sought and received
as infallible by all actors and lovers of the drama. My husband unfortunately did not become acquainted with him for some years afterwards ; but so high an opinion did he entertain of Mr. Leigh Hunt's

a "new broom." The very best thing, perhaps, in the *Theatrical Examiner* (so the papers were headed) is the motto from the *Spectator*, No. 370 :—

> "It is with me a matter of the highest consideration what parts are ill or well performed, what passions or sentiments are indulged or cultivated, and consequently what manners and customs are transfused from the stage to the world, which reciprocally imitate each other."

Of *The Tatler*, established in 1830, Leigh Hunt himself gives the following brief and almost pathetic account :—

> "It was a very little work, consisting but of four folio pages, but it was a daily publication; I did it all myself, except when too ill; and illness seldom hindered me either from supplying the review of a book, going every night to the play, or writing the notice of the play the same night at the printing-office. The consequence was that the work, slight as it looked, nearly killed me; for it never prospered beyond the coterie of play-going readers to whom it was almost exclusively known; and I was sensible of becoming weaker and poorer every day. When I came home at night, often at morning, I used to feel as if I could hardly speak; and for a year and a half afterwards, a certain grain of fatigue seemed to pervade my limbs, which I thought would never go off. Such, nevertheless, is a habit of the mind, if it but be cultivated, that my spirits never seemed better, nor did I ever write theatricals so well, as in the pages of this most unremunerating speculation."

In the interval of nearly twenty years during which the critic had practically laid down his pen, great events had happened in the theatrical world. The older generation of the Kembles, all but its youngest member, Charles, had passed away, and it fell to Leigh Hunt to criticise, not too enthusiastically, the early appearances of Fanny Kemble, who was still among us only the other day.

sound criticism of dramatic talent, and his superior mode of writing upon the subject, that whenever he found himself an object of praise to that gentleman, he was much gratified."

Hunt had been in prison for nearly a year when Edmund Kean made his first appearance in January, 1814, so that it fell to Hazlitt (see "Dramatic Essays," vol. ii.) to chronicle and celebrate the early triumphs of that wayward genius. He was within two years of his end when Hunt championed him in *The Tatler*. Macready, too, had made his first appearance in 1816, and was now a tragedian of established reputation, though his historic management was still in the future. As regards dramatic literature, the critic's spirit was no longer vexed by the ineptitudes of Reynolds, Dibdin, and Cherry ; but a generation of hack playwrights, scarcely, if at all, superior to them, had taken their place. Sheridan Knowles was the only dramatist of real note who had come to the front in the interval; Douglas Jerrold was just at this time making his first essays in drama, and Bulwer Lytton had not yet turned playwright. The reign of Scribe had already set in, and the stage swarmed with more or less acknowledged adaptations from the French. It is curious to find Leigh Hunt (on April 9, 1831) criticising favourably a translation of *Hernani*, entitled *The Pledge, or Castilian Honour*, in total ignorance of the name of its author and of the literary significance of the work itself. All he says is that it is "understood to have been translated or borrowed from the French by Mr. Kenney." Of the famous "crimson - waistcoat night" at the Théâtre-Français of a year before (February 25, 1830) he has apparently heard never a whisper, and he knows no more of the war of the Classicists and the Romanticists than if it had taken place in Central Africa.

The decease of *The Tatler* brought to a close Leigh Hunt's activity as a theatrical critic. He continued to take an interest in the stage, and his play, *A Legend of Florence*, was produced at Covent Garden in 1840, under the Mathews-Vestris management, with a good deal of success. Another blank-verse play, *Lovers' Amazements*, found its way to the stage in 1857, and he wrote several dramas which were never acted ; but for criticism, during the last five-and-twenty years of his life, he lacked either taste or opportunity, or both.

It remains that we should say something of the principles which have guided our selection both from the " Critical Essays " and from *The Tatler*. We have looked primarily, of course, to interest of subject, and have tried to omit nothing that concerns actors whose names have any significance for modern readers, or plays which are still alive, whether in the study or on the stage. Kemble and Mrs. Siddons, Mrs. Jordan and Elliston are personalities within the ken of every educated man, whereas no one but a theatrical antiquary knows or cares to know about Mr. Raymond, Mr. Henry Siddons, or Mr. Murray. The essays dealing with these minor artists are all brief and perfunctory ; even if space had permitted, their inclusion would have served no purpose. Some articles, however, we have reproduced rather as curiosities than as things of vital interest. The essay on Mr. Pope, for instance (p. 16), is given as a specimen of the uncompromising style of criticism which was possible in those good old days. Such freedom of expression could no doubt be used, by dishonest and malignant men, to the vilest ends, so that we cannot altogether regret the change brought about by our present law of libel and its interpretation in the courts. At the same time, it is impossible not to feel that a little plain speaking, after the manner of Leigh

1 ※ ※

Hunt, would sometimes clear the artistic atmosphere. In order that the reader may judge of the number and importance of our omissions from the " Critical Essays," we reproduce Leigh Hunt's own synopses of the whole, marking with an asterisk those papers which are not included in this volume. We reprint, of course, only a small proportion of the daily criticisms in *The Tatler*, but we believe that nothing of permanent interest is omitted. Then, as now, melodramas, farces, and trivialities of all sorts constituted the staple of theatrical entertainments ; and, as Leigh Hunt was not one of the writers who touched nothing that he did not ennoble, his every-day remarks upon every-night productions are no more worthy of preservation than any ephemeral " notice " in the newspapers of to-day. His style naturally rises with his subject, and Shakespeare, Goldsmith, and Sheridan, Kean, Macready, and Fanny Kemble call forth the best of his powers. In very few instances have we felt any temptation to include an article which we have ultimately omitted for lack of space. For example, though the above-mentioned notice of *Hernani* is in its way a curiosity, we felt that the reader of to-day would readily pardon our omission of what is, in effect, a mere recital of the plot of Victor Hugo's play. On the other hand, we have included two letters addressed to Leigh Hunt by anonymous correspondents, because their publication in the theatrical column of *The Tatler* gave them, so to speak, his sanction, and they seemed to complete, in a very interesting way, the pictures of Kean and Macready given in his own articles.

WILLIAM ARCHER.

CRITICAL ESSAYS

ON THE

PERFORMERS OF THE LONDON THEATRES,

INCLUDING

GENERAL OBSERVATIONS ON THE PRACTICE AND GENIUS OF THE STAGE.

BY THE AUTHOR OF THE

THEATRICAL CRITICISMS IN THE WEEKLY PAPER CALLED "THE NEWS."

Respicere exemplar vitæ morumque jubebo
Doctum imitatorem, et veras hinc ducere voces.—HORACE.

London:

PRINTED BY AND FOR JOHN HUNT, AT THE OFFICE OF "THE NEWS," 28, BRYDGES-STREET, STRAND.
1807.

PREFACE.

————◆————

It will be pardoned me if I speak a little of myself, when
I am going to say so much about others. If I have not
been long intimate with theatrical affairs, I have endeavoured to give them no slight attention. The first time
I ever saw a play was in March, 1800 ; it was the *Egyptian
Festival* of one Mr. Franklin : the scenery enchanted
me, and I went home with the hearty jollity of Mr.
Bannister laughing all the way before me. After that I
was present at the comedies of Mr. Reynolds and of Mr.
Dibdin, and I laughed very heartily at the grimaces of
the actors ; but somehow or another I never recollected
a word of the dialogue. Any schoolboy, who had been
accustomed to nothing but natural objects, would have
admired these comedies just in the same way. Admirable
indeed as they were, they struck me with very peculiar
sensations. It was not that I wished them to be like
the productions of Terence, who had afflicted me, or of
Aristophanes, who had made me sick ; but I had been
accustomed to fancy that the comedies of Beaumont and
Fletcher, of Congreve, and of Sheridan, as far as genius
was concerned, were the true models of writing. I
listened, however, with attention to the new dramas ; I

listened to the applauses of the theatre ; and I began to examine whether Mr. Reynolds and Mr. Dibdin were not the true comic writers. It was then that I discovered what excellent actors we possessed.

If any man, not very fond of music, will reflect a little between the acts of one of the modern comedies, he will find that his chief entertainment has arisen from the actors totally abstracted from the author. The phrases, the sentiments, the fancies will appear to his reason very monotonous and inefficient, when separated from the grins of Munden and the chatterings of Fawcett. By degrees, he will imagine that these actors would make almost any phrases equally facetious. In short, he is very soon convinced that the monosyllable *yes* is as admirable a piece of humour in Mr. Munden's mouth as any other touch of rhetoric in modern comedy.

The authors know this as well as anybody. The habit of recommending the most unmeaning dialogue with the most powerful expression is a great injury to the propriety, and ultimately to the judgment, of an actor ; but it is of the greatest use to the dramatist, and accordingly his principal design in forming a character is to adapt it to that peculiar style of the actor, which the huge farces have rendered necessary to their existence. If there is a countryman, it must be adapted to Emery ; if an Irishman, to Johnstone ; if a gabbling humourist, it must be copied from nothing but the manner of Fawcett. Not to mention, therefore, that all the countrymen, and all the Irishmen, and all the gabbling humourists are alike, the author becomes a mere dependant on the player. The loss of Lewis, for instance, whose gaiety of limb is of so much benefit to modern comedy, would be a perfect rheumatism to Mr. Reynolds ; and the loss of Munden, who gives it such an agreeable variety of grin, would affect him little less than a lock-jaw.

It was this strange superiority of the mimetic over the literary part of the stage, of the organ, in fact, over its inspirer, that determined me to criticise the actors. I intended at first to go through the entire list of both the theatres, and it was not till the tragic section had been printed that I discovered the nameless multitude which this plan would have compelled me to individualise. I am sorry that I did not consider this objection sooner, as there are two or three essays under the head of tragedy which I might have spared the reader. The second and third sections, however, are confined to those performers whom I regarded as the possessors of some exclusive originality. Somebody, perhaps, will still miss his favourite king or his favourite footman; but I have endeavoured to criticise those only who deserve applause, not those who merely obtain it. The work was written by starts and snatches in the midst of better subjects of meditation; but I was induced to continue it, partly by the originality of an enlarged criticism on the theatre, and principally by the hope of exciting an honourable ambition in the actors, who have hitherto been the subjects of mere scandal, or at best of the most partial levity. Criticism written with this levity serves merely to confirm the actor in a kind of hopelessness of respect. It cannot, I allow, be denied, that the profession of the stage has been brought into disgrace by the lives of its members; but this very disgrace has become one cause of the moral negligence of actors: the social nature of their errors confounds the fault with its power of pleasing; the foolish and dissipated are delighted to find themselves at their ease in the company of the most public satirists,

and thus the actors become identified with the most contemptible men, whose habits they ridicule on the stage
merely to practise with more familiar imitation in
private.

As to the contempt that has been cast upon histrionic
genius, it is not worthy an argument. If the knowledge
of ourselves be the height of wisdom, is that art contemptible which conveys this knowledge to us in the
most pleasing manner? If the actor is greatly inferior
to the true dramatist, if he merely tells others what has
been told himself, does the officer deserve no praise who
issues the instructions of his general with accuracy, with
spirit, with an ardour that shows he feels them? For
my part, I have the greatest respect for an art which has
been admired by the greatest critics ancient and modern,
which Horace did not think it beneath his genius to advise,
Addison to recommend, and Voltaire to practise, as well
as protect. That genius cannot be despicable in the eyes
of the most ardent for fame, which, without anything to
show to posterity for its reason, has handed down to us
the memory of Æsop, Roscius, Baron, and Le Couvreur,
and which will transmit to our descendants the names of
Garrick, of Oldfield, and of Siddons. If such an art were
divested of its instruction, it would still be honourable
for its imitation of nature. It becomes mean only when
it degenerates into utter farce. Of a mere mimic, indeed,
the praise seems to be little above that of an accomplished
ape. Such an actor is confined to surfaces and externals ;
he possesses a kind of active acknowledgment of another's
habits, that seems to exist in his powers of motion without any reference to the intellect ; he imitates by this
sympathy without the least pretensions to genius, just as
musical instruments sound at the touch of corresponding

keys. It is thus that natives of New South Wales, who are the most stupid and untractable of mankind, mimic the personal peculiarities of the settlers to a facsimile.

Much has been said of the immoral example of the characters and plays performed ; but the managers, who are sometimes actors also, have always the power to remedy such an evil, by correcting their authors for representation ; and it is in consideration of this duty that I have felt the less scruple in recommending our old comedies to public performance. The managers certainly will not pretend too humble a respect for the authors, when they so often neglect the beauties as well as faults of our greatest writers for the utter deformity of the modern drama. And what is such a respect, when vice is its object ? If the genius of the play rests entirely upon its immorality, it cannot be worth the performance ; if it does not, how can a drama lose any of its beauties by the absence of the worst of faults ? [1]

In fact, the perpetual representation of these wretched dramas, which are called new without the least pretension to originality, is not only hurtful to the immediate repu-tation of the actors, but to their fame and memory with succeeding ages. An actor almost entirely depends upon the dramatist for his future name, he leaves nothing either to the eyes of posterity, like the poet and the painter, or to their ears, like the musician : even if his remembrance outlives his poet, it is little better than an Egyptian hieroglyphic, which the writer, who gave it meaning, has left nothing to explain. I do not a little regret, therefore, that I have been compelled to draw

---

[1] Mr. Kemble might have reasoned a little in this manner, without any peculiar detriment to his originality or precision of thinking, when he revived Dryden's alteration of the *Tempest.*—L. H.

examples of good acting from the worst dramas. The
performer, indeed, never shows himself to more advantage
than in giving brilliancy to dulness; but if he is always
occupied with this task, he shares the danger of the
manufacturer, who in polishing certain metals breathes
an air that is his ultimate destruction.

Upon so perishable a subject I cannot enjoy the hope
of talking to other times; it will be enough for me if I
do them any service by assisting the improvement of my
own. It is this consideration that has always encouraged
me to exercise my best powers, such as they are, against
the barbarities of modern comedy. Succeeding ages
very often acquire an unconscious tone from the most
trifling exertions. Like the child who was awakened
every morning by his father's flute, they rise in the calm
possession of their powers, unconscious of the favourable
impulse that has been given them.

LEIGH HUNT'S SYNOPSES.

[*Those articles not included in this Volume are marked with an asterisk.*]

BANNISTER, Mr., the first low comedian on the stage : engages your attention by seeming to care nothing about you : heartiness, his most prominent expression : his representation of ludicrous distress : his Acres : his versatility : his Colonel Feignwell : his Young Philpot : always natural except in the lively gentleman : his Mercutio : mingles the heart with his broadest humour : his humorous pathetic : his Job Thornberry : compared with Mr. Fawcett's : his Walter in the *Children of the Wood* : his Trappanti compared with Mr. Fawcett's : his Dr. Pangloss compared with Mr. Fawcett's.

*BLANCHARD, Mr., his unassuming nature : his Marquis de Grand-chateau : his perpetual catch of the right arm.

COOKE, Mr., his genius confined to various hypocrisy : his failure in Jaques, Macbeth, and Hamlet : not a great tragedian : his Richard the Third : question whether his hypocrisy ought to betray itself to the audience except in soliloquy : greater in comedy than tragedy : his Stukely and Iago : his Sir Archy Mac Sarcasm : his Scotch dialect duly appreciated : his defects of person contribute to the effect of his best characters.

DOWTON, Mr., fails in low comedy, with the exception of King Arthur : catches feelings rather than habits : his lamentable failure in Dr. Pangloss : his superiority in anger subdued by the patience or the pleasantry of its object : his Capt. Cape and Sir Anthony Absolute : excels in the mixed emotions of anger and of tenderness : his Old Dornton and Abednego : his Dornton compared with Mr. Munden's : Mr. Cumberland's encomium on him.

*Duncan, Miss, placed under the head of Comedy for the same reasons as Mrs. Jordan : her feeling less, and her declamation better, than Mrs. Jordan's : her Florence in the *Curfew* : her great originality, the fashionable lady : her Juliana and Lady Teazle : her singing compared with Mrs. Jordan's : her flourish of acting : the general character of her acting termed imposing : her Maria in the *Citizen*, and Miss Hardcastle in *She Stoops to Conquer* : her vixen countenance and nagging voice in the character of Nell : her performance in male attire injurious to her : her exposition of her person in them censured : her respectability.

Elliston, Mr., his combination of tragic and comic powers : this combination excites incredulity : not so excellent in tragedy as in comedy : his want of heroic countenance : his want of study : his Hamlet : his tragic genius naturally superior to Mr. Kemble's : his vivification of Sir Edward Mortimer : his Octavian compared with Mr. Kemble's : his injudicious sobbing in that character : the best lover on the stage : his Frederick in *Matrimony* : his fashionable gallant : his Sir Harry Wildair : his unrivalled gentility : his little accomplishments : his low humour : his preservation of the gentleman in low humour : this of service to his Archer : his three Singles in the *Three and the Deuce* : his humorous ridicule compared with Mr. Charles Kemble's : his hypocritical austereness : his Duke Aranza : his greatest fault, monotony of voice : considered as the greatest actor of the present day : this claim contested with Mr. Kemble, Mr. Cooke, and Mr. Pope : his versatility duly appreciated : if he performed in tragedy only, would be thought a better tragedian : acts too often.

Emery, Mr., an actor of little variety : his Count Curvoso in the *Cabinet* : his deficiency in the representation of age as great as Mr. Liston's : excels in the habits of rustics, personal, moral, and intellectual : his rustics divided into the serious, comic, and tragicomic ; and illustrated by his Farmer Ashfield, John Lump, and Tyke : a piteous or joyous contempt for others, one of his best rustic expressions : compared with Mr. Liston as a rustic : his Caliban.

*Fawcett, Mr., his mere peculiarity takes the place of genius : that peculiarity defined and exemplified : his Caleb Quotem : his comic singing : does not undertake a single natural character, in which he might not be excelled by his contemporaries : his failure in the

LEWIS, Mr., his vivacity in Rover contrasted with that of Mr. Elliston: frankness, his original excellence: his title to the appellation of Gentleman Lewis questioned: his habitual errors explained and accounted for: his eccentricities in dress censured: the most complete fop on the stage: injuriousness of this excellence to his gentleman.

LISTON, Mr., natural in every sense of the word: the ignorant rustic his happiest performance, and the old man his most inaccurate: general repose of his style: his performance in *Catch Him Who Can*: his Quaker in *Five Miles Off*: his rawness of country simplicity: his country lad in the *Three and the Deuce*: his Jacob Gawky: compared with Mr. Emery as a rustic.

MATHEWS, Mr., praised for avoiding buffooneries he can affect: officious valets and humorous old men, his principal excellencies: his natural cheerfulness: his principal fault a redundancy of bodily motion: this fault a beauty in the *Lying Valet*, &c.: his powers of mimicry: his Don Manuel and Old Philpot: his universal excellence in low comedy: his unaffected seriousness in the Quaker in the *School for Friends*: this character again discussed: his conception of passions as well as habits: his inimitable performance of Sir Fretful Plagiary in the *Critic*: instance of his rivalling Mr. Bannister.

*MATTOCKS, Mrs., her comic powers very discoverable even through her farce: compared with Miss Pope: this comparison illustrated by one between Smirke and Wilkie, the comic painters: never descends to mere caricature except her author compels her: her Miss Clementina Allspice: her chief fault, obtrusive force: her Betty Hint; her satisfactory giggle: her housekeeper in the *Tale of Mystery*.

*MELLON, Miss, possesses nothing of the gentlewoman but the frankness: her vulgar shortness of speech: her Volante: the ease and artifice of her chambermaid or unpolished girl: her Lucy in the *School for Friends*: her Charlotte in the *Apprentice*.

MUNDEN, Mr., his grimace rendered more grinning by the farcical characters of modern dramatists: his representation of drunkenness: in the *English Fleet*: has no simplicity: his Polonius: his Menenius: loses half his proper effect by the very strength of his powers: his picture of a Quaker: his Old Dornton compared with Mr. Dowton's.

*MURRAY, Mr., his genius a correct mediocrity : excels in the pathetic feebleness of old age : his Manly.

POPE, Mr., has not one requisite to an actor but his voice : why he gains applause : his skill in clap-trapping : his excellence as an artist has no effect upon his powers as an actor : his two gestures and two looks : his Othello : his Hotspur.

POPE, Miss, a proof that a comedian may please without buffoonery : her education in Garrick's juvenile theatre no argument for the excellence of such institutions : Churchill's opinion of her, not justified in his comparison of her with Mrs. Clive : justified in its general praise : her genius lasting, because her acting easy : her judicious emphasis : her Mrs. Candour : her dry humour : her Lady Courtland ; her failure in farce.

*POWELL, Mrs., her assumption of Hamlet censured : merely copies Mrs. Siddons.

*RAE, Mr., his Octavian : his correct pronunciation : his Count Almaviva in the *Spanish Barber.*

*RAYMOND, Mr., wants the advantage of countenance : his Macduff : his literary air.

SIDDONS, Mrs., always natural : said to be really agitated with the characters she represents : her only defect is in the amatory pathetic : her Grecian Daughter : copied by Mrs. Powell.

*SIDDONS, Mr. Henry, characterised as respectable : wants importance.

*SIDDONS, Mrs. Henry, her genius entirely feminine : love, her peculiar talent : her Emily in the *School for Friends* : her Juliet : her Belvidera : fails in satire : this failure illustrated in her Belvidera and Emily : her monotonous sweetness of voice : this monotony defensible however in love : her modesty : her only affectation a languishing lift of the eye.

*SIMMONS, Mr., an unassuming and simple actor : his Beau Mordecai : represents little else than feeble intellect : his happiest expression silly importance : his Fainwoud in *Raising the Wind.*

*SMITH, Miss, her detention from the public : her genius for lofty tragedy and low comedy : her failure in Lady Townly and Rosalind : her coldness in love : her Belvidera : her Estifania.

*WEWITZER, Mr., his characters amusing on the stage only ; his excellence in the German, the Frenchman, and the Jew : his Canton : an imitator of habits only : fails in everything English.

CRITICAL ESSAYS.

—◆—

SECTION I.—*TRAGEDY.*

THE drama is the most perfect imitation of human life ; by means of the stage it represents man in all his varieties of mind, his expressions of manner, and his power of action, and is the first of moralities because it teaches us in the most impressive way the knowledge of ourselves. When its lighter species, which professes to satirise, forsakes this imitation for caricature, it becomes farce, whether it still be denominated comedy, as we say the comedies of Reynolds, or whether it be called opera, as we say the operas of Cherry and Cobb : the actors in these pieces must act unnaturally or they will do nothing, but in real comedy they will act naturally for the same reason. In the graver kind of drama, however, their imitation of life is perfect, not as it copies real and simple manners, but as it accords with our habitual ideas of human character ; those who have produced the general idea that tragedy and comedy are equally direct imitations of human life, have mistaken their habitual for their experimental knowledge. The loftier persons of tragedy require an elevation of language and manner which they

2

never use in real life. Heroes and sages speak like other
men, they use their action as carelessly and their looks as
indifferently, and are not distinguished from their fellow-
mortals by their personal but by their mental character;
but the popular conception of a great man delights in
dignifying his external habits, not only because great men
are rarely seen, and therefore acquire dignity from concealment, but because we conclude that they who excel
us so highly in important points can have nothing unimportant about them. We can hardly persuade ourselves, for instance, that Shakspeare ever disputed in a
club, or that Milton was fond of smoking : the ideas of
greatness and insignificance associate with difficulty, and
as extreme associations are seldom formed but by minds
of peculiar fancy and vigorous thought, it is evident they
will be rarely entertained by the majority of the world.
A tragic hero, who called for his follower or his horse,
would in real life call for him as easily and carelessly as
any other man, but in tragedy such a carelessness would
become ludicrous : the loftiness of his character must be
universal. An artist who would paint the battles of
Frederic of Prussia in a series of pictures, would study to
maintain this important character throughout; he would
not represent the chief sitting on horseback in a slovenly
manner and taking snuff, though the snuff-box no doubt
was of much importance at those times to his majesty,
who, as Pope says of Prince Eugene, was as great a taker
of snuff as of towns. So great a violence of contrast would
become caricature in painting, and in tragedy it would
degenerate into burlesque. Tragedy is an imitation of
life in passions ; it is comedy only which imitates both
passions and habits.

A tragic actor, then, is to be estimated, not as he always

copies nature, but as he satisfies the general opinion of life and manners. He must neither on the one hand debase his dignity by too natural a simplicity of manner, nor on the other give it a ridiculous elevation by pompousness and bombast. He cannot draw much of his knowledge from real life, because the loftier passions are rarely exhibited in the common intercourse of mankind ; but nevertheless he should not indulge himself in novelties of invention, because the hearts of his audience will be able to judge where their experience has no power. Much study should strengthen his judgment, since he must perfectly understand before he can feel his author and teach others to feel. Where there is strong natural genius, judgment will usually follow in the development of great passions, but it may fail in the minute proprieties of the stage : where there is not a strong natural genius, the contrary will be generally found. For the common actions of great characters he must study the manner of the stage, for their passions nothing but nature.

MR. KEMBLE.

MR. KEMBLE is a peculiar instance of almost all these essentials to good acting, and at the same time an example how much they may be injured by an indiscriminate application of study. His conceptions of character are strong where the characters themselves are strong, his attention to passions is fixed by large objects, he cannot sufficiently study the minute where minuteness is important, though, as I shall hereafter explain, he can give importance to minutenesses that mean nothing He appears to submit everything to his judgment, and exhibits little of the enthusiasm of genius. The grander

emotions are his chief study ; he attaches a kind of loftiness to every sensation that he indulges, and thus conceives with much force the more majestic passions, at
the same time that he is raised above the pathetic
passions, which always carry with them an air of weakness
and humility.

For the expression of the loftier emotions no actor is
gifted by nature with greater external means. His figure,
though not elegant, is manly and dignified, his features
are strongly marked with what is called the Roman
character, and his head altogether is the heroic head of
the antiquary and the artist. This tragic form assumes
excellently well the gait of royalty, the vigorous majesty
of the warrior, and the profound gravity of the sage : but
its seriousness is unbending ; his countenance seems to
despise the gaiety it labours to assume, and its comic
expression is comic because it is singularly wretched. Of
the passion of love he can express nothing ; the reason is
obvious ; love from its dependent nature must always,
unless associated with some other passion, betray an expression of tender feebleness, and such an expression is
unknown to Mr. Kemble's countenance. The attempt of
Mrs. Inchbald[1] to make Mr. Kemble a lover is more
honourable to her partiality for the friend than to her
affection for just criticism. She says that he can paint
love more vigorously than any other man, though he
cannot love *moderately :* in her opinion, " sighs, soft com-
plainings, a plaintive voice, and tender looks bespeak mere
moderation ; Mr. Kemble," she continues, " must be
struck to the heart's core, or not at all : he must be
wounded to the soul with grief, despair, or madness."

[1] " New British Theatre, with critical remarks by Mrs. Inchbald,"
No. III.—L. II.

But this is mistaking the associated passion for its companion. What a lover is he who can neither speak softly nor look tenderly? No man, according to this idea, can express a perfect love, that is, a love opposed to *mere moderation*, unless he is struck with grief, or desperate, or mad: but by such an association of outrageous passions, the expression of the individual one will not be a perfect, because it is not a simple expression: the actor who cannot express an individual passion without the assistance of others can no more be said to be master of that passion, than a singer can be called a master of his art who cannot sing without an accompaniment.

It is in characters that are occupied with themselves and with their own importance, it is in the systematic and exquisite revenge of Zanga,[1] in the indignant jealousy of Othello, and in the desperate ambition of King John, that Mr. Kemble is the actor. There is always something sublime in the sudden completion of great objects, and perhaps there is not a sublimer action on the stage than the stride of Mr. Kemble as Zanga, over the body of his victim, and his majestic exultation of revenge.

But if he succeeds in the prouder passions, his diligence of study has given him no less success in the expression of impressive seriousness.

The character of Penruddock in *The Wheel of Fortune*[2] is his greatest performance, and I believe it to be a perfect one. It is admirable, not because the tenderness of his love, as Mrs. Inchbald tells us, "appears beneath the roughest manners," but because the very defect which hurts his general style of acting, that studious and important preciseness, which is affectation in all his other

[1] In Young's tragedy, *The Revenge.*
[2] By Richard Cumberland.

characters, contributes to the strength, to the nature of Penruddock. Those who can discern any peculiar expression of tenderness under the roughness of Mr. Kemble's acting mistake their feelings for their observation : it is the tenderness the character is supposed to feel, not what he actually exhibits, it is the tenderness of the author not of the actor, which they discern : if there are one or two phrases of tenderness uttered by the stern recluse, they have a pathetic effect, not because they are expressed with peculiar tenderness by the actor, but because a soft emotion so unexpected in one of his appearance produces a strong effect from the strength of contrast. To give a man imaginary praise is to give him real dispraise. Mr. Kemble himself would never think of valuing his own performance for its tenderness of expression ; he would value it, and with justice, for its severity of expression, for its display of external philosophy, and for its contempt of everything that can no longer amuse.

Wherever this air of self-importance or abstraction is required, Mr. Kemble is excellent. It is no small praise to say of an actor that he excels in soliloquies : these solitary discourses require great judgment because the speaker has no assistance from others, and because the audience, always awake to action, is inclined during a soliloquy to seek repose in inattention. Indeed to gain the attention of an audience is always in some degree to gain their applause, and this applause must cheerfully be given to Mr. Kemble, who by his busy air and impressive manner always attaches importance to a speech of whatever interest or length. To this excellence in particular, and to the general action of the stage, he contributes by an exact knowledge of every stage artifice, local and

temporal ; and I could not but admire the judicious contrivance by which he added a considerable interest to his
first appearance in the season of 1805. The curtain rose
and discovered a study ; it was adorned with the most
natural literary disorder possible : the grave actor appeared writing at a table with open books here and there
about him ; the globes, the library, the furniture, everything had its use, and no doubt its effect, for an audience,
though perhaps insensibly, is always pleased with a
natural scene. Of another necessary stage artifice, which
is called *bye-play*, and which beguiles the intervals of
action by an air of perpetual occupation, he is a perfect
master ; he never stands feebly inactive, waiting for his
turn to speak ; he is never out of his place, he attends to
everything passing on the stage at once, nor does he
indulge himself in those complacent stares at the audience
which occupy inferior actors.

This attention to the minute, however, is often employed
needlessly ; he has made it a study hardly less important
than that of the passions, and hence arises the great fault
of his acting, a laborious and almost universal preciseness.
Some of the instances of this fault are so ludicrous that a
person who had not seen him would scarcely credit the relation. He sometimes turns from one object to another with
so cautious a circumflexion of head, that he is no doubt
very often pitied by the audience for having a stiff neck.
His words now and then follow one another so slowly, and
his face all the while assumes so methodical an expression,
that he seems reckoning how many lines he has learnt
by heart. I have known him make an eternal groan
upon the interjection *Oh!* as if he were determined to
show that his misery had not affected his lungs ; and to
represent an energetical address he has kept so continual

a jerking and nodding of the head, that at last, if he re-presented anything at all, it could be nothing but Saint Vitus's dance. By this study of nonentities it would appear that he never pulls out his handkerchief without a design upon the audience, that he has as much thought in making a step as making a speech, in short that his very finger is eloquent and that nothing means something. But all this neither delights nor deceives the audience : of an assembly collected together to enjoy a rational entertainment, the majority will always be displeased with what is irrational, though they may be unable to describe their sensations critically : irrationalities amuse in farce only. An audience when judging the common imitations of life have merely to say " Is it like ourselves ! "

Perhaps there is not a greater instance of the ill effects one bad habit like this can produce, than in Mr. Kemble's delivery. No actor in his declamation pleases more at some times or more offends at others. His voice is hollow and monotonous from the malformation, as it is said, of his organs of utterance : its weakness cannot command a variety of sound sufficiently powerful for all occasions, nor is its natural extent melodious or pleasing. But a voice naturally monotonous must be distinguished from a monotony of delivery ; the latter neglects emphasis and expression, the former, though it will not always obtain, may always attempt both. No player, perhaps, understands his author better, and such a knowledge will easily impart itself to others : his declamation therefore is confident and exact, he is at all times carefully distinct, and his general delivery is marked, expressive, and even powerful : the art with which he supplies the natural weakness of his voice by an energy and signifi-

cancy of utterance is truly admirable. But the same
affectation, which indulges itself in an indiscriminate
importance of manner, the same ambition of originality
where originality is least wanted, characterises Mr.
Kemble's pronunciation : it has induced him to defy all
orthoepy, and to allow no accent but what pleases his
caprice or his love of innovation.[1] To be novel for the
mere sake of novelty belongs neither to genius nor to
judgment. Mr. Kemble insists that the word *rode* should
be *rod, beard* is metamorphosed into *bird,* he never
pierces the heart but *purses* it, and *virtue* and *merchant*
become in the dialect of the kitchen *varchue* and
marchant. The strong syllable *er* appears to be an
abomination, and is never allowed utterance ; Pope says

> To err is human, to forgive divine—

but Mr. Kemble will not consent to this, he says

> To air is human—

making the moralist say that it is the nature of man to
dry his clean shirt or to take a walk. *Thy* is changed into
thĕ, probably because the sound of *my* is sometimes contracted into *mĕ ;* but mutabilities of pronunciation in one
word never argue for them in another ; people are not
accustomed to say, such a man has a *wrĕ* neck, or that it
is very *drĕ* weather. Dr. Johnson, who had an antipathy
to the pronunciation *wĭnd,* and wished to call it *wīnd,*
attacked the custom by a ludicrous assemblage and mis-
pronunciation of other words, in which the letter *i* is
naturally long, and said with much critical gravity,—"*I
have a mīnd to fīnd why you call that wĭnd.*" But this

[1] See Appendix.

pleasantry did not change the pronunciation in general converse. Let us see how Mr. Kemble would improve the following lines : we will put his improvement after the original, since the beauty of the contrast will be greater :

> Virtue, thy happy wisdom's known
> In making what we wish our own ;
> Nay, e'en to wish what wishes thee
> Imparts the blest reality :
> For since the soul that pierces mine,
> Sweet Myra's soul, is full of thine,
> In my breast too thy spirit stirs,
> Since all my soul is full of her's !

Mr. Kemble's improvement :

> *Varchue, the* happy wisdom's known
> In making what we wish our own ;
> Nay, e'en to wish what wishes thee
> ᴜ Imparts the best reality :
> For since the soul that *purses* mine,
> Sweet Myra's soul, is full of thine,
> In my breast too thy spirit *stares,*
> Since all my soul is full of *hairs !*

This is very amusing, but there is no rule for pronunciation but custom ; as customs change, actors may change ; but no individual should alter what he has no reason for altering, or what has either a bad effect or none at all when altered. There have been several attempts to vary the mode of spelling now in use ; the latest innovation was practised by Ritson,[1] a man of curious and happy research into old English literature, and one who might have boasted a better originality than that of making his words unintelligible. Nobody has adopted a single one of

[1] Joseph Ritson, the antiquary.

these innovations, first because it is painful to depart from old rules and habits, and secondly, because it is still more painful to depart from them without a cause. For the same reasons, nobody will adopt Mr. Kemble's pronunciations ; and if he were to carry his dialect into private life, he would be either pitied or laughed at. But why place his ambition where there are no hopes of original praise? I could mispronounce much better than he when I was a mere infant.

Upon the whole, Mr. Kemble appears to be an actor of correct rather than quick conception, of studious rather than universal or equal judgment, of powers some naturally defective but admirably improved and others excellent by nature but still more so by art ; in short of a genius more compulsive of respect than attractive of delight. He does not present one the idea of a man who grasps with the force of genius, but of one who overcomes by the toil of attention. He never rises and sinks as in the enthusiasm of the moment ; his ascension though grand is careful, and when he sinks it is with preparation and dignity. There are actors who may occasionally please more, but not one who is paid a more universal or profound attention.

MRS. SIDDONS.

To write a criticism on Mrs. Siddons is to write a panegyric, and a panegyric of a very peculiar sort, for the praise will be true. Like her elder brother, she has a marked and noble countenance, and a figure more dignified than graceful, and she is like him in all his good qualities, but not any of his bad ones. If Mr. Kemble studiously meditates a step or an attitude in the midst of passion, Mrs. Siddons never thinks about either, and therefore is always natural, because on occasions of great feeling it is the passions should influence the actions. Attitudes are not to be studied, as old Havard[1] used to study them, between six looking-glasses : feel the passion, and the action will follow. I know it has been denied that actors sympathise with the feelings they represent, and among other critics Dr. Johnson is supposed to have denied it. The Doctor was accustomed to talk very loudly at the play upon divers subjects, even when his friend Garrick was electrifying the house with his most wonderful scenes, and the worst of it was that he usually sat in one of the stage boxes : the actor remonstrated with him one night after the representation, and complained that the talking "disturbed his feelings : " "*Pshaw ! David,*" replied the critic, "*Punch has no feelings.*"[2] But the Doctor was fond of saying his good things as well as lesser geniuses, and to say a good thing is not always to say a true one or one that is intended to be true. To call his friend a puppet, to give so contemptuous an appellation to a man whose powers he was at other times happy to respect, and whose death he lamented as having "eclipsed the gaiety of nations," must be considered as a familiar pleasantry rather than a betrayed opinion. The best way to solve the difficulty is

[1] William Havard (1710–1778) was an actor of considerable judgment and assiduity, but not brilliant.

[2] " Mr. Murphy remembered being in conversation with Johnson near the side of the scenes during the tragedy of *King Lear ;* when Garrick came off the stage he said, ' You two talk so loud you destroy all my feelings.'—' Prithee,' replied Johnson, ' do not talk of feelings; Punch has no feelings.' " Croker's *Boswell* under date, Sept. 21, 1777.

to apply to an actor himself, but as I am not in the way of such an application, I think the complaint made by Garrick will do as well, since he talks of his feelings as the means necessary to his performance. It appears to me that the countenance cannot express a single passion perfectly, unless the passion is first felt. It is easy to grin representations of joy, and to pull down the muscles of the countenance as an imitation of sorrow, but a keen observer of human nature and its effects will easily detect the cheat. There are nerves and muscles requisite to expression, that will not answer the will on common occasions ; but to represent a passion with truth, every nerve and muscle should be in its proper action, or the representation becomes weak and confused, melancholy is mistaken for grief, and pleasure for delight. It is from this feebleness of emotion so many dull actors endeavour to supply passion with vehemence of action and voice, as jugglers are talkative and bustling to beguile scrutiny. I have somewhere heard that Mrs. Siddons has talked of the real agitation which the performance of some of her characters has made her feel.

To see the bewildered melancholy of Lady Macbeth walking in her sleep, or the widow's mute stare of perfected misery by the corpse of the gamester Beverley,[1] two of the sublimest pieces of acting on the English stage, would argue this point better than a thousand critics. Mrs. Siddons has the air of never being the actress ; she seems unconscious that there is a motley crowd called a pit waiting to applaud her, or that there are a dozen fiddlers waiting for her exit. This is always one of the marks of a great actor. The player who amuses himself by looking at the audience for admiration may

[1] In Edward Moore's tragedy, *The Gamester.*

be assured he never gets any.   It is in acting as in conferring obligations : one should have the air of doing
nothing for a return.

If Mrs. Siddons has not every single requisite to a
perfect tragedian, it is the amatory pathetic.   In the
despair of Belvidera, for instance, she rises to sublimity,
but in the tenderness of Belvidera she preserves too
stately and self-subdued an air.   She can overpower,
astonish, afflict, but she cannot win : her majestic presence and commanding features seem to disregard love,
as a trifle to which they cannot descend.   But it does not
follow that a tragedian unable to sink into the softness of
the tender passion is the more to be respected for his
undeviating dignity and spirit : it does not follow that he
has a loftier genius.   Love, though humble, never moves
our contempt ; on the contrary, it adds new interest to a
character at other times dignified.   In real life the greatest
heroes and sages have acquired an extraordinary charm
from their union of wisdom and tenderness, of conquest
and gallant submission : and as we doubly admire the
wise Plato for his amatory effusions and the chivalrous
spirit of Henry the Great for the tenderness of his love,
so on the stage the tragedian who unites the hero and
the lover, that is, who can display either character as it
is required, is the more admirable genius.   Besides, the
figure of Mrs. Siddons is now too large and too matronly
to represent youth, and particularly the immediate passions
of youth ; we hope that by the next season she will have
given up the performance of characters suited neither to
her age nor her abilities.[1]

[1] It is not quite clear to what characters Leigh Hunt is here referring.
In the season 1805-6 Mrs. Siddons played Mrs. Beverley (*Gamester*),
Jane Shore, Mrs. Haller (*Stranger*), Calista (*Fair Penitent*), Euphrasia

After this one defect, I have in vain considered and reconsidered all the tragedies in which I have seen her, to find the shadow of another. She unites with her noble conceptions of nature every advantage of art, every knowledge of stage propriety and effect. This knowledge, however, she displays not with the pompous minuteness of Mr. Kemble, but with that natural carelessness which shows it to be the result of genius rather than grave study. If there is a gesture in the midst, or an attitude in the interval of action, it is the result of the impassioned moment ; one can hardly imagine there has been any such thing as a rehearsal for powers so natural and so spirited. Of the force of such mere action I recollect a sublime instance displayed by Mrs. Siddons in the insipid tragedy of *The Grecian Daughter*.[1] This heroine has obtained for her aged and imprisoned father some unexpected assistance from the guard Philotas : transported with gratitude, but having nothing from the poet to give expression to her feelings, she starts with extended arms and casts herself in mute prostration at his feet. I shall never forget the glow which rushed to my cheeks at this sublime action.

These are the effects Mr. Kemble should study, and

(*Grecian Daughter*), Lady Macbeth, Belvidera, Elvira (*Pizarro*), and Queen Katharine. In the season 1806-7 she repeated most of these characters, and also played Isabella (*Fatal Marriage*), Volumnia, and Lady Randolph. None of these characters need be conceived as more youthful than Belvidera and Euphrasia, both of which the critic selects for special praise. Up to the time of her retirement in 1812 she confined herself to the above characters, with the addition of Zara, The Countess of Narbonne, Hermione (*Winter's Tale*), Constance, and Portia. She had played Imogen for the last time in 1801-2, Isabella (*Measure for Measure*) and Desdemona in 1803-4.

[1] By Arthur Murphy. See Appendix.

not the clap-provoking frivolities of ending every speech with an energetic dash of the fist, or of running off the stage after a vehement declamation, as if the actor was in haste to get his pint of wine. If the brother and sister are compared, the palm both of genius and of judgment must undoubtedly be given to Mrs. Siddons. I question whether she understands her authors so intimately, but she gives double effect to their important passages, and their unimportant ones are allowed to sink into their proper mediocrity : where everything is raised into significance, the significance is destroyed. If an artist would study the expression of the passions, let him lay by the pictures of Le Brun,[1] and copy the looks of Mrs. Siddons.

MR. POPE.

WHEN I place Mr. Pope immediately after Mrs. Siddons, everybody will see I do not criticise the actors according to their rank. But it is for the sake of contrast. If we have just had an example of almost perfect tragedy, we have now an instance of every fault that can make it not only imperfect but disgusting. Mr. Pope has not one requisite to an actor but a good voice, and this he uses so unmercifully on all occasions that its value is lost, and he contrives to turn it into a defect. His face is as hard, as immovable, and as void of meaning as an oak wainscot ; his eyes, which should endeavour to throw some meaning into his vociferous declamation, he generally contrives to keep almost shut ; and what would make

[1] Charles Lebrun, 1619–1690, author of *Conférence sur l'expression des différents caractères des passions* and *Traité de la Physionomie.* The designs in these works have been frequently reproduced.

another actor merely serious is enough to put him in a passion. In short, when Shakspeare wrote his description of "a robustious fellow, who tears a passion to tatters," one would suppose that he had been shown, by some supernatural means, the future race of actors, as Macbeth had a prophetic view of Banquo's race, and that the robustious phantom was Mr. Pope. Here is an actor, then, without face, expression, or delivery, and yet this complication of negative qualities finds means to be clapped in the theatre and panegyrised in the newspapers. This inconsistency must be explained. As to the newspapers,[1] and their praise of this gentleman, I do not wish to repeat all the prevailing stories. Who does not know their corruptions? There is, however, an infallible method of obtaining a clap from the galleries, and there is an art known at the theatre by the name of *clap-trapping*, which Mr. Pope has shown great wisdom in studying. It consists in nothing more than in gradually raising the voice as the speech draws to a conclusion, making an alarming outcry on the last four or five lines, or suddenly dropping them into a tremulous but energetic undertone, and with a vigorous jerk of the right arm rushing off the stage. All this astonishes the galleries ; they are persuaded it must be something very fine, because it is so important and so unintelligible, and they clap for the sake of their own reputation.

One might be apt to wonder at Mr. Pope's total want of various expression, when his merit as an artist is considered. It should seem that the same imitative observation, which gives so natural an elegance to his portraits on canvas, should enliven and adorn his portraits on the stage : that the same elegant conception which enables

[1] See Appendix.

3

him to throw grace into the attitudes and meaning into the eyes of others, should inspire his action with variety and his looks with intelligence.

It is in the acknowledgment of gesture and attitude, but more particularly in the variation of countenance, in the adaption of look to feeling, that the actor is best known. Mr. Pope, in his general style, has but two gestures, which follow each other in monotonous alternation, like the jerks of a toy-shop harlequin : one is a mere extension of the arms, and is used on all occasions of candour, of acknowledgment, of remonstrance, and of explanation ; the other, for occasions of vehemence or of grandeur, is an elevation of the arms, like the gesture of Raphael's *St. Paul preaching at Athens*, an action which becomes the more absurd on common occasions, from its real sublimity. If Mr. Pope, however, is confined to two expressions in his gesture, he has but two expressions in his look : a flat indifference, which is used on all sober occasions, and an angry frown, which is used on all impassioned ones. With these two looks he undertakes to represent all the passions, gentle as well as violent ; he is like a quack who, with a phial in each hand, undertakes to perform every possible wonder, while the only thing to be wondered at is his cheating the mob. The best character he performs is Othello, because he performs it in a mask : for when an actor's face is not exactly seen, an audience is content to supply by its own imagination the want of expression, just as in reading a book we figure to ourselves the countenance of the persons interested. But when we are presented with the real countenance, we are disappointed if our imagination is not assisted in its turn ; the picture presented to our eyes should animate the picture presented to our mind ; if either of them differ, or if the former is less lively than the latter, a sensation of discord is produced, and destroys the effect of nature, which is always harmonious.

The pain we feel at bad acting seems, indeed, to be entirely the result of a want of harmony. We are pleased when the actor's external action corresponds with the action of his mind, when his eye answers his heart, when all we see is the animated picture of all we feel: we are displeased whenever the passion and the expression are at variance, when the countenance does not become a second language to the dialogue, when moderate tones express vehement emotions and when vehement tones express moderate emotions, when, in short, Mr. Pope is not Rolla [1] or Romeo but Mr. Pope. A musician who tells us that he is going to play a melancholy movement, and then dashes his harp or his piano in a fury, cannot disappoint us more than this actor, when he raises from language merely sorrowful an expression of boisterous passion. The character of Hotspur has been reckoned a proper one for Mr. Pope, because it is loud and violent ; these are good reasons certainly, and we would rather hear him in Hotspur than in Hamlet, for noise, like any other enjoyment, is delightful in its proper season only. But to act Hotspur well is a mark of no great talent ; of all expressions, violence is the most easily affected, because the conception of violence has no sensation of restraint, it has no feelings to hide or to repress, and no niceties of action to study. The gentler passions give us leisure to examine them, we can follow every variation of feeling and every change of expression ; but here we have leisure for nothing ; everything is rapid and confused ; we are in the condition of a man who should attempt to count the spokes of a wheel in a chariot-race.

[1] In Sheridan's *Pizarro* (from Kotzebue).

Mr. Pope, in short, may be considered as an example of the little value of a good voice unaccompanied with expression, while Mr. Kemble is a proof how much may be done by an expressive countenance and manner with the worst voice in the world.

But perhaps as I can say nothing of Mr. Pope as a tragic actor, I may be expected to say something of him as a comic one, for he does act in comedy. Any one, however, who examines this double gift, will discover that to act in comedy and to be a comic actor are two very different things. Mr. Kemble performs in comedy, but who will call Mr. Kemble a comic actor? Who will reckon up the comic actors, and say, "We have Bannister, and Lewis, and Munden, and Kemble?" If Mr. Pope acts in sentimental comedy, what is called sentimental comedy is nothing more than a mixture of tragedy and comedy, or, if Dr. Johnson's definition is to be allowed, it is sometimes entire tragedy, for he calls tragedy "a dramatic representation of a serious action." There may be very often a serious character in humorous comedies, such as a sober merchant, a careful father, or one of those useless useful friends who serve as a kind of foil to a gay hero; but the actor who performs these characters never excites our livelier feelings or our mirth, and therefore cannot be called a comic actor. Lord Townley, for instance, in *The Provoked Husband*, is merely a tragic character who has stepped into comedy: Mr. Kemble represents Lord Townley with much gravity and stateliness; yet nobody in the pit ever said at seeing this character, "Really that is very comic!" It is necessary to a comic actor that he should be able to excite our laughter, or at least our smiles; but Mr. Pope never excites either, at any rate not designedly. It is for this reason that he has been placed among the tragedians, and that Mr. Charles Kemble, Mr. Henry Johnston, Mr. Murray, and Mr. Siddons [1] will be placed among them too. All these gentlemen might undoubtedly be called comic actors, as Robin Hood's companion, who was seven feet high, was called Little John ; or we might say such a man was as comic as Mr. Kemble or Mr. Henry Johnston, just as we say such a thing is as smooth as a file. But upon plain subjects I would rather be plain spoken.

[1] The essays on Mr. Johnston, Mr. Murray, and Mr. Siddons are not included in this edition. See Introduction. The essay on Charles Kemble appears under Section iii.—"Tragedy and Comedy."

Section II.—*COMEDY.*

I could write a long treatise upon comedy ; I could tell my readers that its name is derived from the Greek ; that the ancients did not know as much of it as the moderns ; that some paltry writers, such as Congreve, Dryden, and Voltaire, have defined it to be a natural picture of human follies ; and that divers great geniuses, such as Reynolds, Dibdin, and Cherry, insist it means nothing but farce ; but this I leave to Miss Seward,[1] or Mr. Pratt,[2] or some other original writer, who says a number of good things quite foreign to the subject. I am writing not upon authors, but actors.

It has long been a question whether as great a genius is required in comic as in tragic acting. This question must be agitated with respect to the best actors only, for I have no doubt that mediocrity is more easily attained in tragedy : a distinct utterance and a grave indifference of visage, which is the look of common life, will qualify a man to make sublime speeches on the stage, and to call himself a tragedian ; he need not have any face whatever ; all that is necessary is to saw the air alternately with the arms and to identify every syllable, and the newspapers will tell him he is a most respectable performer. But to

---

[1] Anna Seward 1747–1809, the " Swan of Lichfield."

[2] Samuel Jackson Pratt, 1749–1814, " Courtney Melmoth."

22

be comic it is absolutely necessary to have a command of feature and of tone : comedy deals much in equivocation, the humour of which is enforced by the opposite expressions of look and of tone, or by an agreement of both differing from the speech itself. I could bring twenty tragedians, that without either look or tone, except a vacant seriousness and a hollow monotony, shall go through twenty speeches in a very respectable manner ; but show me a single comedian that can do such a thing without being hissed.

Nevertheless, it appears to me that a great tragedian is a finer genius than a great comedian. Passions are more difficult of conception than habits ; tragedy is wholly occupied with passions, and though comedy is occupied both with passions and habits, yet it is principally with the latter. The passions of comedy are more faint than those of tragedy; they are rather emotions and inclinations ; for if they strengthen into a powerful character they become tragic. Thus sentimental comedy, in which the passions sometimes exert all their strength, is nothing more than an alternate compound of comedy and tragedy, just as the *Orlando* of Ariosto or the *Lutrin* of Boileau is a mixture of seriousness and pleasantry.

It is more difficult to conceive [1] passions than habits,

---

[1] I would not be understood in the following argument as using the words *conception* and *imagination* indiscriminately. *Conception* is a dependent and passive capacity, that receives ideas suggested by others, and therefore belongs principally to the *actor*, who displays the ideas of the *poet*. *Imagination* is an original and active power, that forms its own images and impresses them upon the minds of others : it belongs therefore more to the *poet*. But actors have sometimes to imagine as well as to conceive, for if the suggestions of the poet are few and feeble, they must be invigorated by the additional ideas of the actor, who in this instance *imagines* as well as *conceives*. Thus the sublime action

principally because the former are less subject to common observation. In comic characters we generally recognise the manners or peculiarities of some person with whom we are acquainted, or who is at least known in the world; but of the deeper tragic passions we have only read or heard. We never see in society an impassioned character like Macbeth, or King Lear, or Hamlet. Such characters exhibit themselves on great occasions only, their very nature prevents their appearance in common life; but habits appear nowhere else; the idea of passion, therefore, requires more imagination than that of habit.

Imagination, then, is the great test of genius; that which is done by imagination is more difficult than that which is performed by discernment or experience. It is for this reason that the actor is to be estimated, like the painter and the poet, not for his representation of the common occurrences of the world, not for his discernment of the familiarities of life, but for his idea of images never submitted to the observation of the senses. In the polite arts imagination is always more esteemed than humour: humour presents us with visible objects, imagination

> . . . bodies forth
> The forms of things unseen, . . .
> . . . and gives to airy nothing
> A local habitation and a name.

Both Smirke[1] and Hogarth are great geniuses, yet who

related of Mrs. Siddons in page 15 was entirely the result of imagination, as the author had given no suggestion whatever of such an idea. If the characters in modern plays were represented with the mere action and spirit which the ideas of the authors suggested, they would never disgrace the stage for a whole season instead of a single night.—L. H.

[1] Robert Smirke, R.A., 1752-1845, painted subjects from *Don Quixote*, Shakespeare, &c.

will say that Smirke is as great a genius as West,[1] or
Hogarth as Michael Angelo? Congreve knew all the
elegancies and Butler all the eccentricities of wit, and
both were intimately acquainted with the follies of mankind ; yet who will compare the author of *Hudibras* with
the author of *Paradise Lost,* or the humour of Congreve
with the sublimities of Shakspeare? Swift is most probably the greatest wit that ever lived, but he will never
obtain a reputation equal to that of Milton or Shakspeare.
It is observed even of schoolboys, that those who surpass
their companions in humour and mimicry do not promise so great a genius as those who exhibit a serious and
romantic disposition, who are fonder of Homer and
Sophocles than Terence and Plautus, and who, in their
themes and declamations, wander from familiar expression
into far-fetched and even extravagant language. Humour
surprises and wins, but it never elevates ; it meets with
too great familiarity our common ideas, and, while it
amuses us with its powers, leaves us sufficient contentment
with our own. Imagination surprises, wins, and elevates
too ; it carries us off from our level with earthly objects
and ordinary cares, it bears the mind to its highest pitch
of ascent, transports us through every region of thought
and of feeling, and teaches us that we have something
within us more than mortal. A tragic actor, therefore,
as he displays more imagination, possesses a more *poetical*
genius than a comedian. This epithet, if it is allowed in
its present application, might finish my argument ; the
word *poetical,* when applied to genius, always indicates the
highest genius, and it is observable that those arts to which
the epithet can with propriety be given, are superior to

---

[1] Benjamin West, P.R.A., 1738-1820, painted "The Death of
General Wolfe," and other pictures in the heroic style.

those which, disagreeing with its implied qualities, have not sufficient *mind* to deserve it. Thus a great painter is a finer genius than a great musician, because he displays more imagination and consequently more of the *poetical ;* Handel, who rises to the sublime in music, is a more *poetical* genius than Reeve,[1] who deals in the quirks and jollities of the humorous ballad ; and the lowest musician is a more *poetical* genius than the maker of a musical instrument, because the former requires some degree of imagination while the latter is a mere manufacturer. By the same reasoning, Mrs. Siddons, who excels in the sublime and the pathetic, which require a lofty imagination and powerful sensibility, is an actress of a *poetical* mind ; but we can never say that Mr. Lewis, who represents common life and is employed principally in mere copy, is of a genius rising to the *poetical*, though he is an excellent comedian.

Another argument for the superior genius of the tragic actor is his superiority of taste : he delights in the highest of intellectual pleasures, the pathetic and the sublime : he turns from the familiar vanities and vulgarities of common life to the contemplation of heroism, of wisdom, and of virtue : he is occupied with the soul only. The comedian, on the other hand, has little to do with the intellectual properties of human nature ; his attention is directed to the lighter follies of men, to fashions and habits, to the familiar domestic manners, in short, to trifling and adventitious qualities rather than to inherent character. This superior taste will always be found united with superiority of genius : nobody will deny that Milton possessed a greater taste than Butler, Corneille than

[1] William Reeve, 1757–1818, composer of many musical pieces for Astley's, Covent Garden, Sadlers' Wells, &c.

Rabelais, or Dante than Tassoni : Raphael, who studied the most beautiful objects, and excelled in the simple dignity of nature, and Guido, who dipped his pencil in tears, strike us with their noble taste more particularly after we have seen the grotesque postures and monstrosities of Callot, or the historical attempts of Hogarth, who, great as he was in humorous character, and discriminative of fine taste in others, certainly displayed no fine taste in his own serious works.

I have always thought it an argument for the superiority of poetry over the other polite arts, that it is more productive of polite manners than either painting or music. There is not a poet, whose life is recorded by Dr. Johnson, nor indeed any great poet with whose private history we are acquainted, who did not bear the character of a gentleman ;[1] we cannot say this of painters, and certainly not of musicians. I do not mean to argue that politeness is always a mark of genius, for I meet with polite fools every day of my life, though to be polite at all times and upon all occasions, or, in other words, to be perfectly well-bred, is the effect of no mean sense : but as good breeding among men of genius is generally found to be proportionate to their mental excellence, we may conclude that the superior manners of tragic over comic actors in private life is some proof of their superior genius. A tragedian, being always occupied in the study of noble manners and in the contempla-

---

[1] I could never exactly understand what Addison meant, when, in answer to a correspondent who desired to know the *chief* qualification of a good poet, he replied " *To be a very well-bred man.*" But we may certainly gather from this reply that he had a very high opinion of the general manners and polite character of great poets. *Spectator*, No. 314.—L. II.

tion of great ideas, naturally acquires a personal behaviour superior to that of the comedian, who can seldom escape the contagion of the familiar and ridiculous manners which he delights to represent. Mimics cannot always get rid of their mimicry ; those who are fond of imitating stutterers are often well rewarded by becoming stutterers themselves. It is true, I advance this argument concerning the politeness of actors not so much from my own experience as from public opinion. But when public opinions are lasting they are seldom wrong.

The public, indeed, might always settle disputes about public men, if we could obtain its general opinion ; and I have no doubt that it conceives a higher character of tragic than of comic genius. An audience who on the same evening should see Mr. Kemble in King John and Mr. Bannister in Young Philpot,[1] would feel no hesitation in thinking the former the greater genius, though it might be more delighted with the latter. There are some people in the world, full of careless good-nature and merriment, whom everybody calls *jolly fellows*, and with whom everybody thinks himself on a level, because though they always amuse they never elevate the mind. Such is the admiration an audience feels for a comic actor : there is something of respect wanting. The dignity of the tragedian, on the contrary, as it is elevated above common life, is elevated above our familiarity, and is contemplated with respect as well as pleasure.

Nevertheless, a comic genius requires no common fancy and no common observation of life. There are tricks and shadows of character, which are so rarely exhibited in the world, that they are to be deduced from

[1] In Murphy's farce, *The Citizen.*

the probable effects of general character rather than from known peculiarities, and must therefore be left to the imagination. The chief qualification of a comedian is an instantaneous perception of everything that varies from the general seriousness of human nature, or from that behaviour which is contemplated with a serious indifference. This variation must nevertheless be found in real life, or it becomes farcical ; and as the actor shows his genius in the conception of humorous character, so it is in the nice division of comedy from farce that he shows his judgment. Such a division is a mark of his genius also, for however an able comedian may some-times indulge in forced humour, a perpetual caricature is always a mark of a lesser genius : it is like bombast in tragedy, it paints to the senses not to the heart, and diverts the attention of the audience from too close an examination into the player's imitative talent. When the actor is to represent the *Merry-Andrew* drolleries of Reynolds, let him, in the name of good-nature, do as much as he can for the author by all the grins and grimaces his jaws can contrive ; but let him preserve in their noble simplicity of shape the natural images of Shakspeare and of Congreve. When we see the nature of these fine geniuses distorted, it is like contemplating a deformed person once beautiful ; we think of nothing but the beauty it originally possessed, we cannot laugh, we feel sorrow and pity.

MR. BANNISTER.

WHEN I write the name of Bannister, a host of whimsical forms and humorous characters seems to rise before me, and I had much rather lay down my pen and indulge myself in laughter. But there is a time for all things; laughter is a social pleasure, and as I have got nobody to laugh with me, I had better be composed.

Mr. Bannister is the first low comedian on the stage. Let an author present him with a humorous idea, whether it be of jollity, of ludicrous distress, or of grave indifference, whether it be mock-heroic, burlesque, or mimicry, and he embodies it with an instantaneous felicity. No actor enters so well into the spirit of his audience as well as his author, for he engages your attention immediately by seeming to care nothing about you. The stage appears to be his own room, of which the audience compose the fourth wall: if they clap him, he does not stand still to enjoy their applause; he continues the action, if he cannot continue the dialogue; and this is the surest way to continue their applause. The stage is always supposed to be an actual room, or other scene, totally abstracted from an observant multitude, just like the room in which I am now scribbling: an actor, therefore, who indulges himself every moment in looking at the audience and acknowledging their approbation, is just as ridiculous as I should be myself, if I were to look every moment at the reflection of my own smiles in my looking-glass, or make a bow to the houses on the other side of the way.

Though I hardly know which excellence to prefer in Mr. Bannister's general performance, yet upon the whole I think his expression of jovial honesty, or what may be called *heartiness*, is the most prominent. There is no actor who makes the slightest approach to him in this expression, and therefore no actor equals him in the character of a sailor. Mr. Munden gives us all the *rough*, but none of the *pleasant* honesty of a sailor, and he has at all times too much grimace for natural jollity : the heart does not study to torture the countenance. Mr. Bannister possesses all the firmness with all the generous good-nature of the seaman ; his open smile, his sincere tone of voice, his careless gait, his person that seems to have undergone all that long and robust labour that must gain the sailor a day of jollity. In short, every action of his body and his mind belongs to that generous race, of whom Charles the Second observed they "got their money like horses and spent it like asses."

But this is not the only expression in which this natural actor is unrivalled ; there is another in which he is, if possible, still less approachable by any performer : that of *ludicrous distress*. It is extremely difficult to manage this expression so as to render it agreeable to the spectators, because it is calculated to excite their contempt : the only method is to unite with it an air of good-nature, for good-nature is a qualification, in the possession of which no degree of rank or of sense can be altogether unpleasing. Bannister's natural air of sincerity easily gives him this recommendation. Who, in the midst of laughter, has not felt for the well-meaning Marplot [1] whining at his unfortunate interferences, or at the blusterous Acres quaking in the manfulness of his duelling? I cannot conceive a more humorous scene than that in *The Rivals* where Acres is waiting with a pistol in each hand for the man he has challenged : the author's dialogue between the challenger and his second possesses an exquisite humour, but it is doubly enlivened by the consummate bye-play of Bannister, who, as the

[1] In Mrs. Centlivre's comedy, *The Busybody*.

hour of combat approaches, begins to show personal symptoms of terror, gradually loses the affected boldness of his voice, and trembles first in his hands and knees and then in his whole body. No description of mine could represent the ludicrous woe of his countenance, when he is coolly asked by his second whether, in case of a mischance, he would choose a snug grave in the neighbouring church, or be pickled and sent home to the country; nor can any action be more humorously imagined than his impotent endeavours to pick up his hat which he pushes about with his quivering fingers.

There is yet a third excellence in which he would still have had no competitor, if the stage had not lately been enriched by the acquisition of Mathews, an actor of whom it is difficult to say whether his characters belong most to him or he to his characters. The greatest comedians have thought themselves happy in understanding one or two comic characters, but what shall we say of Bannister, who in one night personates six, and with such felicity that by the greater part of the audience he is sometimes taken for some unknown actor? If he never acted in any other play, his performance of Colonel Feignwell in *A Bold Stroke for a Wife* would stamp him as one of the greatest and most versatile comedians. Of his five transmigrations, into a Beau, an Antiquarian Traveller, a Dutch Merchant, an Old Steward, and a Quaker, the first is his least happy metamorphosis, because he cannot affect an air of jauntiness: his imitation of an awkward beau, in the character of Acres, for instance, is perfectly happy; but the robust person and the robust manners, which render this *awkward* imitation easy, prevent him from giving a real picture of finical showiness. The

Antiquarian Traveller I do not pretend to criticise; Bannister makes it amusing, as he does everything; but the authoress, Mrs. Centlivre, has made it like nothing upon earth. That a man in a long beard should pretend, in an age like this, to come to an antiquarian with a story of his wonderful travels and of a girdle that makes him invisible, and that he should put this girdle on the antiquarian and persuade him that he is not to be seen, is a story fit for Mother Bunch's Tales only. If such a traveller were to come to one of the most doting antiquaries living, he would be sent to Bow Street for an impostor. But I am afraid I am wandering too much upon Mrs. Centlivre, who without doubt wrote the most entertaining dramas of intrigue with a genius infinitely greater, and a modesty infinitely less, than that of her sex in general, and who delighted, whenever she could not be obscene, to be improbable. If our Antiquarian Traveller, however, is not to be found in real life, the Dutch Merchant is a very natural personage, and is most naturally represented by Mr. Bannister. Every citizen in the Pit must feel his heart grow warm when he sees the substantial Dutchman come lounging, with a sort of dignified roll, into the Stock Exchange, with one hand in his breeches pocket and the other grasping a huge tobacco-pipe, with an air, in short, expressive of pocket-warmth and of a sovereign contempt for every one void of a good conscience and of stock. This is another excellent specimen of Mr. Bannister's idea of good-natured bluntness and plain dealing, to which his natural air of sincerity, that cannot be too often admired, so forcibly contributes; it is a faultless imitation; his very coat, reaching almost down to his heels and swinging as he walks, has something warm and monied in it. The

4

transformation into the Quaker is not very difficult to
any actor ; an unmeaning sedateness of countenance, and
an inflexible stiffness of limbs, are all that is requisite : for
this reason any of our indifferent comedians can assume
this image-character, and there is a man of the name of
Dormer, who, though he can do nothing else, performs
Obadiah Prim very insipidly and very naturally. But
Mr. Bannister's metamorphosis into the decrepid Old
Steward whining for the death of his master is as
admirable as it is difficult. The state of old age is a
condition of which no man perhaps can enter exactly
into the personal feelings : it has no desire of motion ;
but a player is always wishing to be in a state of action,
and acquires a habit of exercising his limbs momentarily,
as may be seen sometimes in his gestures off the stage.
The principal deficiency in the representation of old age
generally arises from this propensity to motion. Thus
an indifferent player, who naturally thinks that a stick
will add to the decrepid appearance of age, forgets his
support in the eagerness of winning applause by a show
of energy, and thumps the floor or amuses his chin with
it. An actor named Purser, who is very well when he
plays the fool, and then only when the fool is a footman,
sometimes misrepresents old age in this manner, and
beats his mouth with his cane when he would affect an
attitude of thought, like a young beau in a room who
does it for want of thought. But Mr. Bannister in his
old age is not Mr. Bannister in his manhood : he loses at
once all his natural vivacity and robustness of manner,
and sinks into that dependent feebleness which seems at
once to fear and to look for protection from every
surrounding object. Other old men on the stage take
off their hats or pull out their handkerchiefs as com-

posedly as young men ; but Mr. Bannister has the
perpetual tremulousness and impotent eagerness of
superannuation : if he takes out a paper he quivers it
about before he can open it, and if he makes a speech
of any length he enfeebles it by frequent breaks of
forgetfulness and weariness, with that sort of pause,
which seems as if it were recollecting what had already
been said, or preparing for what remained to be said.
One admirable mark of the feeble impatience of age
must ever be remembered as one of the most natural
originalities in Mr. Bannister's personation of the Old
Steward. In thanking the heir of his deceased master
for continuing some family favours to him, and in
promising to overcome the violence of his grief for so
heavy a loss, he trembles through four or five words
with tolerable composure ; but suddenly bursts out into
a weeping of impatient recollection and exclaims with
rapidity—"But when I think of my poor master my
tears will flow." An inferior actor would have added
these words to his promise of patience in the same
tone ; but Mr. Bannister understands that violent grief
becomes only the more violent from temporary repression.

But to enumerate all the original excellencies of Mr.
Bannister's comic genius would be to enumerate every
comic character he performs, and I must not linger on
the recollection of his mischievous boyishness in Tony
Lumpkin, his good-humoured vulgarity in Scrub,[1] or his
strutting vanity as the footman Lissardo,[2] when he
delights himself and torments his neglected mistress
by displaying his new ring, or endeavours with an important interference to settle the disputes of the two

---

[1] In Farquhar's *Beaux' Stratagem.*
[2] In Mrs. Centlivre's comedy of *The Wonder.*

maid servants in love with him. There is one performance, however, of which it is impossible not to indulge
myself in the recollection. It is that of Young Philpot
in Murphy's comedy of the *Citizen :* if anything can
excel the grave moniedness he affects in order to cheat
his father, it is his description of the garret-author, of
that miserable pamphleteer who, holding one baby on his
knee and rocking another in the cradle with his foot,
is writing a political essay with his right hand while he
occasionally twirls round a scrag of roast pork with his
left : during this description the mirth of the audience
becomes impatient to express itself, till the admirable
mimic having wound up his climax by a picture of the
author's wife washing clothes in a corner to the song of
Sweet Passion of Love, it bursts into a tempestuous
approbation. As this description is introduced by the
author of the *Citizen* as a mere anecdote related by
Young Philpot, a common actor would have told it in a
passing way as anecdotes are commonly related : Bannister puts himself in the situation of the belaboured
pamphleteer, he dandles his child, then writes a line,
then rocks the other child, then writes another line, then
gives the griskin a twist ; his handkerchief is taken out
and he becomes the author's wife, accompanies the dabs
and scrubbings of the washing-tub with *Sweet Passion of
Love,* and as its ardour grows more vehement screams
out the tender love-song to the furious wringing of her
small linen. I am afraid I am a little prolix here, but
what we remember with delight we are always precise in
describing, lest we should not tell the story as well as it
was told us.

Mr. Bannister, in short, in his comic character is always
animated, is always natural, except when he assumes the

lively *gentleman :* the attainment of this character does not appear to be in the nature of his broad vigorous style of acting : he is a giant bestriding a butterfly. His Mercutio is not gay, but *jolly ;* it exhibits, not the elegant vivacity of the *gentleman,* but the boisterous mirth of the *honest fellow :* the audience immediately feel themselves on a level with him, and this familiar sensation is always a proof that the *gentleman* is absent. The passion for affecting this character is, unfortunately, almost as universal on the stage as it is in real life : an actor thinks he has nothing to do but to dress himself fashionably and clap a cocked hat under his arm, and he becomes the *gentleman.* Thus the stage is crowded with *genteel* comedians, from Mr. Henry Johnston, who is nothing less than a tragedy hero in a round hat, down to Mr. John Palmer, who looks as if he had just emerged from a kitchen ; and yet, after all, there are but two actors who are happy in an elegant vivacity.

But it is worthy of greater praise to catch the feelings than the manners of men. Mr. Bannister contrives to mingle the *heart* with his broadest humour, and it is this union of things so often remote that constitutes his most solid praise : Foote could imitate everybody, but he was a mere mimic though an admirable one : few of our modern comedians have any feeling ; Fawcett has very little, Simmons has none, Lewis fritters his away, and Munden mocks his own pathetic with a thousand wry faces. The most pleasing excellence is that which is performed with the least effort ; to mingle feeling with humour, and humour with feeling, seems to be Mr. Bannister's nature rather than his art ; this felicity gives him another praise, which he must be content however to share with Dowton, an actor whom I conceive to be one of the first comic geniuses our stage has produced. For the qualification, to which I allude, I do not know that there is any name : the Italians, whose motley productions have given them a knack at verbal compounds, may have an appellation for it that I have not discovered. It cannot be called tragi-comedy, for though it breathes a gentle spirit of humour, its essence is really serious ; it differs widely from *ludicrous distress*, for though it raises our smiles, it never raises our contempt, but in the midst of our very inclination to be amused absolutely moves us with a pathetic sympathy ; perhaps it may be defined the *humorous pathetic*, the art of raising our tears and our smiles together, while each have a simple and distinct cause. But I shall explain myself best by example.

In the play of *John Bull*,[1] which glimmers with the hasty genius of an author who could do better, the principal character, called Job Thornberry, is a country tradesman of an excellent heart and much natural sense, who being forsaken by a seduced but amiable daughter, is overwhelmed alternately with indignation at her fault and pity at her misfortune ; there is a vulgarity about the man, but it renders his grief more natural ; his thoughts, unrestrained by refinement, suggest no concealment of emotion, and therefore he is loud and bitter in his sorrow. This abandonment to his feelings, acting upon manners naturally coarse, produces now and then a kind of awkward pathetic, at which we cannot but smile : the actor's skill, therefore, should prevent the pathetic from degenerating into a mere laughable eccentricity, it should interest our feeling while it provokes our risibility, in short should depress while it enlivens

[1] By George Colman the younger.

and enliven while it depresses. This union of opposite effects requires some portion of tragic as well as comic powers, and Bannister's Job Thornberry is respected with all its bluntness, and pitied with all its oddity ; the tears and the smiles of his audience break out together, and sorrow and mirth are united. When the spectators are inclined to be merry, he recalls their sympathy with some look or gesture of manly sorrow ; when they are fixed on his grief, he strikes out their smiles by some rapid touch of peevish impatience or some whimpering turn of voice. It is thus that he holds the balance of tragic and comic feeling in the character of Walter in the *Children in the Wood,*[1] though in his representation of that honest servant as well as of the dishonest one in the drama of *Deaf and Dumb,*[2] he shows that he can divest himself entirely of his mirth, and though he assumes nothing of the dignity of tragedy, can express its homelier feelings with a strongly continued effect. When he returns home, in the *Children in the Wood,* after having lost the infants, and careless of his inquiring friends, drops with a stare of mute anguish into a seat, he produces as true a feeling in the audience as Mrs. Siddons would produce in loftier characters. Then again his natural coarse cheerfulness, struggling with his sorrow, breaks forth in some quaint reply or ludicrous habit of gesture. This is the true art of acting. A player who gives none of these touches and varieties of character is like a Chinese painter, whose men and women are mere outlines, with indistinct dashes for features.

[1] A Musical Entertainment by Thomas Morton. It is the story of the Babes in the Wood with a happy ending.

[2] A drama from the French of Bouilly, by Thomas Holcroft.

Bannister would really be an unexceptionable actor, if he could think no more of the man of fashion and elegance. What Voltaire said to Congreve, when the latter hoped he was not visited as an author but as a gentleman, may be said with sufficient politeness by the town to Mr. Bannister, "If you were nothing but a gentleman, sir, depend upon it I should not take the trouble of coming to see you."

MR. LEWIS.

It is not necessary to turn hermit and live upon roots in order to gain a healthy and animated old age ; temperance is the strengthener of existence equally in the city and in the field ; if old Parr, when he was upwards of a hundred years old, stood in a white sheet for an offence not very possible to old age, the great Newton, at a period of life little less advanced, reviewed and corrected the most profound productions of the human mind. The powers of Mr. Lewis at the age of fifty-seven will not astonish those who have considered these matters, but they will astonish every one who has an impaired memory or a shaking hand, they will astonish those old young men who cannot carry a glass of wine to their lips without making all the angles in Euclid.

It must, however, be universally surprising that of the only two actors on the stage who can represent the careless vivacity of youth, an old man is the most lively. Elliston gives us an excellent picture of youthful animation, but it is an animation corrected by an attention to *the gentleman :* Lewis is all heart, all fire ; he does not study forms and ceremonies, he is polite from a natural wish to please, and if he is not always the gentleman nobody doubts what he could be. This comparison will be well understood by those who have seen the two actors in the character of Rover in *Wild Oats*.[1] In the scene where the young rustic expresses his admiration of Rover's theatrical talents, and at parting shakes his hand with good-natured familiarity, Elliston in the midst of his reciprocal good humour has too much the air of one who condescends ; Lewis gives the bumpkin as hearty a shake as if it had been his brother, and forgets everything but the honest soul of his new acquaintance.

It is in characters like these, full of frankness and vivacity, that Mr. Lewis claims an original excellence. I do not see by what propriety he has been called by the exclusive title of *Gentleman* Lewis ; perhaps it is because he never acts vulgarly, and without doubt vulgarity seems totally impossible to an actor of his manners : but it does not follow that he who never acts vulgarly should always act with refinement. The character of a complete gentleman is a very difficult one to define. Perhaps it consists in the power of pleasing refinedly ; but this refinement is the consequence of an habitual study to please, and the careless good-nature of some characters represented by Mr. Lewis, of *Rover* for instance, does not please by its refinement but by its innate goodness of heart. That this last qualification is not necessary to the gentleman is a melancholy truth which every one who has seen the world must acknowledge : Car, Earl of Somerset,[2] was the most polished as well as the most abandoned man of his time, and that courtly scoundrel, the Earl of Chesterfield, who would have made his own

[1] By John O'Keeffe.

[2] Robert Carr, or Ker (died 1645), the favourite of James I., convicted of the murder of Sir Thomas Overbury.

son a hypocrite and a liar, was the finest gentleman in
Europe.

As it is impossible, however, in real life to find a man
without his defects, so if we meet with one on the stage,
who has every excellence of mind, he may still exhibit
the defects of habit or of trifling affectation. The
habitual errors of Mr. Lewis seem to be the effect of
a too lively rather than a too dull conception of
character. His two principal defects are a shaking of
the head and a respiration of the breath, expressive of a
kind of self-satisfaction at a cunning, or what is called a
knowing, idea. These expressions moderately used might
throw much meaning into his manner ; but the more
natural they are when considered as the effect of a
sudden happiness of thought, the more unnatural they
become when they endeavour to throw vivacity into dull
or indifferent speeches, since it is not the manner should
enliven the thought but the thought should enliven the
manner. Perhaps the chief reason why Frenchmen
appear so frivolous to us, is the perpetual vivacity of
their manner upon the most unimportant occasions and
during the most inanimate speeches ; and the worst of
this habit is, that when these vivacious gentlemen really
do mean to be peculiarly impressive, they have no more
effect upon us than at any other time, because their
manner cannot be more important than it has already been
upon trifles. It must be observed, however, that Mr.
Lewis's extreme vivacity is an error attributable to the
great interest he takes in his characters, and not, like the
errors of Mr. Kemble, to that abstracted artifice which
induces the actor to study his audience more than his
character.

But for the other defect of this actor, his eccentricities

in dress, I know not how to account. Of all ridiculous
characters on the stage, the modern beau should be the
most accurately dressed, because his attention to dress is
one of his most ridiculous failings, and because we observe
it every day in real life. Mr. Lewis in such a character
not only dresses himself in waistcoats and breeches in
which nobody else dresses himself, but very frequently
astonishes us by flaming in coats ribbed and coloured ; if
he could divest himself on such occasions of his native
elegance of manners and would merely stick a nosegay in
his breast, he might pass for an ancient French dancing-
master, he might look like a lord mayor's footman, but
he never will be a fashionable beau. The only reason
we can possibly imagine for such an extravagance is the
same that induced the late Mr. Murphy to wear a bag-
wig to the day of his death, and that still induces a certain lady of rank to cumber herself with the sacks and
hoop-petticoats of the last reign ; perhaps chequered coats
were the fashion in Mr. Lewis's youth, and as he was
much admired in them at that time, he considers his
powers of pleasing as some way connected with a Harlequin jacket still. This is the only drawback on the
excellence of Mr. Lewis's beau, which in every respect of
mind (if the word mind may be used when speaking of
beaux) wants nothing of perfection.

Mr. Lewis is without doubt the most complete fop on
the stage : he inimitably affects all the laborious carelessness of action, the important indifference of voice, and
the natural vacuity of look, that are the only social dis-
tinctions of those ineffable animals called loungers.

Yet from this very excellence arises a defect in his
general style of acting. That which is the chief employ-
ment of our minds, generally gives a turn to all our ideas ;

the same habit, which makes the shopkeeper so often allude to his business in common conversation, induces Mr. Kemble to carry his natural important stiffness into all his characters, and gives a tinge of the beau to Mr. Lewis in his most finished portraits of the gentleman. In his elegant sentiment, in the very seriousness of his love, there is a flippant airiness, a vivacious importance, a sort of French flutter, that hurts the sincerity of his manner and looks more like a study to recommend himself than to please others for their own sakes. The less he has to do with the polished gentleman, the less does he practise this frippery, and the little which he preserves at all times adds to the harmless nonsense of some of his characters, and gives to his less refined ones an affectation by no means unpleasing. If his Squire Groom in *Love A-la-mode*, who is a Newmarket hero, has now and then a little too much of refined action for the *blood*, it must be recollected that the Squire is paying his addresses to a lady, and may therefore be allowed to affect something a little out of his sphere.

With this character in *Love A-la-mode*, if I were writing a panegyric instead of a criticism, I would sum up my highest praises of Mr. Lewis. Who should fear the approach of old age, should dread its debility of frame and its dissolution of intellect, when they see what temperance can perform? For my part, when I see an old man, who wears a star and is called *His Grace*, tottering and coughing upon a bolstered poney, and another old man, whom nobody can discover to be old, sporting on the stage with all the vivacity of youth, I bless my good fortune that I have to labour for my future livelihood, and say to myself " It's much better to keep one's health than to keep a seraglio."

MR. MUNDEN.

ONE of the most amiable effects of the modern drama is to injure those to whom it is most indebted for support. If the principal characters of Reynolds and of Dibdin are always out of nature, their representation, as I have already hinted, must be unnatural also ; and as our comic actors are perpetually employed upon these punchinellos, as they are always labouring to grimace and grin them into applause, they become habituated and even partial to their antics, and can never afterwards separate the effect from the means, the applause from the unnatural style of acting. The extravagance, therefore, of look and gesture, so necessary to the caricatures of our farci-comic writers, they cannot help carrying into the characters of our best dramatists, to which it is every way injurious.

This is the great fault of Mr. Munden, who is unluckily one of the strongest supports to our gigantic farces, and whose powers, like his features, have been so twisted out of their proper direction, that they seem unable to recover themselves. Almost the whole force of his acting consists in two or three ludicrous gestures and an innumerable variety of as fanciful contortions of countenance as ever threw woman into hysterics : his features are like the reflection of a man's face in a ruffled stream, they undergo a perpetual undulation of grin : every emotion is attended by a grimace, which he by no means wishes to be considered as unstudied, for if it has not immediately its effect upon the spectators, he improves or continues it till it has ; and I have seen his interlocutor disconcerted, and the performance stopped, by the unseasonable laughter of the audience, who were conquered into the notice of a posthumous joke by this ambitious pertinacity of muscle.

All this suits admirably well with a character entirely farcical, or with one that has no intrinsic humour, and I recollect no actor, who by the mere abuse of his features could gain so much favour for a modern comedy. If ever such an abuse becomes natural, it is in the deformity of drunkenness. Mr. Munden, therefore, whose action is as confined as his features are vagrant, excels in the relaxed gesture and variable fatuity of intoxication. His most entertaining performances are always of this kind, as that, for instance, of Crack in the *Turnpike Gate* and the Captain's servant in the musical puppet-show called the *English Fleet.*[1] His attitude and looks in the latter piece, when he receives a ring from a lady as a reward for some courageous service, his tottering earnestness in contemplating the honour on his finger, and the conscious glance which he turns now and then at his captain behind him, exhibit a masterpiece of drunken vanity. These are the touches which brighten the miserable daubs of our dramatists, which throw life into their inanimate figures, and character into their half-formed countenances. Mr. Munden, in his imitation of an intoxicated man, always shows his judgment by standing as much as possible in one place. Our actors in general seem to forget that a person under the influence of liquor, unless he is almost insensible, always attempts a command of himself and restrains his motions as much as the weakness of his limbs will permit ; they are too fond of reeling round the stage, and jerking up one leg at every step, like a tavern blood affecting his six bottles.

[1] *The Turnpike Gate* was a Musical Entertainment by T. Knight ; *The English Fleet* was by Thomas Dibdin.

I have heard that the late Mr. Suett used always to be really drunk when he performed a drunkard, but the generality of our performers may certainly be exculpated from such a charge: perhaps the only actor who approaches Munden in this exquisite display of brutality is Mr. Robert Palmer. Truly we stage-critics treat of lofty matters !

But of simplicity Mr. Munden shows not a shadow ; and as old men in general, and particularly old soldiers and citizens, have long forgotten the antics of schoolboys, this perpetual mouth-making destroys his natural representation of age : no man in years accompanies his whole conversation with this harmony or rather this discord of feature ; an old soldier would despise it as boyish, and an old citizen as unprofitable : an old courtier, perhaps, if his king is fond of buffoonery, is more likely to accommodate his countenance to the sallies of those about him, but when Mr. Munden represents Polonius, he forgets he is in a gloomy court, where the king and queen are afflicted with melancholy and the young prince Hamlet supposed to be deranged. In his performance of Menenius in *Coriolanus*, this buffoonery is still more inconsistent. Menenius was a man of wit and prudence, and is celebrated in history for his fable of the belly and the members, with which he appeased the discordant divisions of the people : Shakspeare, taking advantage of the familiarity of that popular address, has perhaps rendered the language and the manners of Menenius too generally familiar, and given the comedian an opportunity of displaying his merriment rather too broadly ; but it should never be forgotten that Menenius was not only of the patrician order, a class of men proverbially haughty, but that he was the intimate friend of the haughty Coriolanus, who was the proudest man in Rome and not very likely to associate with buffoons. If Shakspeare, there-fore, in his fondness for generalising the character of men, and in his determination to avoid what may be called a chronology of nature, has represented Menenius in the light of a merry old modern nobleman, the actor would show his art and his classical judgment in preventing his mirth from extravagance by every possible temperance of action, so that the man of humour might not entirely overcome the man of rank. At any rate Mr. Munden should endeavour to moderate the restlessness of his muscles in representing a patrician and a senator. But then the galleries would not laugh.

This actor, in short, loses half his proper effect by the very strength of his powers : he brings as much expres-sion into his face for an emotion or even an inuendo, as he ought for the liveliest passions : thus he rarely gives us the shadows or gradations of feeling, from the mere exertion of his expression : he is a jumper who, in order to leap four yards, takes a spring that inevitably carries him six : he is like that poetical artist Mr. Fuseli, who to exhibit his anatomical skill discloses every joint and muscle of a clothed figure, when he should merely shadow out their appearances.

Strange ! By the means defeated of the ends !

MR. LISTON.

THOSE comedians who are the most happy in their study of nature might very probably, with the slightest atten-tion, become equally happy in caricature, for as they must learn to separate nature from its contrarieties, so they must undoubtedly understand the contrarieties to be separated. Garrick, who understood nature in all its differences, was an admirable mimic, and I can discover no natural comedian of the present day, who is not also an excellent caricaturist, unless indeed we except Dowton, who seems to have no powers but for powerful nature.

A natural actor, however, may be said to be natural in two distinct senses; he may be correct in the representation of nature, or he may be correct in the representation of the deviations from nature, and either of these correctnesses is called natural, for this word is applied to imitations, not in its expression of the qualities of nature only, but in its relation to any appearance in life, natural or artificial, involuntary or assumed; thus we say that Mrs. Siddons is natural in her expression of grief, which is a natural passion, and that Mr. Mathews is natural in his imitation of Punch, who is certainly no very natural personage.

In Mr. Liston's best performances he may be called natural in every sense of the word. His accuracy of conception enables him to represent with equal felicity the most true characters and the most affected habits, and he passes from the simplest rustic to the most conceited pretender with undiminished easiness of attainment. The actor never carries him beyond the characteristic strength of his part; he adds nothing of stage affectation and diminishes nothing of nature; yet his manner is so irresistibly humorous, that he can put the audience into good humour with less effort, perhaps, than any other comedian.

His happiest performances are his ignorant rustics, and his most inaccurate his old men. Of mere old age he represents nothing. If his usual style of acting is of a

still nature, yet it is not able to sink into personal weakness or weariness ; if he is often quaint and dispassionate,
his general simplicity gives him too youthful an air to
represent the experience and the acquired art of a long
life.   His old men, therefore, are old in nothing but their
wrinkles and walking-sticks, and as he cannot see his own
wrinkles and does not in common want a stick to support
himself, his accustomed youthful spirits soon make him
forget both.

In more youthful characters of little vigour, whose
chief quality is a mixture of ignorance and self-complacency, Mr. Liston indulges in his proper feebleness.
There may be observed a general repose of limb and of
intellect in his style of acting exquisitely conducive to
the character of contented folly ; he can seem at ease
with all around him, but most voluptuously so with himself : his smile of conceit is most peculiarly significant
and enjoying, and I think that the happiest picture of
ignorant vanity I ever saw was his representation of the
foolish military inamorato in the disjointed farce of
Catch Him Who Can: [1] nothing could be more irresistible,
when he wished to insinuate any one of his peculiar
accomplishments, than the curvature of his extended
hand, the languid drop of his eyelids, and the thaw of his
usually rigid muscles into an affected easiness of smile.
For his performance of the Quaker in *Five Miles Off* [2] he
is to be praised, if it is only for divesting the manners of
the Quakers of their stage-exaggeration, and contenting
himself with the caricature which their vegetating affectation really produces in itself.   Mathews, perhaps, had
done this before in Miss Chambers's elegant comedy, the
School for Friends, but a good deal depends upon the

[1] By Theodore Hook.   [2] By Thomas Dibdin.

author in these cases, and the picture was so judiciously drawn by Miss Chambers that it was next to impossible to render it extravagant. Mr. Dibdin, with equal judgment, no doubt, always leaves room for the caricaturing fancy of the actor, for he cannot produce a picture even badly finished ; but Mr. Liston made his Quaker like something natural in spite of the farcical speeches put into his mouth, which a Quaker would call profane, and the farcical love-song, which a Quaker, whose sect never sings, would shudder to hear. He neither walked in one undeviating straight line, nor glued his clasped hands to his bosom, nor conversed in the recitative of a parish-clerk, nor rose at every emphasis upon his toes, nor ended all his speeches with a nasal groan. The actors are much mistaken if they think the Quakers do all this even on enthusiastic occasions : a stage-Quaker, like Munden in *Wild Oats*, dances up and down to his own sing-song like a stiff puppet on a humdrum barrel-organ ; but I question whether those well-clothed ascetics would not consider this extreme as approaching to the abominable art of music.

It is in the rawness of country simplicity that Mr. Liston excels all his contemporaries. A mere rusticity is not difficult of conception, for it exhibits itself entirely in personal habits, and those the most easy of imitation, because they require little or no control of limbs or of countenance : but the different expressions of absolute inexperience, its astonishment, its affected incredulousness and real credulity, its utterly false conclusions, and its self-betraying involuntary acknowledgments, require a nice observation and a powerful explanation of countenance and voice. They who have seen Mr. Liston as Jacob Gawky in Miss Lee's *Chapter of Accidents* have

seen all these varieties inimitably separated and expressed.
But his peculiar expression of amazed ignorance shines
with all its stupidity in a singular drama called the *Three
and the Deuce.*[1]   He represents a country lad, who
imagines his sister to have been seduced by a vivacious
gentleman, and accordingly taxes the seducer with his
crime in a very homely way : the gentleman, who is one
of three brothers exactly resembling each other, and who
really knows something of the girl, but wishes to divert
the rustic's attention, starts into one of his usual fits of
gaiety, and seizing his brother's astonished footman, who
had taken him for his grave master, by one hand, and
the rustic by the other, commences a majestic minuet,
which he accompanies with some burlesque song ; the
footman, who had been frequently astonished already by
this merry alteration of his supposed master, is represented by Mathews, who joins in the dance with a countenance perfectly convinced of the man's insanity ; but
Liston, whose faculties seem deadened by this freak, and
who has evidently risen from mere amazement to an
admiration of the gentleman's lively talents, acquiesces
in the movement with a submission most ludicrously
earnest, and follows the steps by a seeming magic, at
once imitating his leader's affected importance, and
appearing totally abstracted from every earthly consideration but his present enchantment : his mouth is
open and fixed, his eyes scarcely staring, but full of a
leaden attention, and his face altogether expressive of an
ineffable mixture of ignorance, admiration, and astonishment.   This is certainly one of the most ludicrous scenes
on the stage, and really provokes one to laughter by the
very recollection.

[1] A Comic Drama by Prince Hoare.

Upon the whole, Liston is a very original and a very unaffected actor ; nor is he of the lower rank of comedians, for he excels in painting emotions rather than habits,[1] and therefore has a more intellectual praise than Fawcett, than Simmons, and even than Munden in his present degenerate farcicality. What Dryden said of Shadwell[2] in an intellectual sense, may be applied to Mr. Liston in an imitative one, for he must be—

Own'd, without dispute,
Thro' all the realms of nonsense, absolute.

MR. EMERY.

IF education, or early habits, or a former profession will sometimes enable an actor to represent any peculiar character to more advantage, the same causes will often prevent his success in others, and it is most likely that for one imitation which they may enliven, there will be several which will insensibly catch the habits of that one and therefore be injured. Thus Incledon the singer, whose merit raised him from the coarse vulgarity of a sea-life, and who has really a finer voice than any English singer on the stage, ever succeeds in descriptions of his former life, but when he attempts a love-song or any other more refined part of his science, he cannot help reminding us of the sailor ; his voice swells into its ancient jollity, and indulges, if I may use the word, in that slang of sound, which expresses at once joviality, confidence, and vulgarity : after the finest tones in the world, and in the midst perhaps of very pathetic words,

[1] A further elucidation of Mr. Liston's theatrical character by a comparison with that of Mr. Emery will be found in the next article. —L. H.
[2] In " Mac Flecknoe," lines 5, 6.

he seems about to slide off into a *Right fol de ra*, or some such energetic burden of ballad-singing.

It is most probably the same with Mr. Emery. I have been credibly informed that he has a touch of country dialect off the stage, and as his early life is the most likely cause of such a habit, it may certainly be presumed that it is the cause also of his theatrical deficiency in variety, and of the obstinate contradiction which this dialect makes to the truth of all his characters but his country-men.

Mr. Emery is an actor of little variety, however he may attempt it, or however he may be dissatisfied with his exquisite powers of rustic imitation. He does not err so grossly indeed as to attempt young gentlemen, like Fawcett, but even his ungenteel or his vulgar old ones might convince him, if men could ever know themselves, that he can act nothing without rusticity. Independently of his dialect, he cannot shake off his natural activity of body and of mind and compose himself to the feebleness and dulness of age. His old Count Curvoso, in the *Cabinet*,[1] looks like a tall lad with a round ruddy face who had painted his forehead with wrinkles for a frolic ; and it was certainly a strange judgment in the manager of the Haymarket theatre,[2] which gave him the vulgar old peer in the *Heir at Law* and the young countryman to Munden, who has nothing rustic about him, unless indeed some of his grins be like those merry monstrosities exhibited at country fairs through a horse-collar. The same deficiency in the imitation of age I have already observed of Liston, so that our two principal rustics are in this respect unequal to the other good comedians.

[1] Comic Opera by Thomas Dibdin.
[2] George Colman the younger, author of the *Heir at Law*.

It is in the general habits of rustics, personal, moral, and intellectual, that Mr. Emery displays his decided and great originality. To produce all the examples of this ability would be to write a list of all his rustic characters, for I do not know one in which he is not altogether excellent and almost perfect. But when an actor does not excel in many distinct classes of character, I do not think it necessary, in order to estimate his powers, to enumerate a great number of his performances, for there is seldom any difference in his representation of one class of persons but what is made by the difference of dialogue. Emery's class of rustics may be divided into three parts, the serious, the comic, and the tragi-comic, and the three admirable examples which may be produced of this variety will suffice for a multitude of monotonous ones. Of that expression which diverts with its manner while it raises a serious impression with its sentiments, and which is therefore so difficult in its complication, Mr. Emery exhibits a powerful instance in the character of Farmer Ashfield in *Speed the Plough*.[1] Inferior actors indulge their want of discrimination in representing every countryman as a lounging vulgar boor, for, as they catch externals only, they are obliged to exaggerate them in order to supply the deficiency of a more thorough imitation. Mr. Emery understands all the gradations of rusticity: his Farmer Ashfield, though it occasionally raises our mirth by its familiarity and its want of town manners, is manly and attractive of respect: like the master of a family, he always appears attentive to the concerns of those about him, and never breaks out of his natural cares and employments to amuse the audience at the expense of forgetting his character. In an actor who

[1] By Thomas Morton.

excels chiefly in gross rusticity, this species of refinement might have well set bounds both to his own expectation of variety and to that of his audience; but the play called the *School of Reform*[1] gave new light to his genius, and in the character of the rustic villain Tyke he astonished the town by a display of feeling and passion almost amounting to the most thrilling tragedy. His performance in this play I must call tragi-comic, not because he displayed that amalgamation of the humorous and the serious which the word tragi-comedy in our age implies, but because, as its ancient meaning signified, he excelled in alternate scenes of comedy and tragedy. This single display, indeed, would have induced me to rank Mr. Emery with the performers who have gained reputation both in tragedy and comedy, but I recollected that, however critics may talk about the sufficiency of terror and pity to create tragic delight, all ages have agreed by their own measure of approbation to demand a certain degree of refinement as a necessary recommendation of those feelings, and that when Mr. Emery had exhibited a new talent and raised an unexpected wonder for the moment, he had done as much as a tragedy rustic could do, for his dialect and his manners would inevitably have rendered his tragedy comic in a very short time. Hume, in his Dissertations,[2] has thought this refinement so requisite, that he has in a great measure deduced the pleasurable effect of tragedy from the beauty of the poet's language rather than the nature of his characters, though this doctrine seems a curious disproportion of the means to the end, and the object of his inquiry appears to me still

[1] By Thomas Morton.

[2] *Four Dissertations*, 1757. See *Philosophical Works of David Hume.* Ed. Green and Grose, 1875. Vol. iii., Essay xxii. *Of Tragedy.*

undiscovered. That such a refinement, however, is eminently desirable a few familiar recollections would convince us. Those tragic writers, who have ventured farthest into the familiarity of private life, have always elevated their characters above the usual level of common life, particularly with regard to language : and with still greater care would they have avoided any national or local peculiarities of person or habit. George Barnwell, for instance, was a common city apprentice, but does he talk as apprentices usually do ? or to equalise the case more with that of Emery's Tyke, would the author have ventured to give him the cockney dialect ? Would not such a dialect, though it might have been endured at the first utterance and in some scene of peculiar suffering to the speaker, have totally deranged the gravity of the pit in a few moments ? Every tragic effect, however, short as it may be, which is possible to be produced from a vulgar character, Mr. Emery certainly produces from this. Tyke is a villainous rustic, who has not sufficient strength of mind to shake off his depraved habits, though he is occasionally agonised by the tortures of conscience. It is in the scene where he describes the agony of his old father, as he stood upon the beach to witness his son's transportation, that he surprised us with this tragic originality. His description of their last adieu, of his parent kneeling to bless him just as the vessel was moving, of his own despair, the blood that seemed to burst from his eyes, and his fall of senselessness to the ground, was given with so unexpected an elevation of manner, so wild an air of wretchedness, and with actions of such pitiable self-abhorrence, that in spite of his country dialect, which he still very naturally preserved, and the utter vulgarity of his personal appearance, the

audience on the first night were electrified for the moment
with the truest terror and pity. His haggard demeanour
and the outcry of his despair live before me at this instant.

I scarcely know in what class of acting to place his
performance of Caliban in the *Tempest;* perhaps in that
which I have ventured to call the humorous pathetic;
for a great distinction must be made between those two
styles which our language has indiscriminately called
tragi-comedy, between an alternation of the tragic and
the comic, and that disagreement of the language with
the speaker, the effect from the cause, or the end with
the intention, which renders a real seriousness ludicrous.
The humour of Caliban (though I think there are many
persons to whom this monster appears too much perse-
cuted and too revengeful to be at all humorous) must
rise from his roughness of manners and his infinite awe
at the divinity of the sailor who had made him drunk;
and this roughness as well as awe Mr. Emery most inimitably displays, particularly in the vehement manner and
high voice with which he curses Prospero, and that
thoughtful lowness of tone, softened from its usual hoarse
brutality, with which he worships his new deity. Mr.
Emery, notwithstanding the coarseness of style necessary
to the parts he performs, is a truly poetical actor, and in
all the varieties of his poet's flight keeps by his side with
the quickest observation. In this character he again
approaches to terrific tragedy, when he describes the
various tortures inflicted on him by the magician and the
surrounding snakes that "stare and hiss him into madness." [1] This idea, which is truly the "fine frenzy" of the

---

[1] Sometimes am I
All wound with adders, who with cloven tongues
Do hiss me into madness.
                    Tempest, Act ii., Sc. 2.

poet, and hovers on that verge of fancy beyond which it
is a pain even for poetry to venture, is brought before the
spectators with all the loathing and violence of desperate
wretchedness : the monster hugs and shrinks into himself, grows louder and more shuddering as he proceeds,
and when he pictures the torment that almost turns his
brain, glares with his eyes and gnashes his teeth with an
impatient impotence of revenge.

I am afraid it is somewhat like anti-climax to descend
to broad farce after all this display of terror ; but the
most natural excellence of Emery is in the mixture of
rustic ignorance and cunning, and of this mixture his
John Lump in the *Review*[1] is an inimitable instance. In
each successive scene, the fancy of the author has given
him an opportunity of showing his unwearied flow of
nature and of humour. Whether he is recommending
himself to Mr. Deputy Bull as a servant by a list of
unnecessary rustic accomplishments, or bashfully attend-
ing to the supposed overtures of Miss Grace Gaylove, or
felicitating himself, in a vain soliloquy, on the beauty of
his person, he exhibits the same knowledge of every
movement and sensation of gross rusticity. In this last
scene, when he has just parted with the lady, and medi-
tated a little, nothing can be better imagined than his
half-smothered spluttering laughter of triumph at his
fancied importance to the lady's heart. A piteous or
joyous contempt of others, the result of rustic ignorance,
is indeed one of his best expressions ; and he is inimitable
in that peculiarity of gesture which affects a superiority
in sense or artifice, and announces the eagerness of vanity
by preceding its language ; such, for instance, is the pro-
trusion of chin and earnest self-satisfaction with which

[1] A musical farce, by George Colman the younger.

he commences a story or prepares himself to convince another by argument.

If our two stage-rustics, Emery and Liston, are compared, it will be found that the former is more skilled in the habits and cunning of rusticity, and the latter in its simplicity and ignorance. Emery has appropriated to himself the dialects and the personal peculiarities of countrymen ; Liston is the rustic merely because nothing so ignorant and so gaping is ever discovered in town. Emery excels in vain insolence, in the fatigue of comprehending another, and in the meditation of a cunning answer ; Liston in the apparent inability to object, in a hopelessness of perception, and in the fatuity of mere astonishment. Their expression of vanity is in proportion to their expression of ignorance : what is the affectation of superiority in Emery, becomes an important self-conviction in Liston. Emery, full of whim and artifice, is the countryman who has associated with the geniuses of inns, and has preserved his rusticity and his ignorance after acquiring a contempt for both ; Liston is the confirmed, inexperienced, and stupid bumpkin, with all the prejudices of unvaried locality, and with not even sufficient intelligence to imbibe the manner and eccentricities of his neighbours. Upon the whole, Liston is more dry in his humour, more effective with a little exertion and upon inefficient subjects, and altogether more unaffected ; but the greater genius must certainly be allowed to Emery, who exhibits a more discriminative minuteness and variety of expression, and who excels at once in the habits and the passions of the country. In proportion as an actor can pierce beyond externals into the human heart, so is he great in his profession. The actor of habits is a gardener, who raises elegant flowers and distributes gaudy parterres, but knows nothing beyond the surface of the earth. The actor of passions is a miner, who digs into the depth and darkness of the creation, and brings to light its most hidden and valuable stores.

MR. DOWTON.

IF we are to agree with Dr. Johnson, that genius is the power of a naturally strong intellect accidentally directed to one particular object, and that it would excel in any attainment which peculiarly excited its attention, it will be difficult to decide what accident could have directed an universal genius to so many objects at once, what concentration of casualties could have made Garrick so equally excellent in a hundred different characters, or Voltaire so equally delightful in a hundred kinds of writings. The most prominent argument, however, against such a definition is the wrong judgment which men of genius have so often conceived of their own powers : their attention has been directed to object after object without the least success, till at length they have suited their powers where they had neither an expectation nor a wish to suit them. This is the perpetual case on the stage. Mr. Bannister, at one period of his earlier days, almost confined himself to lofty tragedy ; both Mr. Kemble and Mrs. Siddons have flattered themselves they were comedians, and indeed there is hardly a good performer on the stage who has not at some time or other in the same way mistaken inclination for ability.

Mr. Dowton has shared the errors as well as the genius of his contemporaries. If there is no actor living who can represent the testiness of age and the passionate

feeling of impatient honesty with half his felicity, there
is at the same time no actor who imitates his inferiors
with worse success. I recollect but one character in low
comedy, that of King Arthur in *Tom Thumb*,[1] which he
sustains with any power ; and this character is of a
peculiar kind of humour not usual with vulgar comic
actors, and not difficult, I should imagine, even with
professed tragedians ; indeed, if the great requisite in
mock-heroic acting is a serious manner opposed to
ludicrous words, it will not be found very difficult to
any performer. But why Mr. Dowton, who cannot use
his jaws like a piece of indiarubber, should attempt to
grin like Munden, or why, with neither an iron voice nor
a brazen countenance, he should condescend to copy Mr.
Fawcett, is totally inexplicable. In fact, his powers will
scarcely bend to any expression that is not elicited by the
stronger emotions that approximate to tragedy, and which
are comic in proportion only as they are familiar, or
extreme, or unreasonable, or strangely contrasted with
their object. He is therefore a comedian of very superior
powers in his happier characters ; since he catches the
feelings rather than the habits of men, and I really never
lamented an actor's want of self-knowledge so much as
when I saw so true a genius degrading his abilities and
his fame by aping the uncouth levities of Mr. Fawcett in
the part of Doctor Pangloss. His farcical servants and
sailors are not a jot the more natural or more facetious ;
he always appears above them ; his emotions are too
refined, and his faces not even passably monstrous.

But who is so impressive, so striking, so thrilling, as
this actor in scenes of angry perturbation or of anger
subdued by the patience or pleasantry of its object ? His

[1] A burletta, by Kane O'Hara.

Captain Cape, in the *Old Maid*,[1] is a rough miniature of his Sir Anthony Absolute in the *Rivals*, and both are inimitable portraits of a mind naturally good, indulging itself in bursts of extravagant anger. Most actors are content with straining their eyeballs, protruding their lips, and pounding the air with one arm, to express their rage ; in Dowton you see all the approaches, the changes, and the effects of that passion, which becomes impotent by its very power. Most actors are content to stare with stupid inaction at their interlocutor while he is combating or deprecating their rage ; Dowton still preserves the great feature of rage, impatience ; he twists about his fingers, changes his attitude and his gesture, mutters hastily with his lips, turns away at intervals from the speaker with a mouth of contempt, or seems unable to wait for his conclusion. The scene with his son Captain Absolute in the *Rivals*, where he insists on the latter's marriage, is for this reason the masterpiece of extravagant anger. But then, when his son has won upon his feelings or suddenly complies with his demand, who at the same time can drop with such a fall of nature from the height of passion to the most soft emotions and the most social pleasantry ? His expression of satisfaction with another, his grateful shake of the hand, and his hurried thanks breaking through the intervals of overpowering joy, exhibit the perfection of social enjoyment.

But it is not in simple passions only that Mr. Dowton excels ; in the mixed emotions of anger and tenderness, and in the testiness of good-hearted old age, he has proved himself superior not only to the face-making Munden, but perhaps to any actor in the recollection of the present times. Of this union of opposite feelings his

[1] A two-act comedy, by Murphy.

Old Dornton, in the *Road to Ruin*,[1] and his Abednego, in
the *Jew and the Doctor*,[2] are sufficient examples. Munden,
who really has a considerable share of feeling, injures his
Dornton, as he does all his characters, with the most
preposterous buffoonery : he hurts alike his rage and his
tenderness, his violent, his soft, and his comic expression
with this studious farce, because he renders it evident to
the whole house that he is not sufficiently occupied with
himself to give a good portrait of himself, or rather,
perhaps, that he is too much occupied with himself to
give a good portrait of his author's personage. Dowton
thinks of nothing but his immediate character, and this
is a secret by which even indifferent actors might gain a
much better effect with their audience. An actor, in
fact, thinks of two incompatible things at once when he
is representing the author's character and studying his
own personal one, as the droll Mr. Munden, or the merry
Mr. Fawcett : a portrait painter in the act of taking
another's likeness might as well be so infatuated with
himself as to mingle a few dashes of his own : to be sure,
people would then say, "Here is a curious fancy piece
enough !" but what would the intended original say?

Dowton's changes from the irritable to the yielding,
from the angry to the tender, in old Dornton, have so
much nature that a spectator can with difficulty imagine
them to be *designed* for effect. The gradual faltering of
his voice from violence to softness, as he is gradually won
from testiness or anger, is like those beautiful semitones
whose dropping difference is scarcely perceivable in a fine
singer ; and in the same manner, his rise from sullenness
to gaiety is almost as imperceptible in its individual

[1] Holcroft's well-known comedy.
[2] A farce, by T. Dibdin.

gradation as the hundred different tones that melt in ascension on the ear when a vessel is filled at the spring. In Dornton, however, he always preserves the air of the venerable gentleman ; in the Abednego of the *Jew and the Doctor*, he shows with what nature he can still preserve these emotions with even an air of vulgarity. The remonstrances of the humane Jew, when he complains that his visitor has hurt his feelings, his air of honest pride gradually giving way to feelings of humiliation, and his powerless voice at length faltering into tears, are equalled by nothing but the sudden start of consolation and eagerness with which he inquires what *the gentleman asks for his gold-headed cane*. If his Israelitish dialect is not so correct as that of Wewitzer, it is nevertheless inferior to Wewitzer's only, and in every other respect it is the first performance of its kind that I have seen. I must lament indeed that I have not seen either himself or Mr. Bannister in the character of Sheva in Mr. Cumberland's comedy of the *Jew*, since this character, I should imagine, must comprise all the excellencies of his acting, his anger, his tenderness, his united anger and tenderness, and his unaffected force of humour, and it would have been curious to compare the two performers in their full rivalry of excellence. But I mention this comedy, which has done Mr. Cumberland's heart so much honour, to notice the very deserved encomium on Mr. Dowton in the author's memoirs of himself, published last year. The praise is general, and it comes from a writer grateful for assistance, but it is interesting because it is Mr. Cumberland's, and valuable because it is true. "It has also served," says the author, speaking of the part of Sheva, "as a stepping-stone to the stage for an actor, who in my judgment (and I am not afraid of being singular in

that opinion) stands amongst the highest of his profession:
for if quick conception, true discrimination, and the
happy faculty of incarnating the idea of his poet, are
properties essential in the almost undefinable composition
of a great and perfect actor, these and many more will
be found in Mr. Dowton."[1]   I would not be so great a
friend of the bathos as to say anything after this.

MR. MATHEWS.

THOSE comedians are infinitely mistaken who imagine
that mere buffoonery or face-making is a surer method
of attaining public favour than chastened and natural
humour. A monstrous grin, that defies all description
or simile, may raise a more noisy laughter, but as I have
before observed, the merest pantomime clown will raise
a still noisier : laughter does not always express the most
satisfied enjoyment, and there is something in the ease
and artlessness of true humour that obtains a more lasting
though a more gradual applause : it is like a rational
lover, who allows confidence and extravagant mirth to
catch a woman's eye first, but wins his way ultimately
from the very want of qualities which please merely to
fatigue. While such an actor, therefore, as Dowton will
attempt buffooneries in which he neither can nor ought to
succeed, it is no small credit to Mr. Mathews that he has
the judgment to avoid in general what he really can
exhibit with the greater effect. This is the proper pride
of an actor who has a greater respect for the opinion of
the boxes than of the galleries ; this is the laudable am-

[1] "Memoirs of Richard Cumberland, written by himself," 1806,
4to. p. 514.—L.11.

bition that would rather be praised by those who are worthy of respect themselves than by a clamorous mob who, in fact, applaud their own likeness in the vulgarity and nonsense so boisterously admired.

Such a judgment is the more praiseworthy in Mr. Mathews, as his principal excellence is the representation of officious valets and humorous old men, two species of character that with most actors are merely buffoons in livery and buffoons with walking-sticks. His attention to correctness, however, by no means lessens his vivacity, but it is the vivacity of the world, not of the stage ; it seems rather his nature than his art, and though I dare say all actors have their hours of disquiet, and perhaps more than most men, yet he has not the air of one who elevates his sensations the moment he enters the stage and drops them the instant he departs. It is a very common and a very injurious fault with actors to come before the audience with a manner expressive of beginning a task ; they adjust their neckcloths and hats as if they had dressed in a hurry, look about them as much as to say, " What sort of a house have I got this evening ? " and commence their speeches in a tone of patient weariness, as if they contemplated the future labours of the evening. This is a frequent error with Mr. H. Johnston, and a most peculiar one with Mr. C. Kemble, who often seems to have just arrived from a fatiguing walk. Mr. Mathews makes his appearance neither with this indifference on the one hand, nor on the other with that laboured mirth which seems to have been lashed into action like a top, and which goes down like a top at regular intervals. If, therefore, he does not amaze like many inferior actors with sudden bursts of broad merriment, he is more equable and consistent in his humour, and inspires his audience with a more constant spirit of cheerfulness. Such a cheerfulness is the most desirable effect in every comic performer, and this feeling is one of the sensations which render us more truly pleased with comedy than with farce : it is more agreeable to reason, because it leaves room for thinking ; it is removed from violence, which always carries a degree of pain into the more exquisite pleasures : it is more like the happiness that we may attain in real life, and therefore more fitted to dispose us to an enjoyment of our feelings.

The principal fault in the general style of Mr. Mathews is a redundancy of bodily motion approaching to restlessness, which I have sometimes thought to have been a kind of nervousness impatient of public observation ; but I think he has repressed this considerably within these few months, and if it be owing to want of confidence, the stage is not a place to increase any of the more bashful feelings. This fault, however, like Mr. Kemble's stiffness in Penruddock, becomes a beauty in his performance of the restless *Lying Valet*,[1] and of Risk in *Love Laughs at Locksmiths*,[2] who are both in a perpetual bustle of cheating and contrivance. Possibly it may be the frequency of his performance in characters of intrigue that originally led him to indulge it, for there is yet another character, that of the intriguing servant in the farce of *Catch him who Can*, in which he is at full liberty to indulge it. In this servant he gives a specimen of that admirable power of mimicry, in which he rivals Mr. Bannister. I believe there were many in the theatre who had much difficulty to recognise him in his transformation into the Frenchman, and for alteration of manner, tone, and pronunciation,

---

[1] By Garrick.
[2] A farce, by George Colman the younger.

it certainly was not inferior to the most finished deceptions
of that great comedian. As this kind of deception, indeed,
depends chiefly upon a disguise of the voice, one would
imagine it ought not to be very difficult to an actor, one
of whose first powers should be a flexibility of tone ; but
this flexibility becomes valuable on our stage for its rarity,
for it is curious enough to observe that we have not a
single tragedian or female performer who can at all disguise the voice, and of all our comedians, who really
ought to excel in this point, Mr. Bannister and Mr.
Mathews seem the only two who can thus escape from
themselves with any artifice : many of the comic actors,
as Munden, Simmons, Blanchard, Liston, Johnstone,[1]
Wewitzer, and particularly Fawcett, seem blessed with
such honest throats as to be incapable of the slightest
deception.

The old age of Mr. Mathews is like the rest of his
excellencies, perfectly unaffected and correct ; the appearance of years he manages so well, that many of his admirers,
who have never seen him off the stage, insist that he is an
elderly man, and the reason of this deception is evident :
most of our comedians in their representation of age
either make no alteration of their voice, and, like antiquarian cheats, palm a walking-stick or a hat upon us for
something very ancient, or sink into so unnatural an
imbecility that they are apt on occasion to forget their
tottering knees and bent shoulders, and like Vertumnus,
in the poet, are young and old in the turn of a minute.
Mathews never appears to wish to be old ; time seems to
have come to him, not he to time, and as he never, where
he can avoid it, makes that show of feebleness which the
vanity of age always would avoid, so he never forgets that

[1] John Johnstone the Irish comedian.

general appearance of years, which the natural feebleness of age could not help. Our old men of the stage are in general of one unvarying age in all their various characters, as in the case of Munden, for instance, who, though he imitates the appearance of a hearty old gentleman with much nature, is seldom a jot the older or younger than his usual antiquity, whatever the author might have led us to imagine. The two characters of Don Manuel in *She would and She would not* [1] and of Old Philpot in the *Citizen* are sufficient examples of the ease with which Mr. Mathews alters his years and of the general excellencies of his old age. In the former piece he is a naturally cheerful old man, whose humour depends much on the humour of others, and who is overcome alternately with gaiety and with despair, as he finds himself treated by those about him. The voice of Mr. Mathews, were we to shut our eyes, would be enough to convince us of his age in this character, and of his disposition too ; there is something in it unaccountably petty and confined, while at the same time it appears to make an effort of strength and jollity ; and when his false pitch of spirits meets with a sudden downfall, nothing can be more natural than the total dissolution of his powers of voice, or the restless despondency with which he yields himself to a hundred imaginary miseries. When his spirits are raised again and his excessive joy gradually overcomes itself by its own violence, the second exertion of his fatigued talkativeness and of his excessive laughter reduces him to mere impotence ; he sinks into his chair ; and in the last weariness of a weak mind and body, cannot still refrain from the natural loquacity of old age, but in the intervals of oppressed feeling attempts to speak when he has not only

[1] Comedy by Colley Cibber.

nothing to say, but when it is perfectly painful to him to
utter a word. In this character, therefore, Mr. Mathews
exhibits all the gradations of the strength and weakness
of declining years ; in that of Philpot, he settles himself
into a confirmed and unresisting old age : his feeble
attitudes, his voice, his minutest actions, are perfectly
monotonous, as become a money-getting dotard, whose
soul is absorbed in one mean object : his limbs contracted
together are expressive of the selfish closeness of the miser,
and in his very tone of utterance, so sparing of its strength
and so inward, he seems to retire into himself.

From the general performances, however, of Mr.
Mathews, I had been induced to consider him as an actor
of habits rather than of passions ; and as the present essay
originally stood, I had classed him in a rank much inferior
to Bannister and Dowton. But one of his late performances
raised his genius so highly in my estimation, that I
cancelled the original paragraph on purpose to do justice
to his Sir Fretful Plagiary in the *Critic*, to a performance which has proved his knowledge of the human heart,
has given its true spirit to one of the most original characters of the first wit of our age, and has even persuaded
the ancient dramatic connoisseurs to summon up the claps
of former times : nay, some of the old gentlemen, in the
important intervals of snuff, went so far as to declare that
the actor approached Parsons[1] himself. We are generally
satisfied when an actor can express a single feeling with
strength of countenance ; but to express two at once, and
to give them at the same time a powerful distinctness,
belongs to the perfection of his art. Nothing can be
more admirable than the look of Mr. Mathews when the

[1] William Parsons (died 1795) was an admirable actor of old men
in comedy He was the original Sir Fretful Plagiary.

severe criticism is detailed by his malicious acquaintance. While he affects a pleasantry of countenance, he cannot help betraying his rage in his eyes, in that feature which always displays our most predominant feelings ; if he draws the air to and fro through his teeth, as if he was perfectly assured of his own pleasant feelings, he convinces everybody by his tremulous and restless limbs that he is in absolute torture ; if the lower part of his face expands into a painful smile, the upper part contracts into a glaring frown which contradicts the ineffectual good humour beneath ; everything in his face becomes rigid, confused, and uneasy ; it is a mixture of oil and vinegar, in which the acid predominates ; it is anger putting on a mask that is only the more hideous in proportion as it is more fantastic. The sudden drop of his smile into a deep and bitter indignation, when he can endure sarcasm no longer, completes this impassioned picture of *Sir Fretful ;* but lest his indignation should swell into mere tragedy, Mr. Mathews accompanies it with all the touches of familiar vexation : while he is venting his rage in vehement expressions, he accompanies his more emphatic words with a closing thrust of his buttons, which he fastens and unfastens up and down his coat ; and when his obnoxious friend approaches his snuff-box to take a pinch, he claps down the lid and turns violently off with a most malicious mockery of grin. These are the performances and the characters which are the true fame of actors and dramatists. If our farcical performers and farcical writers could reach this refined satire, ridicule would vanish before them, like breath from a polished knife.

MISS POPE.

THE tragic stage is always a step above nature ; for the imitation of tragedy, paradoxical as the phrase may seem, must be somewhat imperfect in its resemblance to real life in order to be pleasing, not only because the spectators would lose sight of the emotion, considered in its imitative powers, from which some critics have deduced all the pleasure arising from tragedy, but because in proportion as they lost sight of this imitation, they would be awake to a sorrow too apparently real to be softened into a pleasing effect. Luckily for nature, indeed, our actors have little occasion to study this elevation above men and manners : for the poet has already lifted them sufficiently, either with his verse, or his declamation, or some other uncommonness of human language, as well as with the intervals of acts, which allow the spectators leisure to collect their thoughts. The tragic performer, therefore, though he attend carefully to the poetry, ought still to imitate nature as closely as possible in passages of emotion and passion, if it were merely to correct the artificial effect of the poet's writing, which is always sufficient to give him the necessary elevation, and, unless softened, would always be in danger of lifting him too abruptly above the standard of humanity.

But in comedy such an elevation is totally unnecessary and injurious ; firstly, because it excites too little passion to carry our enthusiasm beyond a sense of its imitation ; secondly, because if it did thus transport us, the sensations it would inspire would be the reverse of painful and alarming ; and thirdly, because its chief end is satire, and what is not a just picture of human manners will

never be recognised or at least felt as a likeness either by
those whom it is intended to reprove or those whom it
should rouse to a reproof of others. Caricature, for this
reason, is very justly confined by good authors to farce,
which professes nothing but to raise merriment, and
though some writers of huge farces may call their productions comedy, yet the world invariably recognises
them for what they are, and would as soon look for its
own image in their kind of satire, as a beauty would
search for her likeness at the back of her looking-glass.
For the same reason, therefore, the actor should confine
his caricature to farce, otherwise he totally destroys that
end of the poet which it is his business to promote. If
the character, too, is extremely natural and well-drawn,
he contradicts his own sentiments and deeds by farce; and
thus the union between an actor and his character becomes
just as unseasonable and ridiculous, as the assistance of a
boisterous fellow who, to help his friend from the ground,
overturns him by his awkward officiousness.

I have been led into these reflections by a contemplation of Miss Pope's genius, which proves how infinitely a
comedian can please without the least tincture of grimace
or buffoonery, or the slightest opposition to nature. She
exhibits, indeed, such a perfect freedom from the cant and
trick of the stage, that her education in Mr. Garrick's
juvenile theatre allows no argument for the friends of
such an institution, since her excellencies are evidently
the effect of natural genius, and not of any system of
education. A theatre of this kind can be of no use but
to instruct its actors in the mere business of the stage,
and Miss Pope, I believe, is the only good performer
either in England or France that has been thus educated.
Such a stage can never supply that observation of life

which is one of the first requisites towards the representation of men and manners ; it is evident, too, that however excellently children may perform, considered as children, they can never personate a more advanced age for that very reason, and even if they could contrive to imitate men, they would merely disgust us the more because they were no longer children. Of what service, then, is a juvenile theatre ? Why, it hurts the health of children by forcing them into bad hours, it hurts their minds by giving them a premature knowledge of seducing vices, it takes away, in short, that lovely simplicity whose greatest charm is its inexperience, and without which childhood becomes a mere effort at manhood, contemptible for its want of power, and infinitely pitiable for its want of modesty. If Miss Pope has escaped all this, it is owing to that excellent sound sense which has taught her to avoid the most common errors of her profession. But what has become of all the other persons educated in this manner ? If their early habits are not sufficient to make them fit for the stage, they will at the same time render them unfit for almost every other profession, and what is to become of those, especially if they are females, whose very passion for bustle has made them indolent, and for reading, unwise ? I do not speak from momentary consideration, for I have eagerly sifted the subject before. There was an attempt last year to establish in this metropolis what was called an academic theatre ; its proprietors, some of whom were fathers of the children, instructed the infant performers in the most iniquitous plays of our degraded wits, and it will ever be the honest pride of my heart that, by the confession of these very men, its dissolution was materially owing to the ridicule of the *News*.

Neither these dangers, nor the earliest as well as greatest

praise that an actress could receive, have had any effect on the steady, unassuming, and unaffected genius of Miss Pope, of whom Churchill, in the ancient character of poet and prophet united, and in the midst of the most galling satire upon others, spoke his perfect approbation.

> With all the native vigour of sixteen,
> Among the merry group conspicuous seen,
> See lively Pope advance in jig and trip,
> Corinna, Cherry, Honeycomb, and Snip.
> Not without art, but yet to nature true,
> She charms the town with humour just, yet new.
> Cheer'd by her promise, we the less deplore
> The fatal time when Clive shall be no more.
>
> *Rosciad.*

The anticipation of Miss Pope's resemblance to Mrs. Clive, who excelled in hoydens and romps, as well as intriguing chambermaids, does not seem to have been perfectly justified in the former character ; but in the latter we ourselves can witness to that lively nature which seems determined to survive her very powers, and the picture of Mrs. Clive's genius, if not of her characters, might still be drawn for Miss Pope :

> In spite of outward blemishes she shone
> For humour fam'd and humour all her own.
> Easy, as if at home, the stage she trod,
> Nor sought the critic's praise nor fear'd his rod.
> Original in spirit and in ease,
> She pleas'd by hiding all attempts to please.

It has not been my fortune to see Miss Pope in her former days and characters, but if her humour is still so powerful, when her powers of voice and of action have become so weak, it is easy to imagine her former excellence. Her genius, however, is of a very lasting nature, for it does not depend upon bodily exertion. The stage, as Churchill says with respect to Mrs. Clive, appears to be her own room : she never indulges in that excess of action which is intended to supply the want of active countenance, and which would be so astounding to Englishmen in real life ; she never talks to the audience, she does not exhibit all she can when her character will not warrant the display, and with the same judgment she never affects what she cannot do. One of her great beauties is a most judicious emphasis of speech that unites the qualities of reading and of talking ; for it has all the strength of the one tempered by the familiarity of the other. Her general style of acting, indeed, may be termed emphatic, not because, like Mrs. Davenport, who is a very sensible actress in other respects, she digs, as it were, into particular words with her voice and her action, but because she relieves with much art the uniform temperance of her manner by that variety of tone which appears the natural result of a person's obedience to feelings, without any attempt either to repress or to elevate them. This is peculiarly observable in her performance of Mrs. Candour in the *School for Scandal,* in which her affected sentiments are so inimitably hidden by the natural turns of her voice, that it is no wonder her scandal carries perfect conviction to everybody around her. Her humour is perfectly adapted to this affectation of truth, for it is of that dry sort which a person of little judgment might mistake for seriousness, and it is so perfectly equalised with her immediate feelings, that in scenes of cool contemptuous defiance or of anger affecting coolness, as in the character of Lady Courtland in the *School for Friends,*[1]

[1] A comedy, by Miss Chambers.

she never passes those limits at which the actor's adherence to his author ends, and his mere wish to please the audience commences.

In parts of mere farce, like that of stupid Audrey in *As You Like It*, Miss Pope must yield, I think, to Mrs. Mattocks, but in true comic humour and in temperate unaffected nature she yields to no actress on the stage, and it is a very considerable praise to her judgment and her general manners that in the present rare gentility of the stage she is the only natural performer of the old gentlewoman. With features neither naturally good nor flexible, she manages a surprising variety of expression, and with a voice originally harsh and now enfeebled by age, her variety of tone is still more surprising. None of her deficiencies, in short, are acquired, and she contrives that they shall injure none of her excellencies. With perpetual applause to flatter her and a long favouritism to secure her, she has no bad habits ; and when even the best of our actors are considered, it is astonishing how much praise is contained in that single truth.

MRS. JORDAN.

I HAVE placed this charming actress under the head of comedy, notwithstanding her occasional performance in tragedy and her peculiar excellence in the artless miseries of Ophelia. The declamatory parts, which she sometimes sustains in sentimental plays, require, as I have before observed, very little genius on account of their verbal monotony ; and though considerable feeling is mingled with everything Mrs. Jordan does, yet she increases this very monotony by a plaintive undulation of voice, an

alternate rise and fall of emphasis, that seems conscious
of her want of tragic powers and is labouring to impress
upon us something very fine, like a person spouting forth
a laborious quotation. She appears indeed on these
occasions to be reading her part, and proceeds from line
to line with a singing solemnity, like a parcel of milliners,
during their work, taking their turn to read *Romeo and
Juliet* or the *Victim of Sensibility*. As to her excellent
performance of Ophelia, a great distinction must be made
between characters originally and essentially tragic, and
those which become so by some external means that do
not change their disposition ; between characters, in
short, which are tragic on account of what they have
done or felt, and those which become so by what is done
to them. In the former case a general solemnity and
sorrow is necessary in the performer, in the latter the
character may still preserve its sprightliness in its utmost
tragedy, as Ophelia does in her madness, so that the tragic
effect of such a character does not consist in the performer's
powers of tragedy, but in the contrast which its misfortunes
make with its behaviour : the darkness is rather in its
atmosphere than in itself. Nothing can be more natural
or pathetic than the complacent tones and busy good-
nature of Mrs. Jordan in the derangement of Ophelia ;
her little bewildered songs in particular, like all her
songs, indeed, pierce to our feelings with a most original
simplicity ; but as all her actions and speeches are lively
and airy, though unseasonably so, she is nothing but the
comic actress who has become tragic for the reasons above
mentioned.

The immediate felicity of Mrs. Jordan's style consists,
perhaps, in that great excellence of Mr. Bannister, which
I have called heartiness ; but as the matter of this feeling

is naturally softened in a female, it becomes a charming openness mingled with the most artless vivacity. In characters that require this expression, Mrs. Jordan seems to speak with all her soul: her voice, pregnant with melody, delights the ear with a peculiar and exquisite fulness, and with an emphasis that appears the result of perfect conviction; yet this conviction is the effect of a sensibility willing to be convinced rather than of a judgment weighing its reasons; her heart always precedes her speech, which follows with the readiest and happiest acquiescence.

This subjection of the manner to the feelings has rendered Mrs. Jordan in her younger days the most natural actress of childhood, of its bursts of disposition, and its fitful happiness; and as her fancy has not diminished, and her knowledge of human nature must have increased with her years, it would render her the most natural actress still, were it not for the increase of her person. To be very fat and to look forty years old is certainly not the happiest combination for a girlish appearance, and Mrs. Jordan, with much good sense, seems to have almost laid aside her Romps [1] and her Little Pickles [2] for younger performers. So delightful, however, are the feelings and tones of nature, that there is still no actress who pleases so much in the performance of frank and lively youth, in Shakspeare's Rosalind, for instance, and the broad sensibilities of the *Country Girl.* [3] With this frankness, too, she unites a power of raillery, seldom found in a performer of her honest cast. Mrs. Jordan manages this raillery with inimitable delicacy; yet it does not carry with it

[1] Priscilla Tomboy, in the farce of *The Romp.*
[2] In the farce of *The Spoiled Child.*
[3] Garrick's expurgated version of Wycherley's *Country Wife.*

an air of contempt, though such an air is one of the
severest weapons of the ironical humourist; it is not
delivered with an indifferent air, though such an appearance gives irony one of its most excellent reliefs; nor
does it assume an air of gay acquiescence in the proceed-
ings of its object, though the object may thus become
doubly ridiculous in its misconception and unconscious
furtherance of the ridicule. These three kinds of ridicule,
considered with regard to the speaker, form a contrast
with his manner only, since we can always discover his
real meaning and mind, and are not surprised at either;
but raillery becomes much more effective in the mouth
of frankness and simplicity from the contrast it presents
with the usual good-nature of the speaker, and from the
peculiar obnoxiousness of that object which can rouse so
unexpected and unusual a reprover. Mrs. Jordan utters
her more serious ridicule with the same simplicity and
strength of feeling that always pervade her seriousness
when it does not amount to the tragic, and she gives it a
very peculiar energy by pronouncing the latter part of
her sentences in a louder, a deeper, and more hurried
tone, as if her good-nature should not be betrayed into
too great a softness, and yet as if it wished to get rid of
feelings too harsh for her disposition. Her lighter raillery
still carries with it the same feeling, and her laughter is
the happiest and most natural on the stage; if she is to
laugh in the middle of a speech, it does not separate itself
so abruptly from her words as with most of our performers;
she does not force herself into those yawning and side-
aching peals, which are laboured on every trifling occasion,
when the actor seems to be affecting joy with the tooth-
ache upon him or to have worked himself into convul-
sions like a Pythian priestess; her laughter intermingles

7

itself with her words, as fresh ideas afford her fresh merriment ; she does not so much indulge as she seems unable
to help it ; it increases, it lessens, with her fancy, and
when you expect it no longer, according to the usual habit
of the stage, it sparkles forth at little intervals, as recollection revives it, like flame from half smothered embers.
This is the laughter of the feelings ; and it is this predominance of the heart in all she says and does that
renders her the most delightful actress in the Donna
Violante of the *Wonder*,[1] and the Clara of *Matrimony*,[2]
and in twenty other characters which ought to be more
ladylike than she can make them, and which acquire a
better gentility with others.

Why Mrs. Jordan should be so deficient in the lady will,
however, be no matter of surprise to those who reflect, in
the first place, on the levelling familiarities of her profession, and, in the second, on the broad and romping
characters in which she has hitherto excelled, and to
which the manners of any actress, perpetually employed
in those characters, must in some degree unavoidably be
bent. Mrs. Jordan has unfortunately been the finest
breeches-figure, as the newspapers gloatingly call it, upon
the British stage ; her leg is reported to have been copied
into a model for the statuary, and her foot has rivalled the
sublime toes of that modest dancer Vestris, who differed with
the all-conquering Achilles merely as it was the mortality
of the warrior and the immortality of the dancer that lay
in their respective heels, and who one day cried out to his
son, "Here, boy, kiss this foot, which enchants heaven
and earth!" The male attirement of actresses is one of
the most barbarous, injurious, and unnatural customs of

---

[1] The *Wonder, or a Woman keeps a Secret*, by Mrs. Centlivre.
[2] A "Petit Opera," adapted from the French by James Kenney.

the stage ; it has proceeded sometimes from want of invention in the author, sometimes from a spirit of pru- riency, or, if they please, of versatility in the actresses ; for when actors rule authors, as they do in our time, good performers may very often obtain what parts they please. In all cases it is injurious to the probability of the author and to the proper style of the actress, for if she succeeds in her study of male representation she will never entirely get rid of her manhood with its attire ; she is like the *Iphis*[1] of Ovid, and changes her sex unalterably. There is required, in fact, a breadth of manners and demeanour in a woman's imitation of men, which no female, who had not got over a certain feminine reserve of limb, could ever maintain or endure ; and when the imitation becomes frequent and the limbs bent to their purpose, it is impos- sible to return to that delicacy of behaviour, which exists merely as it is incapable of forgetting itself. Vivacity does nothing but strengthen the tendency to broadness by allowing a greater freedom of action ; it merely helps the female to depart more from her former chaste cold- ness of character, from the simplicity of her former mental shape ; it is like attempting to straighten a curled lock by holding it nearer the fire. I cannot but persuade myself, therefore, that Mrs. Jordan's inability to catch the elegant delicacy of the lady arises from her perpetual representation of the other sex and of the romping, un- settled, and uneducated part of her own. It has been the fashion to compare Miss Duncan in the character of a lady with Mrs. Jordan ; but let them be compared with references to their age and situation. The deficiency of Mrs. Jordan arises from bad or inappropriate habits of acting : had she never represented rakes and romps, it is

[1] *Metamorphoses,* bk. ix., fol. 10.

most probable she would have been at least as genteel as
Miss Duncan, for in point of real genius and comic powers
she is as much her superior as she has been in person and
still is in voice. Miss Duncan has undoubtedly the advantage in gentility, and her youth and figure will assist
that advantage : but let her take care of her superiority ;
she has lately been very fond of wearing the breeches, and
she wears them, as Sallust's female danced, much better
than becomes her.

Mrs. Jordan, as a performer who unites great comic
powers with much serious feeling, and who in all her
moods seems to be entirely subservient to her heart, is
not only the first actress of the day, but as it appears to
me from the description we have of former actresses, the
first that has adorned our stage. But if it may be suffered
me to shadow with a little gloomy philosophy the gaiety
of theatric criticism, if it may be suffered me to fancy
myself at some silent distance from the brilliant stage,
undisturbed by its noise and undazzled by its lustre, how
distressing is it to our benevolence, how humiliating to
our powers of pleasing, and to our capacity of receiving
pleasure, that the very tastes and abilities that produce
one of our most rational delights, should corrupt the
source of that delight ; that the stage should at once be
the improver of our manner and the debaser of its own ;
that the most sensitive, the most amiable part of the
creation can scarcely ever venture upon the public imitation of even the most estimable part of their sex, without
losing something of what renders themselves estimable !

MR. ELLISTON.

IF Briareus were to appear on earth with his hundred hands, the world would deny him his powers. There is something in a multiplicity or combination of powers that excites the incredulity of mankind in spite of ocular demonstration. Wonder has been defined to be the effect of novelty upon ignorance, and as ignorance is but a shallow recipient, it is in this case, perhaps, filled above its brim and lost in the torrent. In no instance is this hardness of belief so powerfully exhibited as at the union of tragic and comic excellence. The long disputes and jealousies arising from their combination in Garrick have scarcely ceased at this moment, and they were instantly roused at the appearance of Mr. Elliston, who is the only genius that has approached that great actor in universality of imitation. When Voltaire produced his first comedy, he concealed the author's name because he had succeeded in tragedy : his caution was afterwards proved to be well-founded : the instant he was discovered, the journalists unanimously altered their opinion, for though Shakspeare had done it in England, De Vega in Spain, and Racine in France, yet it was evidently impossible that a man could write tragedy and comedy too. The English are less pardonable when they indulge such an incredulity, since they have had so many excellent examples to persuade their belief. But after all, perhaps, it is the critics only who would convince us of Mr. Elliston's utter incapacity for tragic acting, those amiable journalists, who will abuse one performer merely to please another, who after getting drunk at an actor's table will come and tell us what power he possesses over their senses, and what a want of solidity there is in that man who never invites them to eat his roast beef. These gentlemen, some day or other, will endeavour to argue that the world is divided into mere merrymakers and mourners, and that it is impossible for the same man to laugh and to cry.

Though I do not think Elliston so excellent in tragedy as in comedy, yet I would never be so tasteless as to brush the dew entirely from his laurels and allow him nothing but his dry humour. He is already the second tragedian on the stage, and he wants nothing but study and a more heroic countenance to be at least equal to Mr. Kemble, whom in the true inspiration of his art I think he excels. His person is elegant, but let us examine the deficiencies of his face, his peeping eyes, and his truly English nose, and it will be astonishing to consider what a dignity as well as general variety he can summon to his features, and how infinitely he is superior in general expression to Mr. Charles Kemble and Mr. Henry Johnston, actors blessed with faces of handsome tragedy.

If Mr. Elliston's want of the hero in countenance renders his aspect less imposing in grand characters than that of Mr. Kemble, his want of study renders him considerably inferior to that careful actor in the graver and less active parts of tragedy. He cannot retire into himself with that complacent studiousness, which feels easy in the absence of bustle and in the solitary enjoyment of its own powers ; in soliloquy, therefore, which is nothing but thinking loudly, he is too apt to declaim ; and in this respect he is like those common actors, who think of nothing but their profession, and forget that declamation is of all styles of speaking the most unfit for soliloquies, because they ought never to have the air of being made for effect. For this reason, his Hamlet, which surpasses Mr. Kemble's in humour, and on account of its youth has the advantage also in appearance, is by no means so just a picture of the more philosophical parts of the prince's character, of his sorrow, his profound reflection, and that mingled air of anxiety and repose, which breathes over the manner of a person whose hours are spent in meditating one great purpose. The character of Hamlet, however, seems beyond the genius of the present stage, and I do not see that its personification will be easily attained by future stages ; for its actor must unite the most contrary as well as the most assimilating powers of comedy and tragedy, and to unite these powers in their highest degree belongs to the highest genius only. With all the real respect I have for a true actor, I must rank him in an inferior class both to the great painter and great musician ; and neither of these inspired ones has united comic and tragic excellence. It is the pen alone which has drawn a magic circle round the two powers, and rendered them equally obedient to the master's hand.

That Mr. Elliston's tragic genius is naturally equal, if not superior, to that of Mr. Kemble, may be seen in his quick conception of whatever is most poetical, or, in other words, most fanciful in tragedy ; and it must be recollected that the extravagant character of Sir Edward Mortimer,[1] which darts through every extreme of imagination and feeling, was condemned in its original representation by Kemble, and received with enthusiasm in its vivification by Elliston.   Both these performers have their extremes in madness, but as Elliston's is the violent one, it is less opposite to the frenzied fancy of Mortimer.   Mr. Kemble has too much method in his madness, and in his most fanciful speeches he cannot forget his usual precise nod of the head and preaching abstraction of delivery : he some-times reminds one of the sick barber in the Connoisseur, who supplied his inability to procure medical advice, by putting doctors' wigs on four or five of his blocks and pretending to hold a dialogue with them round his bed : he seems to talk solely for himself, if not to himself, and occasionally exhibits an air of solemn satisfaction at his own speeches that becomes absolutely ludicrous.   As to love, which is the vital principle of another frenzied cha-racter, performed by both these actors, that of Octavian, I have already expiated upon Mr. Kemble's utter want of amatory feeling[2]: his attempts this way may be compared to the ogling of Hogarth's parish clerk in the reading-desk ; for they present a most ludicrous mixture of the clumsy, the serious, and the uncharacteristic.   He seems, indeed, to do everything he possibly can to injure the natural effect both of his own love and the love of others, for it appears by a curious communication to the *News*, that he has absolutely forbidden the actress, who performs

[1] In *The Iron Chest*, a play (founded on Godwin's *Caleb Williams*), by George Colman the younger.   It was a failure on its original pro-duction in March 1796, with Kemble as Mortimer.   In August of the same year Elliston played the part, and the play was a great success. The character was afterwards one of Edmund Kean's greatest triumphs.

[2] See *ante*, p. 4.

his mistress, to express her affection a jot more naturally than he does his own.[1] The fault of Elliston in Octavian is certainly not want of ardour, either amorous or declamatory. If he bursts into his maddening mouthings with the proper vehemence, he sinks into recollective tenderness with as proper a softness; but like a man accustomed to yield to his feelings, he does both with a natural abandonment; though his sensations may be momentary, he is full of them for the time; his feelings follow each other like the buckets on a water-wheel, full one instant and empty the next, now rising with all their rapidity, now disappearing with as rapid a fall. In this quick variety of conception, which requires as quick and various an expression, his management of features not naturally good is astonishing. Sorrows and joys, regret and indulged memory, despair and hope, love and hatred, the collectedness of reason and the scatter of insanity, rush over his features with alternate mastery : if there is any fault in his vehemence, it is the indulgence of that sobbing in which he has been so injudiciously imitated, and which injures the suddenness of his transitions from patience to despair. Sobs may occasionally attend a sudden feeling of grief, but they are never frequent except in a long indulgence of tears : in fact they are a violent effort of nature to regain its strength after an exhaustion of weeping, as we may observe in children ; and we have an excellent example of their proper imitation in hysterical ladies, who, with much knowledge of cause and effect, always keep their sobs for the last touch of the pathetic. But the smile of Mr. Elliston is more natural and winning than any one actor's, and when it suddenly breaks from the midst of his melancholy, exhibits a feeling unknown

[1] See p. 128.

to Mr. Kemble's countenance, whose familiar expression is always accompanied with an air of precise superiority. In most actors you can fancy from their familiar expression what their feeling in private life may be ; you become acquainted with the men, as you do with a poet from his works ; but Mr. Kemble always appear the actor ; you see nothing in his face of what you conceive to be domestic habits and feelings : he is almost a second mystery of the Man with the Iron Mask.

Mr. Elliston's peculiar warmth of feeling has rendered him the best lover on the stage both in tragedy and comedy, and when we consider the theatric dominion of love, this single superiority gives an actor a greater range of characters than any one talent he could possess. Mr. Charles Kemble, indeed, has so much amatory softness, that I once thought him superior to Elliston in the single character of Romeo ; but he has suffered himself of late to be overcome by a most peculiar kind of indolent air, that seems too much occupied with its own ease to possess that attention to another which is the soul of love. When Elliston makes love, he appears literally to live in the object before him ; he shows a most original earnestness in his approach and in his devoirs to his mistress, he enters into all her ideas, he accompanies her speech with affectionate gestures of assent or anticipation, he dwells upon her face while she is talking to another ; in short, he is his fair one's shadow which obeys her slightest movement with simultaneous acknowledgment.—Love leads to pleasure, and I make a natural transition from Mr. Elliston's tragic to his comic powers.

Mr. Elliston's love is equally natural in all its shapes, in the self-tormenting suspicions of Sheridan's Falkland, in the assumed gaiety and side chagrin of Frederick in

Matrimony, and in the affectation of alternate submissiveness and tyranny, the pretended indifference, the dry raillery, and lastly the dignified affection of the Duke Aranza.[1] His performance of the second character is, in my opinion, a perfect specimen of real love affecting indifference and at length yielding to its object, and I am sorry that I did not expatiate in the proper place upon the nature of Mrs. Jordan also, in his wife Clara. The cool manner arising from their unexpected confinement to the same room after a voluntary separation, and the gradual approach of their hearts, divided as they had been by wayward circumstance rather than by loss of affection, are managed with a delicacy superior to any theatric picture of simplicity I ever saw. Elliston's airs of disdain, when his young wife, with sidelong raillery, commences a gay song, are full of natural petulance ; he turns the back of his chair towards her to read his book to himself, then crosses and re-crosses his legs, then listens with some sort of admiration at her voice though with the book up to his eyes, then darts them again with fitful impatience on the book, as he fancies himself observed ; and, lastly, as she draws nearer to him to play her lute in his ear, turns his chair more violently, jerks his head with a pshaw of malicious pity and irritation, and again fixes his eyes on the book as if he were thoroughly absorbed in the perusal, though his overstrained eagerness proves him unable to read a syllable. As this distance, however, is gradually narrowed, the mutual advances are made with the greatest delicacy and under the mask of that common indifference which allows a familiarity without acknowledging a friendship. If the wife ventures in an indifferent tone of voice to ex-

[1] In *The Honeymoon*, by Tobin.

press something like surprise and satisfaction at her husband's re-assumption of hair-powder, he receives the observation with an affirmative equally cool and with a most judicious hasty eking out of the speech, while he feels his head as if to assure himself of a thing so perfectly indifferent to him ; the author, however, with much nature, has made him so far moved as to compliment his wife with rather an earnest kind of civility on her new head-dress, and then Mrs. Jordan, with equal nature and agreeably to female susceptibility, exhibits a rather warmer acknowledgment of the compliment, till at length civility softens into complacency, and complacency melts into tenderness : the performers then very properly indulge in as much social eagerness as they were before distant and slow, for capricious lovers are full of extremes. This is altogether the most complete scene of amorous quarrel that I have witnessed.

If Mr. Elliston, however, is raised by his feeling to this amatory perfection, his observation of habits and manners enables him to assume with equal skill the more external love of the fashionable gallant, that love, in fact, which is a mere love of the world directed for the moment to a single purpose. Much is always said by old frequenters of the theatre, with a very plaintive kind of malice, respecting the inimitable performance of deceased actors, the absence of whom, however great their fame may be, is often lucky perhaps for their comparison with the present stage. You may be amused for a whole evening, not merely with the vivacity of Elliston in Archer [1] and Sir Harry Wildair,[2] but with his variety of countenance, his complete occupation with busy pleasure, and the dry

[1] In *The Beaux' Stratagem*, by Farquhar.
[2] In *The Constant Couple*, by Farquhar.

humour so peculiarly his own, and then an old gentleman
sitting next you, with two flaps to his waistcoat, shall tell
you that Dodd or Garrick was the only man who could
do that sort of character ; that Peg Woffington, the finest
breeches-figure that ever was seen, played Sir Harry
much more *correct ;* and then, offering you his snuff-box
to secure your attention, he exclaims with a sigh, " The
last time I saw Garrick—let me see—ay—was it or was it
not in Don John ? yes, it must have been Don John, because he wore slashed breeches,—ay—in Don John—and
a very noble performance it was—I watched the eyes of
the women, sir, all the time he was playing, and egad,
they followed him about as if they were jealous." Here
the old gentleman looks round to the side boxes, and
shakes his head with a sort of triumphant pity : " Hah !
the boxes are very different things from what they were
in those times—some pretty women to be sure—but no
wits, sir, nobody one knows or reads about—now there
was Doctor Johnson used to be in the boxes when Garrick
played—a very great man—I recollect seeing him when
Garrick did Lear—he was fast asleep all the last act, and
I couldn't keep my eyes off of him—he was a very great
man to be sure—I recollect offering him a pinch of snuff
once—allow me, sir—the true Macabaw, I assure you—
Pray, sir, isn't it your opinion that this theatre has a
certain vile hugeness, as a man may say, in its appearance?
—I often tell Jack Wilkins—' Ah, Jack,' says I, ' it's a
long time since you and—'" At this instant the stage-
bell luckily rings and saves you from a long history of
Mr. John Wilkins and the old gentleman's club, who
were all rampant apprentices and critics in their day, and
as fond of hissing the actors as they are of applauding
their memory. You just snatch an instant to say that

you cannot see how the size of the theatre can hurt its appearance, however inconvenient it may be for the audience, and then busy yourself so entirely with the new scene, that your ancient critic is compelled to let you alone, with an ardent desire, however, that he had you over a pint of wine, to convince you of the hopelessness of the present stage.

But social and vivacious as Elliston is in all his gallant characters, there is always something in his manner of that peculiar self-command of action, which is half the secret of gentility. If this restraint renders him second to Lewis, as I have already observed, in characters of pure heartiness, it gives him an unequalled grace in the polished gentleman. Blessed with the proper medium between the extreme vivacity of that restless actor and the extreme languor and reserve of Mr. Charles Kemble, he appropriates almost exclusively to himself the hero of genteel comedy, that character which attracts the regard of the fair and the fashionable, and that in its happiest point of view unites the most natural attractives of social pleasure with the nicest repellents of gross familiarity. If he is not the "scholar's eye" like Mr. Kemble, he is the "courtier's and soldier's tongue and sword,"

"The glass of fashion and the mould of form;"

and to finish his talents for the gentleman, he exhibits a fund of miscellaneous powers, which enables him to be at his ease in all companies and in all exhibitions of polite acquirement. He is the gentleman of Sir William Jones, who reckoned every little art, that added to mental or bodily grace, an object of ambition to polished leisure.

If dancing is going on, he joins in the step ; if fencing, he leaps into his posture ; if singing, he takes his part in the harmony. The effect of this spirit is particularly distinguishable at those times, when the actor mingles more familiarly with his audience and talks to them in his own person : thus there is no performer, who gives a prologue such social elegance, or addresses the house upon managerial topics with so neat and natural a strength.

His gayer versatility, however, is not strictly confined to the varieties of genteel comedy ; he can descend with very excellent mimicry below his sphere, as in his disguises of a Jew and a common soldier in *Love Laughs at Locksmiths*, and in many other low characters which his pride or his policy has laid aside, since his possession of the theatric throne at Drury Lane. It must be confessed at the same time that he descends with some of his radiance about him, for he certainly does not so entirely get rid of the gentleman as he should. He is not in this respect like Garrick, of whom a wild story is related respecting a young lady that fell in love with him while he was performing *Ranger*, and who was very judiciously taken by her parents, a few nights afterwards, to see him in the part of *Abel Drugger*, which he acted with so natural a grossness as turned the lady's love almost to antipathy. Mr. Elliston's gentlemanly pertinacity, however, is of use to him in one disguise, which Garrick's consummate versatility seems to have led him at once to perfect and to abuse : I believe it was Dr. Johnson, who accused him of assuming the livery with too accurate a vulgarity in the character of Archer in the *Beaux' Stratagem*.

The performance which allows the greatest versatility

to Elliston, while it leaves him his proper gentility, is
that of the three brothers in the *Three and the Deuce*.
In order to explain his acting in this singular drama, it is
necessary to explain the author a little. The story turns
upon the adventures of three brothers of the name of
Single, who are of very different manners and dispositions,
but so perfectly alike in appearance that none but their
most intimate relations can distinguish them separately.
One of them is a serious gentleman, another a lively
beau, and the third an idiot, a most improper object
certainly for any kind of drama. Mr. Elliston represents
this triple likeness with a felicity, which it is little praise
to say no other actor could approach. The serious Mr.
Single has a servant,[1] who resides with his master at the
same hotel, of which the other brothers, without the
slightest suspicion of family neighbourhood, happen to be
inmates. Upon this poor fellow turns the attraction of
the piece. He is joked and beaten about by the merry
brother, who does not know what to make of his misplaced attention ; the grave brother, who is equally at a
loss to understand his remonstrances and accusations of
levity, treats him as a drunkard ; and the idiot gives the
climax to his astonishment by manifesting a total ignorance
of his office and person. Into these three different characters and their aspects, with the assistance of three kinds
of hats and as many modes of buttoning his coat, Mr.
Elliston changes himself with an alternation as perfect as
it is rapid : in the gay brother, with his cocked hat and
huge frill, he dances, and sings, and fences, and plagues
the strange footman, and darts about into a thousand
ideas and attitudes : in a moment you find him with the
gravest of all possible faces reproaching his servant for his

[1] See page 52.

fancies, and deliberately convincing himself of the man's intoxication : in an instant he waddles forward under a white beaver, with a wide grin upon his countenance and with a stupid lisp that breaks every now and then into as stupid a giggle. One does not know which to admire most, his bustling importance in the first character, his real importance in the second, or his silly earnestness and gaping pretensions to importance in the third. When he boasts of his riches to the Welsh maid-servant, with an idiotic undulation of whine, he reminds you of the half-breathing pomposity of a little girl whispering about her new shoes.

In this triple character Mr. Elliston exhibits with its usual effect that dry expression of humour, which is so peculiarly adapted to his genius and countenance, and which is in fact his great originality. All art acquires its greatest effect from contrast, and particularly the art of humorous ridicule, which in a grave dress pursues an end to which its means are apparently inadequate. It is full of contrast : its manner is easiest when its intention is most violent ; it appears to be absolutely indifferent when it is absorbed in attention ; it says one thing when it evidently means another ; and its meaning, instead of being dissipated, is peculiarly embodied and enforced by this confusion. It might appear, at first, like attempting to reach a goal by running away from it, or endeavouring to grasp a sword by putting your hands in your waistcoat pockets ; but in an instant the goal is reached, the active sword is grasped.

The end of an actor, in the management of this humour, is to talk in two languages ; one, the language of the tongue ; and the other, that of the manner and aspect united. Charles Kemble sometimes exhibits much nature in the lighter intermixture of these opposite effects : he assents, for instance, to a ridiculous proposition with a very easy gravity that contradicts its necessity by its indifference : but he cannot reach the perfect conviction of Elliston, who with half-shut eyes, an opened mouth, a shake of the head, and a nasal depth of affirmation, perfectly cheats his interlocutor without deceiving the audience a jot. His representation of Captain Beldare in *Love Laughs at Locksmiths*, affords an excellent specimen of his skill in dry humour ; but in no character does he display it with such felicity as in that of the Duke Aranza in the *Honey Moon*. As this character at the same time allows him also his lively gentility, his imposing dignity, and his amatory fire, it is altogether his finest performance. No actor, except Mr. Kemble, can elevate himself to so marked as well as natural a height from the rest of the dramatic persons, or, in other words, can exhibit with such strong propriety that distinct character which the author intends for his hero. The Duke Aranza of the poet is the prominent point upon which everything in the play turns and is beheld : the Duke Aranza of Elliston possesses the same relief, is the same central point, gives everything the same prominence and distinction ; but all is natural. When he courts his mistress, it is with the gallant obeisance of the prince ; when he commands his wife, it is with the firmness of one who knows his duty and his right ; when he joins in the rustic dance, it is with that familiarity of the gentleman, which in its utmost condescension avoids the air of condescending ; when he ironises his peevish wife, or pleads sarcastically before his own servant, he does it with a dignified conviction and seriousness that awes the lady while it enrages her.

Every body, who has seen the *Honey Moon*, must recollect his consummate union of dignity, satire, and good humour, when he convinces the mock-duke, before whom his wife had brought him, how easily she might have perceived the difference

"Between your grace and such a man as I am."

In short, I have no hesitation in pronouncing his representation of this character a perfect performance ; and there are but two other performances of note in my recollection which I consider as deserving the same epithet, Mr. Kemble's Penruddock and the Queen Katharine of Mrs. Siddons.

With all this variety of conception and of representation, it is remarkable that Mr. Elliston's greatest fault is an occasional monotony, which indulges in a pompous depth of voice and a singular snatching of the breath at the end of his more energetic words. These snatches sometimes amount to a sort of grave sobbing, ludicrously abstracted from everything like sorrow. His words seem to burst out with majestic emotion, and then to retire into themselves to enjoy their achievement. From whatever cause this error may arise, whether it really proceeds from the self-complacency of declamation, or whether it be not rather a recollection of the speech-making schoolboy who affects a certain manly depth of utterance to astonish the lower forms, it is a mere habit of speaking which Mr. Elliston ought to renounce with the greater ease, since it is owing neither to confined powers of voice nor to a confined range of ideas.

In spite of this fault, however, I consider Mr. Elliston, not only with respect to his versatility, but in his general excellence and in the perfection to which he has brought some of his characters, the greatest actor of the present day.

Mr. Kemble's friends, Mr. Cooke's, and Mr. Pope's all speaking at once.	" Bless my soul, sir, you have totally forgotten	that great actor Mr. Kemble ! " that excellent, unsophisticated actor Mr. Cooke ! " that lofty, energetic, and surprising actor, Mr. Pope ! "

Excuse me, gentlemen. Mr. Kemble is certainly an actor of consummate study ; Mr. Cooke has a genius natural and powerful, though confined ; and Mr. Pope is an excellent miniature painter. Let everybody possess his due honours. It is my firm conviction that if Elliston possessed the fine countenance of Mr. Kemble, he would instantly outshine him in everybody's opinion, even in the character[1] which Mr. Kemble at present calls his own. Mr. Kemble's studiousness damps his enthusiasm ; Mr. Elliston's enthusiasm overcomes his study : if the one has more judgment, the other has more genius. Mr. Cooke, like Elliston, is a greater comedian than tragedian ; and in his peculiar walk undoubtedly displays a firm and original step ; but neither in comedy nor tragedy is he at the height of the drama, for he is confined to hypocrisy and sarcasm. As to Mr. Pope, he is, as I have said before, a very excellent artist : Mr. Elliston, at least as far as I know, is no artist at all. They are therefore at issue : there are no points of comparison between them.

With respect to Mr. Elliston's versatility, it is much

---

[1] So in original edition ; no doubt a misprint for " characters."

the fashion for certain critics to insist that if he performs twelve distinct species of character tolerably, he does not succeed in any one of them, so well as the actor of that particular character ; he is great, they say, in the aggregate only : if his bundle, in short, is strong, his sticks are easily broken one by one. Now, though his comedy is, in my opinion, generally unrivalled, yet I have granted that he is not so great in tragedy as Mr. Kemble, merely for want of manner, not for want of genius. But if these gentlemen desire perfection with versatility, let them observe that Mr. Kemble wants versatility and perfection. Mr. Kemble is by no means at the height of tragedy, since his best performance is Penruddock, which is of that mongrel declamatory genius that belongs half to tragedy and half to comedy. If this actor be suffered to want perfection, who has to attain it in one or two species of character only, Mr. Elliston may certainly be suffered in a greater degree, who has to attain it in many. If it be allowed a man not to reach the goal who runs in one straight road, it may certainly be allowed another who runs through fifty devious paths.

The powers of versatility unluckily weaken each other's effect, and were a performer able to represent ten characters to perfection, he would run the hazard of being thought inferior to ten other actors, each of whom was perfect in only one of them. A lady in four gauze cloaks of the brightest colour with a yellow one underneath might not boast half the amber radiance of a female dressed in nothing but the same yellow, but her colours would be really as bright and at the same time of a much richer variety. There are many of these unitarian critics, who think Milton a more sublime poet than Shakspeare, merely because his fancy is generally grave and employed

upon sublime subjects, not to mention that he is totally
void of humour. Shakspeare, unfortunately for himself,
can not only elevate our imagination, but can familiarise
us with the business of life, nay, what is still more
unlucky, he can make us laugh heartily, and has an
inexhaustible fund of gay wit and humour. But it would
be difficult to produce a sublime thought in Milton which
should not be at least equalled by one as sublime in the
great dramatist : and unhappily for these gentlemen,
Milton is almost utterly deficient in one great part of the
sublime, which is carried to its perfection by Shakspeare : it might be questioned whether he ever excited a
tear.

In short, if Mr. Elliston performed in tragedy only, he
would be thought a much better tragedian, not only
because the critics would more willingly allow him his
single claim, but because his comic powers would no
longer present their superior contrast. It must be confessed, at the same time, that he acts too often : his busy
frequency of appearance injures him doubly ; it familiar-
ises his powers of pleasing too much with the town, and
it leaves him too little leisure for study. They whose
value partakes much of the personal, whether kings or
actors, should yield themselves as sparingly as possible to
public exhibition. Mr. Kemble knows this well.

MR. COOKE.

Mr. Cooke is the Machiavel of the modern stage. One
would imagine that if he had been in the French theatre
during the revolution, when actors became legislators, he
might have become the most finished statesman of his

day. He can be either a gloomy hypocrite, like Cromwell, or a gay one, such as Chesterfield would have made his own son. He can render all his passions subservient to one passion and one purpose, and can

> ". . . smile, and smile, and be a villain."

Like most statesmen, however, he can do nothing without artifice. His looks and his tones invariably turn him from the very appearance of virtue. If he wishes to be seriously sentimental, he deviates into irony ; if he endeavours to appear candid, his manner is so strange and inconsistent that you are merely inclined to guard against him the more. It is for these reasons that his gentlemen in sentimental comedy become so awkward and inefficient, that his Jaques in *As You Like It*, instead of being a moralising enthusiast, is merely a grave scoffer, and that his Macbeth, who ought to be at least a majestic villain, exhibits nothing but a desperate craftiness. Of his Hamlet one would willingly spare the recollection. The most accomplished character on the stage is converted into an unpolished, obstinate, sarcastic madman.

Mr. Cooke is, in fact, master of every species of hypocrisy ; and if he is a confined actor, it must be confessed that his powers are always active and vigorous in their confinement. He is great in the hypocrisy that endeavous to conceal itself by seriousness, as in Iago and Stukely,[1] in the hypocrisy that endeavours to conceal itself by gaiety and sarcasm, as in Sir Archy M'Sarcasm,[2] and lastly in the most impudent hypocrisy, such as that of

[1] In *The Gamester*, by Edward Moore.
[2] In *Love à la Mode*, by Macklin.

Sir Pertinax M'Sycophant[1] and of Richard the Third. I do not think he can be called a great tragedian, though he performs Richard so excellently. Much of this character is occupied by the display of a confident dissimulation, which is something very different from the dignity of tragedy. If Cooke performs the more serious part with success, if we are attentive to his misfortunes as well as to his prosperity, it is because our attention has been so fixed by the fraud that produced them : we see the punishment of hypocritical ambition fallen upon its proper object. Kemble has more dignity in the character, but he entirely wants its artifice, and he has done singular honour to his judgment and forbearance in relinquishing the crafty usurper to the most crafty of actors.

In the more humorous parts, however, of Mr. Cooke's Richard, and indeed in all his hypocritical humour except when it soliloquises or confesses itself, it may be questioned whether he ought to betray his deception to the audience by so manifest an hypocrisy of countenance. It is evident that a consummate hypocrite in real life would attempt a look the very reverse of apparent fraud, otherwise he would render himself liable to detection, and, in fact, be no true hypocrite. To those who would object that if hypocrisy be thus divested of externals, an actor capable of mere gravity would succeed best in deception, it may be answered that there are always times in a play when a hypocrite must talk to himself either by side-speeches or by expressive meditation ; in soliloquies especially, he will lay aside the mask, and give a loose to his enjoyment or vexation by setting his features at liberty. The best excuse, however, that can be given for the carelessness with which Mr. Cooke's

[1] In *The Man of the World*, by Macklin.

hypocrisy looks out of his countenance, is the unconscious enjoyment which deceitful villainy cannot help expressing at the anticipation or attainment of success; and it must be confessed that any vice long indulged generally stamps its peculiar character on the countenance.

A performer like Cooke is necessarily greater in comedy than tragedy, because hypocrisy is not only one of those baser passions which excite our contempt, but because it deals much in equivocation and sarcasm, which are among the first beauties of comedy. Stukely in the *Gamester* is tragic in the effects produced by his villainy, but in the pursuit of this villainy he is merely grave or sentimental; and everything like cheating has a principle of the ridiculous in it: Rochefoucault, perhaps, would account for this in the superiority which we give our own sagacity over the person cheated. With all Cooke's assumed meekness of countenance in this character and in that of Iago, with his fits of thoughtfulness so inimitably familiar, and his sudden sighs of pitying conviction, he is always greater as he approaches comedy, and his most finished performance is, in my opinion, Sir Pertinax M'Sycophant in the *Man of the World*. The author's Sir Archy M'Sarcasm is merely a slight outline of this corrupt satirical Scotchman; and therefore it is nothing but a smaller sketch in the hands of the actor.

Sir Pertinax would be a perfect piece of acting if Mr. Cooke's action was more various. By giving the person represented a manner, it is sometimes, indeed, more impressive in its effect, especially when the character is an eccentric one; but our love of genius will sometimes make us displeased with a beauty itself when we know the performer cannot help it, though Mr. Kemble's

Penruddock may be a proof to the contrary; and in the case of Sir Pertinax a variety of action would be much more natural, since he is of so various and sanguine a temper, so various in his contrivances, and so various in his behaviour. A monotony of any kind must be un-usual with active hypocrisy.

But you may see all the beauties and all the faults of Cooke in this single character; and this proves, perhaps, that it is his favourite one, since he feels inclined to in-dulge all his habits in its representation. The Scotch dialect which he so inimitably assumes is in vain under-valued by those who persuade themselves that he was born in Scotland. In the first place, to be merely born there is nothing to the purpose, for a man born upon the sea might as well be expected to talk like a dolphin. If he was educated by or with Scotch people, it is merely wonderful that he does not talk Scotch in his English characters, for he gives them none of those compressed vowels and liquified consonants, none of that artlessness and undulation of tone so ludicrous in Sir Pertinax. It is this artlessness of tone that renders a hypocritical Scotchman or Welshman more humorous on the stage than any other hypocrite, and more successful, perhaps, in the world. Sir Pertinax, however, conceals an unavoid-able ludicrousness, which might sometimes injure his cause, by apparently delighting in his dialect and by possessing much intentional humour. If Cooke bows, it is with a face that says "What a fool you are to be deceived with this fawning!" If he looks friendly, it is with a smile that says "I will make use of you, and you may go to the devil." A simple rustic might feel all his affections warmed at his countenance, and exclaim "What a pure-hearted old gentleman!" but a fine observer would descry under the glowing exterior nothing but professions without meaning, and a heart without warmth.

The sarcasm of Cooke is at all times most bitter, but in this character its acerbity is tempered with no respect either for its object or for himself. His tone is out-rageously smooth and deep ; and when it finds its softest level, its under monotony is so full of what is called hugging one's self, and is accompanied with such a dragged smile and viciousness of leer, that he seems as if he had lost his voice through the mere enjoyment of malice.

It is thus that in characters of the most apparent labour as well as in a total neglect of study, this excellent actor surpasses all his contemporaries. His principal faults are confined to his person, for they consist in a monotonous gesture and a very awkward gait. His shrinking rise of the shoulders, however, may give an idea of that contracted watchfulness, with which a mean hypocrite retires into himself. His general air, indeed, his sarcastic cast of countenance with its close wideness of smile and its hooked nose, and his utter want of study joined to the villainous characters he represents, are occasionally sufficient to make some people almost fall out with the actor ; but it must be recollected that if Garrick was disgustingly vulgar in Abel Drugger, he displayed the most fascinating manners in private life, and that if Mr. Davenport [1] the actor always looks like a man whose gouty leg has been just kicked, he is said to be a man of much benevolence.

[1] Mr. Davenport was a comedian of considerable ability, whose wife was a noted actress. He retired from the stage in 1812, and died in 1814.

MR. CHARLES KEMBLE.

I DO not know what thoughtlessness or forgetfulness could have possessed me when I proposed to class this elegant actor with the tragedians only. I must have been seized with a little of that languor, which is his worst affectation, and which is as infectious in an actor as in a supper of lettuces. But how could I forget his occasional vivacity, his occasional dry humour, and his inimitable pictures of intoxication, so natural and yet never disgusting ; not to mention his frequent awfulness of frown, which is infinitely droll, though he does not know it ?

Mr. Charles Kemble excels in three classes of character : in the tender lover, like Romeo, in the spirited gentleman of tragedy, such as Laertes and Faulconbridge, and in a very happy mixture of the occasional debauchee and the gentleman of feeling, as in Shakespeare's Cassio and Charles Oakley in the *Jealous Wife.*[1]

In theatric love, in that complaining softness with which the fancies of young ladies adorn their imaginary heroes, Mr. Charles Kemble is certainly the first performer on the stage. He seems resolved to make up for his brother's utter deficiency in this respect. His performance of Romeo would undoubtedly be superior to that of Mr. Elliston, could he shake off his indolent languor. Fondness of attitude and looks of abstracted endearment acquire an additional charm from his dignified and graceful aspect, and from that reposing command in the air of his head and shoulders, which reminds us of the placid dignity of the Antinous. But this languor is occasionally so unhappy that his attention

[1] By George Colman the elder.

to his mistress appears to be a painful effort, and instead of being tender from amatory feeling betrays a kind of civil pity for the poor lady, the true *comis in uxorem* [1] of Horace.

That this weariness or affected patience of manner is not natural to the actor, but the mere result of bad habit, may be easily seen in the animation of his Laertes and his Faulconbridge. If in the former character he has little to display but personal spirit, in the latter he exhibits a very bold spirit of raillery, a gay insolence justified by the contemptibility of its object. It is with much skill that he suddenly bursts into a proud ridicule of the Duke of Austria, without indulging in the flourish of fist which common actors mistake for indignation : he does not, like a South-sea warrior, waste half his strength on the enemy by a preliminary bravado of gesture. All great effects are produced by contrast. Anger is never so noble as when it breaks out of a comparative continence of aspect : it is the earthquake bursting from the repose of nature.

One could not well excuse, even in tragedy, that perpetual lightning of frown with which Mr. Charles Kemble pierces the pit ; and as to his perpetual bite of the lips, it is allowable to nobody but a young lady preparing her rosiest looks for company, or to a malicious and mean villain suddenly detected, or to a schoolboy, perhaps, when he is winding up his top. But this cloudiness of face, this system of frowning and biting is wonderfully misplaced in comedy ; the νεφιληγίρετα Ζεύς, the cloud-compelling Jove, is not the god of levity. What with the lamps and the rouge, his eyes may indeed acquire much ferocious decision and brightness, but he

[1] *Epistles*, bk. ii., 2, l. 133.

would lose no reputation by leaving to Mr. H. Johnston [1] the judgment of turning mere " meditation to madness." A frank youth, like Frederick Bramble in the *Poor Gentleman*,[2] a character which Mr. C. Kemble otherwise performs with most appropriate spirit, never thinks of this gloomy stare, which amounts to the expression of an afflicted conscience ; nor does a gay villain, like Plastic in *Town and Country*,[3] make his resolutions with a countenance that might betray him to the slightest observer.   Mr. C. Kemble's ironical contempt of Reuben Glenroy's advice in this character, and of Sir Charles Cropland in Frederick Bramble is in the happiest wonderment of tone : his languor becomes a beauty when thrown into the careless slur and patient acquiescence of his replies.   Any cool humourist would talk in the same way.   But what should we think of a man who, when he was meditating on the choice of a watch-string, should dart into the most terrific side-frowns ; or when he was asked whether he preferred pudding or pie, should knit his brows into an agony of logical doubt ?

Guest, (after frowning with downward meditation). Madam, I will take a little pie.—(*Aside, after receiving the pie and frowning with awful study*).   I am not sure that pudding wouldn't have been better.

I was sorry to see that Mr. C. Kemble could not help carrying this ludicrous fault into his most careless intoxi·cation : his representation of a superior sort of drunkard would otherwise be perfect.   It is this representation

---

[1] Henry Johnston is blamed by Leigh Hunt (in an essay which we do not reprint), for " indulging himself in all the mute cant of the stage, rolling his eyes, and frowning most terrifically."

[2] By George Colman the younger.

[3] By Thomas Morton.

which renders his Charles Oakley and his Cassio such
finished and original performances. To amuse us, and
at the same time to maintain our respect in intoxication,
might be thought an impossibility, if he did not do both
in these characters. But with all that relaxation of limb,
which seems so destructive of gentlemanly appearance,
with all that relaxation of countenance which is the very
reverse of sensible expression, with all that gay disdain
of common customs and civilities which wine inspires, he
contrives not only to appear respectable, but even to
interest our feelings. I have seen him, when representing
a fond husband who had been seduced into a debauch,
absolutely borrow a pathos from this odious vice, and, in
the midst of his careless nonsense, turn to his wife with a
voice so quarrelling with himself, so broken between
gaiety and remorse, so painful in its attempt to be strongly
affectionate, that the contrast of his graces with his
defects, of his powers with his wishes, of his love for his
wife and his heartfelt inability to express it, reached all
the domestic feelings of his audience. It is the same with
his Cassio, whose remorse appears so much the stronger
from his inability to rid himself of the debauch which he
abhors. There is no actor who imitates this defect with
such a total want of affectation. All the other performers
wish to be humorous drunkards, and by this error they
cannot help showing a kind of abstract reasoning which
defeats their purpose. They play a hundred antics with
legs which a drunkard would be unable to lift, they make
a thousand grimaces which the jaws of a drunkard could
not attempt from mere want of tone ; they roll about from
place to place, though his whole strength is exerted to
command his limbs ; they wish, in short, to appear drunk,
when the great object of a drunkard is to appear sober.

Mr. Charles Kemble is upon the whole a very gentlemanly and useful actor, with much of graceful mediocrity, and with an occasional display of great genius. It appears to me that his unfortunate languor hides his real ability, and that, like a giant oppressed with sleepiness, he sinks to the level of feebler men. When I call him a useful actor, I do not apply the epithet like those newspapers who bestow it on every actor that can do a number of things tolerably and nothing well. Not that I would question, as to matters of stage convenience, the utility, much less the genius, of any gentleman who would undertake to read a book at a moment's notice : but Mr. C. Kemble is useful to the audience, as well as to the managers ; if he undertakes a character not originally his own, he gives us its moral effects as well as its discourse ; he gives us not only the face but the soul of his person, not only its gesticulation but its proper impulse. A bad actor may be defined as an animal who utters a certain number of sounds to exercise the patience of a certain number of people.

APPENDIX.[1]

EXTRACTS FROM *THE NEWS*.

JOHN KEMBLE'S MISPRONUNCIATIONS.

WE are amazed that the audience do not contrive some means of noticing Mr. Kemble's vicious orthöepy. He appears to alter the pronunciation of his words merely for the sake of alteration. There is no rule for pronunciation but custom, and this rule he perpetually violates in a manner that would be highly amusing, did it not injure some of the finest sentences of our tragic poets. This defect has gradually increased on the stage, and the other actors, thinking it, perhaps, a mark of their invention to clip and coin in this way, are sometimes totally unintelligible. A man who utters one of these affectations in company would be set down by his hearers as a person unfortunate in a country dialect. Let us conceive for instance two gentlemen in conversation, making use of the language of Mr. Kemble and these other actors, and the astonishment of a third person overhearing them. We will suppose that an officer of the regiment which has just been ordered to let the beard grow on the upper lip is accosted by a fashionable friend :--

[1] The titles to these articles are supplied by the editors, except where otherwise noted.

A. Ha, Captain how dost? The[1] appearance would be much improved by a little more attention to the[2] bird.[3]

B. Why, so I think: there's no sentimint[4] in a bird.[5] But then it serves to distinguish the soldier, and there is no doubt much military vartue[6] in looking furful.[7]

A. But the girls, Jack, the girls! Why the[8] mouth is enough to banish kissing from the airth[9] etairnally.[10]

B. In maircy,[11] no more of that! Zounds, but the shop-keepers and the marchants[12] will get the better of us with the dear souls! However, as it is now against military law to have a tender countenance, and as some birds,[13] I thank heaven, are of a tolerable quaality,[14] I must make a vartue[15] of necessity, and as I can't look soft for the love of my girl, I must e'en look hijjus[16] for the love of my country.

———

Is it not a pity that an actor, who can give such dignity to what is worthy of being dignified, should by an indiscriminate importance level it with meaner matter? The following lines were delivered with almost as heroic a resolution as the last: Coriolanus means to be familiar; but Mr. Kemble is—what shall we say? is still Mr. Kemble:—

> *Cor.*　　　　　　　I will go wash:
> And when my face is fair, you shall perceive
> Whether I blush or no.

The word *fair* might positively have been measured by a stop-watch: instead of being a short monosyllable, it became a word of tremendous elongation. We can describe the pronunciation by nothing else than by such a sound as *fay-er-r-r*. Luckily for our fastidious, or as Mr. Kemble would say, our *fastijjus* ears, we had no opportunity of hearing *bird* for *beard;* but it was in vain to expect any repose in orthöepy, when Mr.

[1] Thy. [2] Thy. [3] Beard. [4] Sentiment. [5] Beard. [6] Virtue. [7] Fearful.
[8] Thy. [9] Earth. [10] Eternally. [11] Mercy. [12] Merchants. [13] Beards.
[14] Quality. [15] Virtue. [16] Hideous.

Kemble had gotten such a word as *Aufidius* to transmogrify. This he universally called *Aufijjus*, like a young lady who talks of her *ojus* lover, or the *ojus* month of November. The name, too, of Coriolanus is divided by Mr. Kemble with syllabical precision into five distinct sounds, though the general pronunciation, as well as Shakspeare himself, shortens the *rio* into one syllable, as in the word *chariot:* the alteration is of no effect, but to give a stiffness to what is already too stiff, and to render many of the poet's lines harsh and unmetrical. It is unlucky for Mr. Kemble's audience that he never meets with a line in which this absurdity would be too frequently glaring to be endured. We should like to hear Mr. Kemble repeat the following lines: we will suppose he is in the manager's room addressing a rascally Jew with a thin beard, who wishes to purchase some of the worn-out seas and thunder of the stage :—

> *The varchue,* Jew, is scanty as *the bird,*
> *Ay-y-y,* and *the* heart as black ; *the* very cloaths bag,
> Pregnant with rottenness, is *fay-er-r-r* unto't,
> Though stuff'd with all the *furful marchandise*
> Of shirt purloin'd, or shoes, or milk-white shift,
> Once wrapping heav'n, now wrapp'd with *airthly* things,
> Nankeens perchance, or buckskins saddle-proof,
> Or plush, or worse than all, rough corderoys
> Six-stringed, that on the musical knock-knees
> Of 'prentice-boy seducer, toiling fast
> Through dust and sunshine to the hill of Greenwich,
> Charm'd with *melojus* creaks the easy maid.
> Nay, get thee gone : I've nothing for thee, Jew,
> Nor tinsel crown, nor tyger wheel-embowell'd
> *Furful* with painted deal-board, nor the steeds
> Centaur revers'd, prancing on human legs,
> Nor mine heroic sheep's-blood, nor the hosts
> Of pasteboard war, nor mustard-bowl, nor bullet
> ' Grating harsh thunder," nor an ounce of rosin
> Pow'rful alike on billowy seas of tin
> To flash dread light, or soften fiddle-strings.
> Nay, get thee gone !—
> It doth abuse my mother tongue to talk wi'thee,
> *Ojus, insijjus, hijjus,* and *perfijjus !*

AN ESSAY ON INVENTION IN PRONUNCIATION.[1]

> *Coriolanus.*   So shall my lungs
> Coin words till their decay.—*Shakspeare.*

The critics from time immemorial have agreed that invention
is the first qualification and mark of genius ; but it is certain
they have not thoroughly comprehended the nature of this
invention.   Those who would confine it to what is usually
understood by the word *originality* are evidently mistaken ;
for by this simple definition they would persuade us that none
were great geniuses but Homer, Milton, Shakspeare, and a few
other originals ; but the fact is, that invention displays itself by
two beauties instead of one, *originality* and *singularity;* though
it must be confessed that the nature of these beauties is essentially the same, their possessors equally agreeing to differ from
the rest of mankind.   It is inconceivable how infinitely this
true definition of genius will increase the literary glory of Great
Britain ; the drama, for instance, will be proud not only of
Congreve, Wycherley, and Sheridan, but of D'Urfey, Shadwell,[2]
Reynolds, Cherry, Dibdin, and a thousand others, whom the
malice of ignorant critics would have condemned to eternal
oblivion.   In fact, a new world of genius will burst upon our
view ; in Doctor Mavor[3] we shall find an excellent biographer,
in Mr. Robert Heron[4] a most dispassionate historian, in Mr.
Capel Loft[5] a critic amiably impartial ; to be brief, in every
street-ballad the spirit of wandering Homer, and in every stupid
pretender a genius of consummate modesty.

[1] So entitled by Leigh Hunt.

[2] Leigh Hunt is rather unjust to Tom D'Urfey (died 1723) and Thomas
Shadwell (1640-1692). Both were dramatists of great ability, and the
latter especially wrote some comedies of striking merit.

[3] William Fordyce Mavor (1758-1837) of spelling-book fame, author
(among many other things) of a " Universal History " in 25 vols. (1801).

[4] Author of a " New General History of Scotland " (1794-99) ; " Memoir
of Burns" (1797) ; and " Letter to Wilberforce on the Justice and Expe-
diency of Slavery (1806). Died 1807.

[5] Capel Loft (1751-1824) author of " Eudosia, a Poem of the Universe "
(1781) ; " History of the Corporation and Test Acts " (1790), &c.

If by these means we discover a great number of geniuses in writing, we shall find a still greater number in speaking. That oratorical body, the mob, has always exhibited a peculiar felicity in the invention of dialects, as the writer of the " Cant-Dictionary " has elegantly exemplified; but in pronunciation few have excelled the daring imagination of Mr. Kemble, of Covent Garden, who seems determined not only to render himself altogether unintelligible, but to introduce a new language on the stage, and make Shakspeare and Congreve as difficult of comprehension as if they had written in Coptic or Hindostanee. The reason of this is very simple : Mr. Kemble is determined to be thought a genius in all possible ways, and while he displays a happy originality in some of his stage performances, is determined to be *singular* where no man can be *original*. One circumstance would be a little unfortunate for Mr. Kemble, if, with a spirit truly magnanimous, he did not take a pleasure in difficulties. There will always be some envious critics obstinate enough to maintain that no man can pretend to dictate to society its mode of pronunciation ; that if Sheridan, or Walker, or Jones were to give his opinion in the course of conversation on the pronunciation of any word, this opinion would be no more than that of an individual not very learned ; and, therefore, that no such man, nor indeed any other, either in public writing or speaking, is warranted to insist on a favourite mode of his own ; for as intelligibility of speech is the concern of the majority, the majority alone can decide what is convenient or inconvenient to their mutual understanding. But, like other superior geniuses, Mr. Kemble despises the majority, and is ambitious of pleasing the chosen few only, who, without doubt, if there be any such, are very few indeed, and very great linguists. What but very learned ears could have found any possible meaning in Mr. Kemble's conversion of the word *aches* into *aitches?* If Mr. Kemble wishes to show his regard for Shakspeare's metre by giving the proper quantity of syllables to the line,

Fill all thy bones with aches, make thee roar,

it is somewhat strange that he should so often put the poet's feet out of joint in *Coriolanus.* Were we to reason from analogy, and to divide the word *aches* into two syllables at all, we should certainly call it *a-kes*, since in words derived from the Greek,[1] the *ch* before a vowel is, we believe, invariably pronounced like *k*, with the exception of *charity, archer*, and *schism.* But to supply all deficiencies of Shakspeare's metre is a task for those verbal slaves only who would make Chaucer's lines as exact as Swift's, and as Mr. Kemble in his very systems is a daring rather than a plodding genius, and does not use this pronunciation from a regard either for Shakspeare or the audience, we must attribute it to that self-possession or self-confidence which in all ages has enabled great men to be perfectly satisfied with themselves, though the whole world were unable to tell why.

Those facetious gentlemen, the lottery-office-keepers, whose newspaper advertisements afford so many fine specimens of the bathos, have with their usual disinterested fancy indorsed the play hand-bills with divers literary eccentricities, that instruct us, when we have thrown away half our money at Mr. Reynolds's farces, how to throw away the rest elsewhere. This example, we have had some thoughts of turning to account in our publication of the following Lexicon, so that every lady or gentleman, who should purchase a play-bill, might find a list of the performers on one side of it, and the means of understanding them on the other :—

aches,	- - - -	aitches.
beard,	- - - -	bird.
cheerful,	- - -	churful.
conscience,	- -	conshince.
earth,-	- - - -	airth.
err,	- - - - -	air (and so in every recurrence of the syllables *er* and *ir*).
farewell,	- - -	farwell.
fearful,	- - - -	furful.

---

[1] "Ache" is of Saxon, not Greek, origin. Leigh Hunt adopts the derivation given by Johnson, to whose authority the substitution of *ache* for the earlier spelling, *ake*, is mainly due.

fierce, - - - -	furse.
hideous, - - -	hijjus.
insidious, - - -	insijjus.
innocence, - - -	innocince.
infirmity, - - -	infaremity.
leap, - - - - -	lep.
leisure, - - - -	leasure.
melodious, - - -	melojus.
merchant, - - -	marchant.
odious, - - - -	ojus.
perfidious, - - -	perfijjus (and so in all adjectives ending with *dious*).
pierce, - - - -	purse.
prudence, - - -	prudince.
quality, - - - -	(the first syllable like that in the word *aliment*).
rode, - - - - -	rod.
sovereign, - - -	suvran.
stir, - - - - -	stare.
thy, - - - - -	the.
virgin, - - - -	vargin.
you, - - - - -	ye (that is, the plural for the singular number).
ye, - - - - -	*jee*, after words ending with *d*, as *demanjee*, for *demand ye :* or *chee*, after words ending with *t*, *hurchee* for *hurt ye*.

We are afraid that all our readers will not exactly agree with the arguments we have produced in favour of Mr. Kemble's genius for orthöepy. The English have an awkward conciseness about them, very unfavourable to these far-fetched eccentricities of genius; and the same spirit that makes them prefer a short cut through a lane to a circuitous walk round a fine street, will render them disgusted at these slow approaches of meaning, however pompous their manner and language. We have more than once felt for the distinct speaker, as he gave his dialect its most methodical utterance, for

> There still remains, to mortify a wit,
> The many-headed monster of the pit ;

and we should not be at all surprised if, on some tragic night, while Mr. Kemble's genius is indulging itself, a few marks of illiterate contempt should produce an awkward catastrophe.

"THE GRECIAN DAUGHTER."

Murphy's tragedy of the *Grecian Daughter* was rendered interesting by the energetic performance of Mrs. Siddons, who like all great performers contradicts the old adage, *ex nihilo nil fit ;* for in this character she certainly makes a great deal out of nothing. Her sudden start towards Philotas and mute prostration to the ground to thank him for saving her father's life was sublime. Murphy was no poet ; his only talent, which was an excellent one, lay in humour, and he will be for ever remembered as the author of the first farce in the English language, the *Citizen.* His tragedy of the *Grecian Daughter* is one tissue of commonplace ideas, and commonplace expressions; the incidents which he has borrowed from tradition are affecting, but he has very little else of tragedy except its language, which abounds in pompous lines and hackneyed invocations to the gods. If there are any good sentiments they are not his own ; Murphy was a man of learning, and has called Homer and Plato to assist him in sentimentalising his tragedies, as he made Plautus and Terence laugh for him in his pieces of humour. There is but one original thought, at least we believe it to be original, in this whole tragedy ; it is the idea of Philotas on hearing that Evander had been saved from starvation by his daughter's milk :—

All her laws
Inverted quite, great Nature triumphs still !

This sentence, which would have been passed over amidst innumerable beauties in Shakspeare, shines like a star from the cloudy dulness of Murphy's tragedy.

PLAYWRIGHTS AND THE PRESS.

The reason of the production and reproduction of modern plays is at present not a little obscure. It can hardly be the interest of the managers, for their views in that case are never attained ; it cannot be the beauty of the author, for beautiful authors there are none ; it cannot be the pleasure of the town, for the town cannot be pleased with what it invariably condemns. Let us lift the curtain a little, and glance into the machinery of theatrical politics. Paucity of contribution is certainly not the cause of these miserable productions, for the manager has his chest full of manuscript dramas ; all of these he cannot bring to light, and it is well no doubt that most of them are locked up in everlasting sleep, fated never to give sleep to others. But in all this mighty mass is there nothing worthy of consideration, is there nothing that can deliver us from such dramatic opiates as the *Delinquent* and the *Prior Claim*, and teach us to keep our eyes open, instead of yawning out our disapprobation and wishing for our nightcaps? No doubt there is, but the manager can do nothing : we must suppose, indeed, that he can distinguish good writing from bad, for if he cannot he is not fit for his situation ; but he may find twenty good pieces, acknowledge their merit, and yet he shall do nothing. We will explain this. A bad writer, who cannot trust to the intrinsic merit of his productions for their success, has a thousand manœuvres to supply the deficiency. In the first place, he scrapes acquaintance with all the actors, one after another, invites them to dinner, takes tickets on their benefit-nights, and praises their jokes; these habits beget familiarity, familiarity is the twin-brother of confidence, and in the glow of some fifth pint after dinner our author produces a manuscript written by himself *purposely for the display of the peculiar talents of his theatrical friends :* his theatrical friends are enchanted, he becomes a haunter of the green-room, and the manager at length accepts his piece, though he knows no more of the talents of the writer than his drollery at a dinner, his turn of a pun, or his slapping the actors on the shoulder and calling them Dick, Jack, and Harry. Our author has now nothing to think of but the first night ; every goose that he hears reminds him of the pit, and every oath of damnation ; he flies to the newspaper offices, and scrapes acquaintance with those good-natured paragraphists who cheat the town by false criticism out of pure love for their friends, or what is the same thing, their friends' suppers : one he invites to a bottle, a second he praises for his learning and wit, and to a third he whispers, "*Box tickets—no reserve—all your friends !*" Having thus secured all quarters, and well stocked the galleries with those strong-lunged idlers who for the consideration of a few tickets are always at the service of a timid author, he ventures his piece on the public : the actors exert themselves to admiration, the applause that follows is given not to the excellence of the dialogue, but to the excellence of its delivery, and the good-natured audience, in spite of a few discerning hissers, are unwilling to send supperless to bed the miserable scribbler, who begs and prays them so hard in his prologue. The next day all the papers are in raptures, and the old obliging criticism comes forward :—" *Last night a new piece—from the fertile pen of Mr. So-and-so—wit—genuine nature—dialogue piquant— incidents chaste—originality—Mr. —— was excellent—Mrs. —— looked charmingly—great eclat—crowded house—promises to be a great favourite.*" In two weeks the piece creeps into its grave ; the author, however, being a friend of the actors, and, as it were, *naturalised* in the green-room, grows like a bad habit upon the manager, and toils every year to be applauded by the papers and to be forgotten by posterity. Such is the origin of the Reynoldses, the Dibdins, and the Arnolds of the day, and such are the reasons that influence managers in their studies to please the public. Such, too, must have been the influence of Mr. Lewis in prevailing on the managers to revive his prosaic tragedy. This gentleman is more successful as a follower of Mrs. Radcliffe in the fields of romance. Though his genius at times appears to have been nourished in a charnel-house, and he too often mistakes the disgusting for the terrific, yet it is some praise to a modern romance-writer that he can throw interest into hobgoblin-stories and alarums of the nursery. In an age, however, that can boast but three genuine poets, Mr. Lewis has no pretensions to the Parnassian laurel ; his genius forsakes him when his steps begin to tread metrically, and his tragedy of *Alfonso*, in its antiquity of imagery and its inanity of language, serves but to add another proof to the melancholy truth, that there is no British tragic poet existing. Of the universal decline, indeed, of the English drama, every day brings stronger conviction, and it becomes the duty of the conductors of the stage to discourage the future attempts of those who are hastening its declension. We yield to no nation upon earth in the glory of the conqueror's laurel, why should we in that of the poet's? If the manager would say that it is impossible to find a dramatic genius, he will not say the truth: let encouragement but call them forth, and they will appear. The profoundest ages of ignorance owed all their sleep, not to the actual decline of the human mind, but to circumstances that narrowed its scope of action. The ministers of France in the seventeenth century loved the arts, and they raised what is called the Age of Lewis the Fourteenth: Augustus wished to be immortal; he opened the sunshine of his court to literary genius, and his reign is immortalised under the title of the Augustan Age.

It has been said that we are sometimes too severe in our dramatic strictures. To be severe is not our will but our necessity; the fault lies not in us but in those unhappy authors who

in spite
Of nature and their stars will write.

It is ludicrous enough that a man should produce something contemptible and then quarrel with us for our contempt: a criminal who had been found guilty at the bar might as well express his astonishment at the want of feeling in the judge. Let the managers present the public with something that shall do honour to their own judgment, and the town would see with what pleasures we should give them the sanction of ours. It is the boast of the writer of this article that his opinions have been guided by nothing but a regard for truth, for the real pleasure of the town, and for the literary reputation of Englishmen; and it is his happiness that these opinions have been approved by the public. He was severe indeed with the *Prior Claim*, when the daily papers were not; he ridiculed the *Delinquent*, when the daily papers saw nothing ridiculous in it. Who was right?

The *Prior Claim* died in a few days after his criticism, and the *Delinquent* has followed it to the grave. It is time to rescue the critical character of the public prints from the charge of carelessness, of ignorance, and of corruption; they are the directors of the public taste and the correctors of its depravation, and they should study to deserve the confidence of those whom they would instruct. As long as there is nothing to praise, the Dramatic Critic of the *News* must continue to blame : the task of correcting the stage in its present vitiated state is no doubt a difficult one, but if he shall have contributed to crush one wretched play, or to shame one wretched author, his efforts will have been sufficiently rewarded ; and he is resolved that if the somniferous dramatists will suffer him to keep his eyes open and hold his pen, and while he is honoured with the public attention,

> no dull dramatic knave
> Shall walk the stage in quiet to his grave.

RULES FOR THE THEATRICAL CRITIC OF A NEWSPAPER.[1]

In the first place.—Never take any notice whatever of the author of a play, or of the play itself, unless it be a new one : if the author be living, it is most probable you will have no reason to speak of him more than once, and if he be not living, you have no reason to speak of him at all, for dead men cannot give dinners.

Secondly.—Indulge an acquaintance with every dramatic writer, and with every actor, and you will have a noble opportunity of showing your fine feelings and your philanthropy, for you will praise every play that is acted, and every actor that plays ; depend upon it, the world will attribute this praise solely to your undeviating benevolence, which is a great virtue.

Thirdly.—If an audience should not possess this virtue equally with yourselves, but should barbarously hiss a new piece merely because it could not entertain them, say in your next day's criticism, that it would have been infinitely more

[1] Leigh Hunt's title.

entertaining if a little had been added, or a little had been taken away, a probability which few will dispute with you. No man of real feeling will think of damning another merely because the latter cannot succeed in every attempt to please him. If the exclamation *bravo!* will make a man enjoy his supper and put a few pounds into his pocket every winter, who would not cry out *bravo?* Suppose an ugly, whimsical fellow were to accost you in the streets and to say, " Sir, I'd thank you to tell me I am handsome, or I shall be miserable for months to come," you would undoubtedly say, " Sir, I am enchanted with your appearance, and entreat you to be perfectly happy." In the same manner it is easy to say to Mr. Reynolds, or Mr. Dibdin, or Mr. Cherry, " Your play was excellent," and the poor fellow will be as comfortable as if it were really the case.

Fourthly.—If you do not exactly understand how to conceal your evil opinion of men's writings or performances, but find yourself occasionally apt to indulge in maliciously speaking the truth, always say the direct contrary of what you think. The following little glossary, collected from the most approved critics, may be of service to you in this case ; you will of course make use of the first column :—

A crowded house——a theatre on the night of a performance, when all the back seats and upper boxes are empty.

An amusing author—an author whose very seriousness makes us laugh in spite of himself.

A successful author—an author who has been damned only four times out of five.

A good author——the general term for an author who gives good dinners.

A respectable actor—an insipid actor ; one who in general is neither hissed nor applauded.

A fine actor——one who makes a great noise ; a tatterdemalion of passions ; a clap-trapper : one intended by nature for a town-crier. This appellation may on all occasions be given to Mr. Pope, who has the finest lungs of any man on the stage.

A good actor——the general term for an actor who gives good dinners.

A charming play——a play full of dancing, music, and scenery ; a play in which the less the author has to do the better.

Great applause——applause mixed with the hisses of the gallery and pit.

Unbounded and universal applause—applause mixed with the hisses of the pit only. This phrase is frequently to be found at the bottom of the play house bills in declaring the reception a new piece has met with. The plays announced in these bills are generally printed in red ink, an emblem, no doubt, of the modesty with which they speak of themselves.

There was once a kind soul of an author who could not bear to use a harsh word, even when speaking of villains ; he used to call highwaymen *tax-gatherers*, pickpockets *collectors*, and ravishers *men of gallantry*. This gentleman would have made an excellent theatrical critic ; he would have called Reynolds Congreve, and Cherry Shakspeare, and everybody would have admired his invention.

Fifthly, and lastly.—When you criticise the performance of an old play, never exceed six or seven lines, but be sure to notice by name the fashionables in the boxes, for such notices are indispensably requisite to sound criticism ; there is a choice collection of sentences which have been in use time immemorial with newspaper critics, and are still used by common consent, just as we universally allow one style for a note of hand or a visiting letter. Your observations, therefore, will generally be such as these :—

DRURY LANE. —Last night the *beautiful* comedy of the *Rivals* was performed with great eclat to an *overflowing* house : Bannister was excellent—Mrs. H. Johnston looked *beautiful*. Among the company we observed the Duchess of Gordon, the Duke of Queensbury, Lady Hamilton, and many other *amiable* and *beautiful* personages. There was a quarrel in the pit.

What can be more concise, more explanatory, more critical, than such a criticism? Grammarians undertake to teach a language in five months, musicians, the whole theory of music in five weeks, and dancing-masters all sorts of steps in five hours, but by these rules a man may be a profound critic in five minutes. Let Aristotle and Quintilian hide their huge volumes in dismay, and confess the superiority of a criticism, which, like the magic word *Sesame* in the Arabian Nights, opens to us a thousand treasures in a breath!

STAGE COSTUME.

The majority of an audience were certainly never deluded into a belief that events represented on the stage were realities. The best actors, who are the most likely to produce such a delusion, are always the most applauded ; but it is evident they would gain no applause, were their assumed character forgotten ; for in common life we do not clap any incident that pleases us in the streets, nor cry out " bravo " at a pathetic circumstance in a room. A rustic, perhaps, who knew nothing of the machinery and trick of the stage, might be momentarily deceived ; but the dream would soon be removed by the frequent cessations of the entertainment, and particularly the alteration of scene, so badly managed at the theatre, where you see two men running violently towards each other with half a castle or a garden in their grasp. Though it is impossible, however, and indeed generally considered it would be unpleasant, to maintain this impression of reality, the imitation of life and manners should be as exact as possible, for the same cause that we are pleased with our just resemblance in a glass, though we are convinced that it is a mere resemblance. But the most consummate actor gains but half his effect, if his eloquent imitation is not assisted by the mute imitations of dress and of scenery. A man, for instance, who in his countenance and his action could display to perfection the mind of the great Alfred, would make a singular impression, if his dress were made after the fashion of the reign of George the Third, and his room after that of Queen Elizabeth's. Yet the chronological absurdities of the present stage are scarcely less laughable than such a compound. Alexander, indeed, does not rave now in a cocked-hat and jack-boots ; Timoleon does not frown in a profusion of periwig ; nor does Cleopatra

wanton in an enormity of hoop-petticoat. But though times
and countries are not set at this open defiance, their proprieties
are unaccountably neglected.

Perhaps there is not a single performer, who knows how to
dress with perfect propriety, except Mrs. Siddons, who is
excellently classical and just in this respect. Mr. Elliston, and
Mr. Kemble and his brother Charles are more attentive to
their apparel than the generality of actors ; but the second is
at all times too fond of a glare of ornament, and we have seen
both the brothers, in the parts of modern gentlemen, flaming in
court dresses on the most common occasions. As to the
other actors, their absurdities in dress are innumerable, and
are observable every night of a performance. Old men of the
present day are hardly ever without the laced coats and flapped
waistcoats of the last century. The ladies wear spangled
gowns and ostrich feathers upon all occasions, and the beaux
appear in the streets with frogs instead of plain buttons, cocked
hats instead of round ones, and swords when nobody wears a
sword but at court. Of all beauish dressers, however, Mr.
Lewis is the most faulty and the least excusable, because he is
an actor of great experience as well as genius ; this gentleman
seems to delight in uncouth habiliments, and not unfrequently
astonishes the audience by appearing as a beau in a coat
chequered with ribs and enlivened with variegated colours : of
what age or of what country such coat may be we know not ;
all that we can discover is, that it is more like the dress of an
ancient French footman than of a modern English gentleman.

KEMBLE AND MRS. ST. LEDGER.

We have received a very curious letter from a defender of
Mrs. St. Ledger, convicting us of a mistake respecting her performance of Floranthe in the *Mountaineers*, and making some
other observations on our criticism upon that lady. We take
the first opportunity of acknowledging our error. Our readers
will recollect that we accused Mrs. St. Ledger of inanimation

and want of feeling in the scene where Octavian faints at the sight of his mistress. The defender of Mrs. St. Ledger gives the following singular but conclusive reason for this apparent fault in her performance : " It is well known in the theatre, that during the whole of that scene, Mrs. St. Ledger is acting in direct opposition to her common sense, that she is not permitted to stir or breathe but by Mr. Kemble's direction, that she is expressly forbid to go near him when he falls, to assist him when he rises, to kneel to him or embrace him ; in short, she is obliged to appear an automaton." It is supposed that " she would disconcert or put trammels on Octavian, and by that the audience would lose in one moment from Mr. Kemble more than would have been repaid in the whole life of Mrs. St. Ledger."

We never before heard such an absurd instance of Mr. Kemble's disregard of theatrical propriety, or such a disgusting one of his vanity : he had better send all the actors about him from the stage, in scenes of this kind, that he may have room to astonish the audience at his leisure. His conduct reminds us of an ancient fable, in which the Great Bear wished to put out all the other constellations in order to shine by itself. It is to be hoped that the public will no more receive with their usual indulgence so flagrant a violation of nature and propriety. Actors are for the audience, not the audience for the actors ; and Mr. Kemble should pay a little less deference to his own conceit, and a little more to their judgment.

AN ESSAY ON THE APPEARANCE, CAUSES, AND CONSEQUENCES OF THE DECLINE OF BRITISH COMEDY.[1]

Sect. 1.—*On the Appearance of this Decline.*

The chief object of the following criticism is to expose in a mass the errors of the present Comic Drama, to show that they

[1] Leigh Hunt's title.

are as obnoxious to serious argument as to ridicule, and to
convince those readers, who have not immediately witnessed
the faults of our dramatists, and might therefore be amazed at
the perpetual peal which this paper rings upon their names,
that a love of our country's literature and honour is a sufficient
reason for the exposure of such writers. The vanity of these
writers, who cannot imagine that any critic should unceasingly
object to their manœuvres without personal hostility, has
rendered it necessary on our part to disclaim such a feeling
entirely, and we repeat that we know nothing of these men
but their dramatic attempts : we hope and believe that they
are good private characters ; but they are doing all they can to
ruin the British drama, and they must be treated as the public
violators of literature. It must be understood at the same
time that when we speak of them as the distinct race of
modern dramatists, we confound with them neither Sheridan
nor Cumberland ; the former of these gentlemen, who is one of
the first wits that this or any age has produced, belongs to
former times, for he has long ceased to write : the latter has
for some time been in the dotage of literature, has been as fond
of writing as other old men are of talking, and has written to as
little purpose : we will not judge of the colour of his head when
it is become grey.

Even the present dramatists, however, might be endured, if
they would confine themselves to the praise of that farce with
which they have so besotted the stage, if they would be content to follow better writers with little pieces of avowed
caricature ; they might occupy, indeed, the chief honours of
Sadler's Wells or the Circus, without a single wish on our part
to interrupt their exclusive possession. But when they usurp
the rank of comedy, when they seat themselves in the chairs
of those great comic writers who have won the palm from
Spain and from Italy to divide it with France, we are filled
with indignation and contempt. A royal jester is a very harmless and a very merry sort of personage, but when the King's
jester places himself on his master's throne, it is time for the
courtiers to look to the royal dignity.

It is the observation of all Europe that the British drama is rapidly declining. Of tragedy, indeed, we have nothing; but this subject will be considered hereafter. Every foreigner who visits England confirms the amazement and contempt of preceding travellers; the Spaniard wonders that we can exclaim against the hasty farces of his favourite Lope, and the German finds a rival of the melancholy absurdities of his own stage in the merry monstrosities of ours. So manifest indeed are the successive tricks of the dramatists, and their utter want of everything solid, that a person new to theatrical entertainments has nothing to do but to guard himself, as he would in a juggler's room, against anything that might cheat him into applause; and it is in vain, when he leaves the theatre, that he would recollect one single witticism or logical sentence that is worth remembrance, one remark on men and manners that could so meet the acknowledgment of the closet as to pass into a maxim, as hundreds have done in our old comic writers, as thousands in Shakspeare.

A comic writer of the present day may be immediately distinguished by his dislike of all those difficulties which oppose a writer ambitious of imitating the best models; the whole object of his pen seems to be the attainment of applause in the easiest manner possible, and he accordingly writes for the galleries, or, in other words, for that part of the audience which is the least capable of judging, but the nosiest in declaring its judgment. He appeals, therefore, to the eye and to the ear, because they are the soonest pleased with the least reason; a new piece of scenery or an uncouth dress conquers the visual faculties of the spectators, and a volley of puns is the signal for the author's triumph. This artifice of punning, which has become a perfect system with the dramatists, is the method by which the author rids himself of the difficulty of wit, as his flowery language, when he becomes what is called sentimental, is his device to forego the necessity of thinking. By these means language becomes separated from ideas, since mere punning is nothing but an unexpected assimilation of sounds, and mere floweriness, like a harlequin jacket, is nothing

but a surprising combination of colours. The incidents and
characters of his pieces always agree in one alternative : they
are either of very manifest commonplace, or they are clad in
the most monstrous disguises to gain the appearance of
novelty ; they remind us of the tricks practised, according to a
modern traveller, at some of our country fairs, where a vulgar
woman has been dressed in catskins and a tumultuous periwig,
and exhibited as a wild Indian, not to mention a shaved bear,
who, in a check shirt and trousers, gained a great deal of
applause as an Ethiopian savage. If he exhibits a character
that has been too often handled to stand inquiry, he gives a
new tone to its appearance by some prominent peculiarity of
manner, which, however ill-adapted it may be, immediately
catches the attention by the mere force of oddity, and depre-
cates your censure for the sake of the laughter it creates. This
peculiarity generally consists in some hackneyed phrase or cant
maxim, which is used upon all occasions, seasonable and unseasonable, and is very often as suitable to the mouth of
the speaker as a tobacco-pipe would be in the lips of the Venus
de Medicis.

The author, however, is not content to do everything for the
sake of pleasing the more easy part of the audience, but in
order that they may be more interested in his behalf, he tells
them, in the most abject terms, how entirely he is their most
humble servant : he literally begs them to be blind to his
errors ; that is, to care more about his nonsense than the
literary reputation of their country ; and for this purpose two
petitions, in the shape of Prologue and Epilogue,[1] are generally
presented to the audience, the one to bespeak their kindness,
and the other to secure it. In the interval, however, of these
petitions, the house is assailed in the masterpiece of these
seductive playwrights, by a profusion of encomiums on the spirit,
the loyalty, and the invincibility of the British nation. It is
never considered that everybody could roar out these encomiums
with an ardour quite as literary, and that everybody may feel

---

[1] Prologues and Epilogues were still in vogue at this time. They continued in fashion til' about 1825.

a patriotic pride in his country, without swelling with self-importance at the flattery of a cunning author. If the author can get applause, he does not care whether the applause be consistent either with his pretensions or our dignity : he gives praise for praise ; and while he is exalting our invincible wisdom, is considering into what sort of a clap he shall conquer us.

The art of a modern dramatist, then, consists in a series of deceptions on his audience; and he manages, like a true juggler, to make the audience assist in the very tricks with which he contrives to astonish them. The least use of common perception, however, will always distinguish his artifice, and he will be detected either in the partial, or more often in the indiscriminate exercise, of the following errors, which, in fact, compose the whole of a modern comic writer's genius :—

An inveterate love of punning.

A deformed alteration of common characters and incidents.

A dialogue either extremely flowery or extremely familiar.

An affectation of ardent loyalty, and, consequent to this affectation, a gross flattery of his audience.

Lastly, as flattery and timid meanness generally accompany each other, a most abject system of begging the favour of the house, particularly in prologue and epilogue.

Sect. 2.—*On the Causes of this Decline.*

We do not know which should afford better subject for astonishment, the origin or the toleration of this dramatic corruption. The evil, perhaps, would be less endured, if its causes were detected ; for it is one of the inconsistencies of human nature to reject error, not so much for its effect as its cause. We do not always blush at acting wrongly, but we blush most painfully when we find that our reason for it has become ridiculous, or unfashionable, or perhaps out of date. Literature has its modes like dress, and all popular changes are apt to rush into extremes : the beaux of Charles the Second's age suddenly retreated into a forest of peruke, because the Puritan's had valued themselves upon their own lank hair; the English drama broke out into mere farce, because it began to despise the solemn foppery of sentimental comedy. But we have now no reason for extremes, either in the appearance or the productions of our heads; let us get rid of our dramatic perukes and exhibit something like a natural pericranium.

The causes of the decline of comedy, or, in other words, of the present predominance of farce, are certainly not to be attributed to the present writers. Literary delusions never become lasting with a literary people, unless they are supported by the authority of real genius. There are always so many comparative models of writing, that none but writers capable of giving good examples can recommend bad ones. It was Lucan and Seneca, men in other respects of true genius, that encouraged the Romans into bombast, and not Nero and the poetasters of his court, who were inspired with nothing else. It was Donne and Cowley, writers of original wit, that recommended the conceits of the Metaphysical Poets, and not such grotesque pedants as Cleveland and Flatman. The modern farci-comic writers would never have been elevated into their present sway, had they depended solely on themselves. Like the drunken tinker in the play, they must have been carried by more rational beings than themselves upon that throne, which, like him, they disgrace by their vanity and buffoonery. Sheep have been found on the tops of oaks, but it is the eagle that has borne them thither. In short, we must attribute the farcical decline of English comedy to the indignant haste of Goldsmith in overthrowing sentimental comedy, and to the farcical extreme in which he was followed and even outrun by his immediate successors.

This species of writing, which from its imitation of the more chequered fortunes of life might be rendered the most natural picture of mankind, was, indeed, in a most desponding way in Goldsmith's time. It began with Kelly and others to make those appalling faces, which mark the unmeaning sorrows of infancy, and prepare us for a tempest of weeping,

and it advanced rapidly in misery with Mr. Cumberland,
who has since been so ably seconded by Mrs. Inchbald. Its
full growth, however, was reserved for Mr. Morton, who with
an observation of life worthy of better cultivation, has indulged
in so furious a mixture of the laughing and the weeping, that
he has thrown comedy into absolute hysterics. Such a style of
writing possessed in itself the means of its destruction, for the
house was divided against itself. Goldsmith, however, saw
nothing in the unnatural struggle but the death of all comic
humour, and out of pure pity he became extravagantly merry,
just as the celebrated Dr. Radcliffe, to cure a patient of the
quinsey, endeavoured to make him laugh by playing all sorts
of unseasonable antics.[1] The farce succeeded ; the extravagant,
though delightful vagaries of *She Stoops to Conquer*, like the
touch of the painter, turned the weeping face of the town into
a laughing one ; O'Keeffe, a man of much humour, afterwards
kept up the peal, till it became mere noise and grimace with
Mr. Reynolds and his brother merry-andrews Messrs. Dibdin
and Cherry. Inattention, or haste, or very possibly exhausted
powers, gave a strong support to these writers in the pen of Mr.
Colman, a man who, with the dramatic reputation of his father
to urge him to his proper goal, the hopes of good writers to

[1] This argument, in which Goldsmith is represented as heading a re-
action against the sentimental comedy of Kelly, Cumberland, Morton, and
Mrs. Inchbald, seems to proceed in defiance of chronology. Hugh Kelly's
first play, *False Delicacy*, was not acted until 1768 ; while *The Brothers*,
Cumberland's first comedy of any moment, dates from 1769, and *The
West Indian* from 1771. Now Goldsmith's first play, *The Good-Natured
Man*, in which the characteristics of his comic style are quite as fully
developed as in *She Stoops to Conquer* (1773), was produced in 1768, only
six days later than Kelly's *False Delicacy;* so that we can scarcely take it
as marking a reaction against Kelly, and still less against Cumberland,
who was at that time practically unknown. As for Mrs. Inchbald and
Thomas Morton, they did not come to the front until long after Goldsmith's death—the former in 1785, the latter in 1792. It is no doubt true
that Goldsmith's works marked a reaction against sentimental or tearful
comedy, but it was the comedy of an earlier generation (see Forster's
"Goldsmith," bk. iv. chap. i.). John O'Keeffe (1746-1833) was a prolific
farce-writer during the last quarter of last century.

invite him, and a great fund of natural humour to support him
in his attempt, has deserted the cause of literature, and does
not blush, not only to join in a debauch of merriment which
he must despise, but like a true literary rake, to defend his
companions by the most miserable merry sophistry. This
gentleman, in a prologue that does and does not deserve to be
remembered, says, if we recollect rightly,

> If we give trash, as some few pertlings say,
> Why flocks an audience nightly to our play?

We answered him in a distich of our own :—

> If there's no merit in six yards of haunch,
> Why flock the town to gaze on Lambert's paunch?

But we are almost ashamed to refute an argument, which is
contradicted by every pantomine exhibition, by every petty
show, nay, by every house of bad reputation in town.

Such, we imagine, is the simple cause of the decline of our
comedy. The great *existing* reason is the mere want of
critical opposition. If the newspapers were unanimous, they
might overthrow the farci-comic writers in a few months. As
the body of the people is always much too void of reflection to
ask itself why it is satisfied, the dramatic taste of the town is
at the mercy of any set of men that can control the majority of
the periodical prints, and it is somewhat unlucky for good letters,
that the greatest number of these editors are too much occupied
with politics to care, much less to know, anything about the
drama. The playwrights either procure the favours of their
careless critics by an eager advance of all their little powers of
accommodation, or worm themselves into their gay hours of
confidence ; and what is more philanthropic than the maudlin
sympathy of a second bottle? By these means the newspaper
editors certainly become the true friends of the dramatists ; for
while the latter trust their critics with all the tricks and
dependencies of theatric authorship, the former keep them a
profound secret from the town, and would rather tell us any
falsehoods than betray their trust. Till the evil, therefore, out-

grows concealment, it is natural enough that the majority of the town should be willing to believe the majority of its critics. Critical opinion is like madness : if it is confined to an individual, everybody is alarmed : if it influences a sect or a party, attention is scattered by its generality.

Sect. 3.—On the Consequences.

The good disposition which men of little judgment manifest towards our present dramatists may in some measure be attributed to the harmlessness of their drama, which can certainly offend nobody by its satire : the ignorant and the vicious find themselves safe from chastisement, and they will naturally assist those who insure their safety. But this very kind of harmlessness gives the last finish to the stupidity of the farci-comic writers, and produces a general effect the total reverse of harmless ; for in consequence of their monstrous caricature and its perfect inapplicability to human manners, the end of comedy, which should satirise the lighter vices and follies of mankind, is utterly destroyed. They paint rakes, indeed, and coxcombs, and cheats ; but the characters lose so many of their proper characteristics in their attempt to be facetious, that it seems the endeavour of their life to afford amusement, and thus their natural character is perpetually struggling with their theatric one : the rake is vicious merely as far as he thinks he can be pleasant ; the coxcomb is taught to think more of the galleries than of himself ; the cheat pursues his iniquities merely that they may be agreeable tricks ; the selfish, in short, live wholly for others ; and the author thinks, not how he may improve his audience by painting its likeness, but how he may flatter it by making its features beautiful, or amuse it by showing how merrily he can distort them. As nobody, therefore, finds his likeness on the stage, nobody is improved by it ; virtue is not encouraged by the representation of its *unpresuming* countenance, nor is vice alarmed at the deformity of its passion-tortured features. The scene is so far drawn forward, as it were, into the part appropriated to the

audience, or, in other words, it is so evidently the intention of
the author, and consequently of his actors, to stand before the
spectator as mere candidates for applause, that the stage becomes literally abstracted from its abstraction ; its professed
absence from an overlooking multitude is forgotten, and this is
the reason why the actors so perpetually enter the scene with
their hats off in the open air ; they forget the fields and the
forests, they imagine themselves entering a room full of company, and they are as full of respect as a showman, who comes
into a parlour on a winter's evening to amuse the children with
his grotesque shadows.   The theatres, therefore, should take
down those inscriptions over their stage, which invite us to
contemplate the representation of ourselves, since that magnificent, that polished mirror, which reflected all our features with
so animated a resemblance, which obeyed the momentary
varieties of our attitude, and glanced forth the nicest movements
of our countenance, has been exchanged for a glass full of
excrescences and undulations, in which the human figure becomes a mere laughable monstrosity, a thing of grimace and
distortion, a shadow that mocks the spectator with fantastic
ugliness.

The vicious fashionable have been so happy in the security
they enjoy during this sleep of satire, that they start with dismay at every little movement of its hand indicative of waking,
and the managers of Drury Lane Theatre have still to explain
why a comedy, called the *Faro Table*,[1] which was reported to
contain a fine satire on gaming, and to have been written by
the late celebrated Mr. Tobin, was suddenly withdrawn from
the public expectation, not only after its announcement, but
after its complete study by the actors.   We have already expressed our indignation at this incident, which argues a control
over the drama and a timidity in the managers, not to be

[1] This play was announced on October 16, 1806, for production on
October 20 ; was advertised on October 18 as postponed on account of the
illness of a principal performer, and on the 22nd was said to be unavoidably
postponed for a few days.   It was then dropped, and was not heard of till
November 5, 1816, when it was produced under the title of *The Guardians.*

endured in a nation so free and comparatively so virtuous as ours. Such a circumstance displays at once all the ridiculous imbecility of our usual comedies, which are suffered to exist merely because vice itself can laugh at them without feeling unpleasantly.

It must be mentioned, at the same time, in praise of Drury Lane, that it has at least promised to become *rational* next season, and that it has never been so totally occupied with farci-comedy as Covent Garden. Why the grave manager, Mr. Kemble, who, with all his faults, is a man of judgment, and possesses a discriminative relish of our great writers, should suffer the everlasting antics of the modern merry-andrews about him, is an enigma we never could solve ; the idea of him under these circumstances is as ludicrously incongruous as it would be to see the statue of William Penn surrounded by carved dancing dogs.

At any rate, let us always repeat to ourselves what Mr. Gifford, a man of vigorous learning and the first satirist of his time, has said of the present comic writers—"*All the fools in the kingdom seem to have risen up and exclaimed with one voice*—LET US WRITE FOR THE THEATRES !"

CRITICISMS

FROM

"THE TATLER"

*A DAILY PAPER OF LITERATURE, FINE
ARTS, MUSIC, AND THE STAGE
1830—1831.*

CRITICISMS FROM "THE TATLER."

DOWTON AS FALSTAFF.

October 4, 1830.

WE do not like to see an actor such as Dowton in a new character, and not think the performance excellent. But we must out with it—his Falstaff is a failure. It wants richness; it wants filling up; it wants geniality. Mr. Dowton cannot but interest the audience in particular passages: he is too clever not to do that; but his Falstaff is a common shrewd man, behaving, for the most part, like other men, and peculiar only in an occasional vivacity and a general abdomen. If Mr. Dowton thinks this the *rationale* of the character, he is greatly mistaken. Falstaff's size, which is thought to be the greatest part of him, is the least. It is only a gross help towards the comprehension of him by the vulgar. It belongs to him, we allow. He cannot do without it, seeing the quantity of sack he drinks: but his real superabundance is in his animal spirits: the festivity of his soul is his most unctuous plentitude : he has an enormous capacity for making the most of life, and swallowing every satisfaction that comes in his way : and this is the reason why we like him : we cannot be melancholy in his company. Of any grave or ordinary contradiction to his mirth, he is incapable : his anger has a spice of something pleasant as well as biting : his cups of calamity, like his other cups, have a sugar at bottom. He cannot drown but he talks of his "alacrity in sinking." Now Mr. Dowton wants the *habitual* Falstaff, and in wanting that, he wants everything. There is not the ease of perpetual joviality about him : he is silent, and sudden, and pleased, and angry, after the fashion of other men : you do not see, underneath it all, the jolly sensualist, incapable of anything but self-complacency and enjoyment. A misconception of the same kind, though it appears different, leads Mr. Dowton to give what he thinks great force to the amorous anticipations of the fat knight, when Mrs. Quickly brings him news of the Merry Wives. But Falstaff would not think it necessary to break out into those overt acts of capering and gaping, which in truth are more like a gloating idiot than a tavern wit. Falstaff is too much accustomed to such ideas to vent them in that manner.

The ordinary stage conception of Falstaff's character is the right one, if actors could but act up to it. It is probably handed down from Shakspeare's own time. It purports to represent a puffing and blowing, swaggering, chuckling, luxurious, fat-voiced " tun of a man," gathering corpulency from every dish and goblet as he rolls, for ever mirthful and shameless, making a jest of danger in the apprehension, and anxiously getting out of it when it comes, but above all things witty and festive, unable to admit care or to give it, making his moral enormities appear as natural and jovial a part of him as his fat ; in short, a perpetual feast to himself and to his beholders. Now easy as this character appears to sustain, and sure of the good-will of an audience beforehand, it has been found one of the most difficult on the stage ; and the reason we take to be, that it requires an actor remarkable both for intellectual address (to meet all the wit of it) and a merry blood of his own (to hinder any misgivings in the jollity). The man who should stand a chance of performing it best, would be one who had himself "laughed and grown fat," and acquired a character among his friends for bon-mots, good humour, and no ambition to be a tragedian. It was that notion of something else besides his genuine propensities, which spoiled Quin for this and all other characters—as we may pretty plainly discern in what has been said of him by friends as well as foes. Garrick's Falstaff may have been an admirable piece of mimicry : we cannot conceive it to have been anything more ; his own character was too bustling and anxious.[1] We never remember a Falstaff well performed, and we have seen it undertaken by all sorts of actors, stuffed and unstuffed. Robert Palmer [2] made a terrible dry business of it. An actor now living knew no more of it than a knife-grinder's wheel.[3] And Stephen Kemble, who performed it without stuffing, left out the other stuffing besides—the sauce to the veal.

[1] In this passage Leigh Hunt shows himself curiously ignorant or regardless of facts. Garrick never played Falstaff, while Quin was recognised by all, foes as well as friends, to be almost an ideal representative of the character.

[2] "Bobby" Palmer, as Charles Lamb called him, was an actor of fops, &c., who must have been quite unfitted for Falstaff.

[3] This may be an allusion to John Fawcett.

Mr. Dowton must give up Falstaff, and treat us again with Sir Anthony Absolute, Colonel Old-boy, and Justice Woodcock. He can be angry always, and jovial as it happens; but his jollity cannot be a mere round of wit and pleasure.

We are sorry we are unable to say much of the rest of the performance, especially as there were some debutantes who sung. We must hope they were frightened and will do better. There is something clever in Mrs. C. Hill, who is unquestionably the female Bartley. Mr. Harley we like, but not in the character of Slender. He is not abstracted and fantastical enough—has not sufficient bye-play, and absorption in his love. When he says "Sweet Anne Page," there seems to be no reason why he should say it: it does not sufficiently come out of the fulness of his emptiness. Neither did Mr. Harley put enough emphasis on his willingness to "do anything with reason," and some other passages where Slender plays the "magnanimous feeble." Mr. B. Hill is in too great a hurry, even for Dr. Caius; otherwise his French seemed as if it could have been heard to some purpose. He darted his head continually from one side to the other, as though he was too anxious to be able to look the audience in the face. The completest performance of the evening, much to our surprise, was Mr. Webster's Sir Hugh Evans: for we had not suspected that his hard manner and voice could have accommodated itself so cleverly to the "gentle senses" of the Welshman. We certainly should not have guessed who it was, but for his name in the play-bills. All the harshness of his manner was gone; and his voice he threw up admirably into the light petulance of the Welsh tones, by means of a falsetto. We could have wished a little more slowness, a few more pauses, filled up with look and action, in the soliloquy previous to the duel ; but upon the whole it was far beyond what we had expected of this actor, clever as we thought him in an inferior way at the Haymarket. And it received the applause it deserved. What particularly pleased us, was his complete understanding of the character *throughout*, and the attention he paid it accordingly to the last moment—as in the instance of his caressing simplicity towards his new friend the Doctor, after they had acquired a regard for each other from the duel. Mr. Webster has taught us to expect a good deal of him ; so he must look to it, and brush up the very hats of his footmen. We do not know that we can allow him to do anything vulgarly in future.

MISS FANNY KEMBLE AS JULIET.

October 5, 1830.

IT is with unaffected pain that we feel ourselves compelled to differ with the measure of admiration which has been dealt out to Miss Kemble, especially after the circumstances under which she was introduced to the public, and the good which she has done the theatre.[1] But as those circumstances were the cause of what appears to us to be an exaggerated opinion of her talents, they must be our excuse. We had a fear lest we should be obliged to think as we do, from the inferior opinion entertained of her in the country, where the causes of her town popularity were not likely to have so much influence : and yet when we saw her first scene last night, we began to feel reassured, and to hope that the original opinion of her was the right one. The

[1] Covent Garden.

reason why we felt so was that she appeared to us the reverse of an artificial person : her manner and tones were natural, her smile equally so ; we thought she was going to trust entirely to her own feelings ; and as we looked at the general expression of her face, could not help quoting to ourselves the words of the old poet,

—simple goodness shined in her eyes.

All this, in her own person, off the stage, we should guess her to be still ; and we heartily wish for everybody's sake, the critics included, that she had had such a natural call to the stage, as to draw upon herself and her own character for some genuine theatrical result.

But the moment she gave us the first burst of feeling, our expectations fell many degrees, and they never rose again. The manner was different in an instant, not as showing more feeling, but as showing less : the regular theatrical start and vehemence were substituted for the natural emotion of the artless girl we had been contemplating : the Nurse was told to go and inquire after the stranger, in a tone, not of pleasant, but of indignant vehemence ; and then commenced the regular conventional tragic style, both in voice and manner, which was maintained with little variation the whole evening, and which has certainly left an impression on our minds that this young lady is entirely an artificial performer, very apt in catching all that may be learnt in tragic acting, but not essentially superior to many that have had but a brief day of repute. She wanted real passion throughout, and variety of feeling. She was not only not the Juliet of the South, but not more the heroine of a love-story than of any other tragedy. Her emotion was loud, her gravity dignified and queen-like, her flow of utterance breathed with a regular vehemence of solemnity, something between the tones of her great kinswoman, Mrs. Siddons, and the mellow monotony of the late Mrs. Powell.[1] Once and away there was a brief passage, a sentence, in that sort of natural manner, which, coming after a great deal of the artificial, appears to be as much got up as any, or more so. But the general character of the performance was certainly no higher than that of an older stager of the better conventional sort ; and this was not only our opinion, but from what we heard from some persons about us, appeared to exist where it did not before. The passages the most applauded were those which are far from doing a performer the most honour, though they appear to produce the greatest effect ; namely, the violent ones, and those which were accompanied by some vehement gesture or sudden rush ; as in the scene where she fancies a vision of her husband suffering, and slides, in a manner, all across the stage, before taking the poison. In short (for we saw little of Miss O'Neil, and do not remember seeing her in this character) we have never yet witnessed a proper Juliet on the stage, and Miss Kemble has unfortunately furnished us with no better. In the Garden Scene she ought to have hung more over the balcony, and varied her tones with a greater mixture of familiarity and archness (all our English Juliets miserably fail in this : they have not faith enough in passion or the poet for it, and are neutralised by the decorums. In the scene where she thinks the Nurse has brought news of

---

[1] Mrs. Powell was a very handsome woman, and a good actress. We are inclined to doubt the accuracy of Leigh Hunt's description of her speaking, for contemporary criticisms speak of her voice as " strong and variable." She retired from the London stage in 1816.

Romeo's death, and finds that he is not dead but banished, she should utter the word "banished" not with the same unchanging despair as she had before been evincing, but should mix with it a passing intimation of relief, even at the moment when she is relapsing into wretchedness for his absence ; for after all, a banished lover is not quite so bad as a dead one, nor did the poet mean to say he was ; though all the performers of Romeo and Juliet make just as much noise about the exile as the death.

Miss Kemble is not handsome ; but there is a goodness in her face, when left to itself, that is very pleasing, and looks like an ingenuous nature.   As an actress, we cannot think at present that she has any genius, properly so called, or will ever establish a reputation for one ; though she may make a very useful, and what is called a highly respectable performer.   The applause, we presume, last night was not so great as it used to be ; there was a waving of hats in the pit, and a vehement welcome, when she appeared : and now and then she received great approbation in the course of the play : but there was no prevailing enthusiasm : nor was she called for after the play.   What is more, we doubt whether a tear was shed in the house ; certainly not in our neighbourhood.

Mrs. Gibbs appeared for the first time as the Nurse. We cannot commend her performance, compared with that of Mrs. Davenport[1] and others.   It wanted the habitual look of age. Her occasional hobble seemed to be volunteered ; and she overdid the rheumatic scene.

---

[1] Mrs. Davenport, who retired in 1830, was the recognised representative of the Nurse for many years, and sustained the part in October, 1829, on Fanny Kemble's first appearance.

Sudden cramps are affecting ; but they may be repeated too often.

Must we speak of Mr. Abbot's Romeo ? We hear he is a pleasant person everywhere but on the stage, and such a man may be reasonably at a disadvantage with his neighbours somewhere. Mr. Abbot has taken it in his head that noise is tragedy, and a tremendous noise he accordingly makes. It is Stentor with a trumpet.

The best performance in this piece is decidedly Mr. Charles Kemble's Mercutio. It wants airiness, both in person and manner ; and a fat Mercutio is like a fat Mercury ; but there is abundance of vivacity. His elaborate mimicries of the fops are particularly good. His *pardonnez moi* seemed at once a joke on the coxcombry it nick-named, and a kick into the bargain.

We stopped the afterpiece in order to see the famous sailor of Mr. T. P. Cooke, and the genuine face of little Cawse in *Black Eyed Susan.* [By the by, what are the Christian names of Mr. T. P. Cooke ? Is he Theophilus Philip, or Thomas Patterson,[1] or what ? or is it necessary to the mystery of his reputation that he should always remain Mr. Tee Pee Cooke, as if he was Captain Cook's son by a Chinese? We have a grudge against these mysteries of initials. What is Miss *Eff Aitch* Kelly ? And why is Mr. Farren Mr. *Double-U* Farren ? We were in pain for the appellation of Miss H. Cawse, till we learnt that her name was Harriett. Harriett is a good name ; but Aitch was a vile precursor.]

We hardly know what to say to Mr. Cooke's sailor. We like it, and yet we can hardly wish to see it at this theatre. Is it because it is so like a sailor, that the man himself seems as if he ought to be further eastward? Or

---

[1] His name was Thomas Potter Cooke.

is it because it wants the investment of genuine acting—
the something besides commonplace nature which the
acting of a Bannister used to give it, and which made his
sailors bring laughter and tears into our eyes, as Mr. Cooke
does not ?   Mr. Cooke gives himself heartily up to the
character ; he looks really affectionate when he means to
look so ; and resigned when he means to look resigned ;
furthermore he is very cordial and plentiful in his
dammes and shakes of the hand ; he sings a good burden
of a song, if not the song very well itself : and he dances
a hornpipe with all the transport of a sailor who has not
had a hop for these five years, and who kicks the ground
as if he would shake himself into it for love.   Yet still
there is something in the performance, which we would
rather see at the Coburg than Covent Garden.   We take
the secret to be, that the mere professional sailor is made
too much of in the piece ; that there is too much sea
jargon and ostentation in it ; and that Mr. Cooke does
not so much appear to love and enjoy what he does as a
man who happens to be a sailor, as a sailor who makes
a point of playing the man.[1]

Harriett Cawse made a nice genuine little girl, such as
any man or sailor might have loved ; and was delicate
enough not to mince the matter or shrink back when the
honest tar took her in his arms : for in those impertinent
decorums lies the real indelicacy of such moments.   They
think or affect to think the matter wrong, and make it
so whether it will be or not ; whereas the genuine honesty
of it does not stand upon ceremony.

[1] So in original.   We do not grasp the distinction sufficiently clearly
to venture upon any emendation.

MISS FANNY KEMBLE AS BELVIDERA.

October 7, 1830.

MISS KEMBLE's performance of Belvidera last night [1] has not altered the opinion we found ourselves compelled to form of her in Juliet. We did not see the first part of the play, or we should doubtless have witnessed some of those simpler tones and looks which engage our regard for her as an individual. We came in while she was sailing on the full stream of her tragedy, and found her bearing herself accordingly, with ease and loftiness, with due theatrical effect of the received order, but with no impulses of her own, no originality; not like the enamoured Venetian, talking with natural passion as she went, but like all the clever tragedy princesses we have hitherto seen, who have not given themselves up to nature. Her great kinswoman, Mrs. Siddons, was not celebrated so much in parts of this kind as in those of loftier heroines; it was a defect even in the more level part of *her* style, that she had a tendency to dole out her words with too formal a solemnity; and we cannot help thinking that, like other imitators on system, Miss Kemble has been better taught to catch the defects than the beauties of her originals. She too doles out her words too much; dwells upon the vowels till they become double, as in the instance of *shaame* for *shame* (which is occasionally natural where some more than ordinary emphasis of passion warrants it, but becomes a trick when used always): in short, she is not the natural woman Belvidera, full of varied emotion and talking with her husband in household tones (as for the most part a true genius for the character would do) but

[1] At Covent Garden.

the Belvidera of the tragedy-reader school, thinking
more of the book than the passion. At the same time
we must own that we never saw a Belvidera of the
kind we speak of. What an effect she would produce!
Perhaps too dreadful a one.

A performer of such a part as Jaffier ought not to have
it said of him that he is quite incompetent to it : yet we
are forced to say as much of Mr. Ward. A pause now
and then, and a self-possessed air always, may be very
good things for a common tragedy gentleman ; but they
are not sufficient to warrant the undertaking such a
character as Jaffier.

Mr. Charles Kemble, as tragic actors go, makes a good
and effective Pierre ; though, judging of him by a standard
proportioned to his reputation with some of the critics,
we think there are considerable objections, on the conventional score, to be made to his tragedy in general.
However, he has much lightened and familiarised his style
of late years, and he is always worth seeing, if it is but for
that air of chivalrous elegance and vivacity which years
try in vain to take from him. Last night, with his yellow
vest and sleeves, his rich girdle, and dark thick rim of
a beard round his handsome face, he looked like one of
the portraits of Titian.

What a beautiful, most painful, and in some respects
disagreeable play is this *Venice Preserved!* Otway's
genius, true as it was to nature, had a smack in it of the
age of Charles II., and of the company of Lord Plymouth
and the bullies. Sensuality takes the place of sentiment,
even in the most calamitous passages. The author de-
bauched his tragic muse ; brings her, as he does his
heroine, among a set of ruffians ; and dresses her in
double tears and mourning, that her blushes may but

burn and her fair limbs be set off the more, to furnish his riotous imagination with a gusto of contrast.

MISS FANNY KEMBLE AS JULIET.

October 12, 1830.

On this occasion we again saw Miss Kemble, and have again to state that our impressions as to her style of acting are unchanged. We feel ourselves called upon to do so by an article in the *Examiner*, in which we are said to entertain too unfavourable an opinion of this young lady, and to have been "indiscreet" and "unfair" in saying that she would "never establish a reputation for an actress." We believe we did not say that, but that she would never establish a reputation for a "genius." Unfairness we cannot acknowledge, because it involves something of wrong intention : but the indiscretion we admit. We grant that it is idle to pronounce what will or will not happen, especially for us who are in the habit of protesting against the favourite phrases "ever was" and "ever will be," and who do not profess to know whether the human being itself will remain in its present state a thousand years hence. We grant also that many performers who have set out with apparent mediocrity, have established high reputations—at least so it is said, and we can believe it of some, though with difficulty of the very greatest. But still we must say that with the exception of that profane peep into futurity, our opinion of Miss Kemble's talent appears to us to be perfectly justified by what we have since witnessed. We doubt not from that ingenuous face of hers, that she is a very nice girl ; and we think she has very cleverly seized what has been taught her ; but we see nothing in her at present that we should not expect to find in twenty others. She has caught the stage manner ; she has a good idea of stage effect ; she possesses a family tone, resembling that of Mrs. Siddons : you might shut your eyes sometimes, and almost fancy you heard her aunt again—but without the genius. It is an imitation so exaggerated that you doubt whether there is any ground of self-reliance. Far from thinking with the critic in the *Examiner* that Miss Kemble has a clever conception of the character of Juliet, we think she is not aware of the very foundation of it ; which is a love so trusting and so joyous, that all its after melancholy is founded on its very hilarity—on the dancing buoyancy of the first flood of youthful passion and delight, suddenly frozen by calamity. It is easy for the critic to fancy the character well conceived, because he knows it to be so in the poet, and is a man of sensibility and good-nature : but we will give an instance to the contrary, and one instance is as good as twenty, where a proper conception of the character would have hindered it. Juliet says, in one of her enthusiastic speeches during her happier moments—

> "Come, gentle night ; come, loving, black-browed night,
> Give me my Romeo : and, when he shall die,
> Take him and cut him out in little stars,
> And he will make the face of heaven so fine,
> That all the world shall be in love with night,
> And pay no worship to the garish sun."

Now if ever there was young love in the world, this speech (which would be a conceit in the mouth of a less trusting and lavish passion) is full of it ; and if there is any speech which should be well and trustingly given by a young actress, such as Miss Kemble has been described, it is one which seems fittest for the enthusiasm of her time of life. Yet we will venture to say she has no sort of faith in it. She thinks it a speech, and that is all ; fine, because it is Shakspeare's ; fit for Juliet, because it is given to Juliet ; but her heart does not go with her words : she has no "conception " of it. She begins it well enough, rises into ordinary declamation as she proceeds, and finishes by uttering the last words with a lingering solemnity and a shake of the head ! " And pay—no worship—" (*shaking her head*)—"to—the—*gaarish*—sun." How then should she repeat it ? Why, rather than in this manner, with a joyous tone throughout ; with an undiminished hilarity ; with her heart dancing in her eyes ; nay, even with an enthusiastic pacing down the stage lamps, looking the audience rapturously in the face, as if she breathed out her soul to the air and to all nature. (What does Mozart, the Shakspeare of music, say ? *A l'aria, a l'onda, ai venti.*) It is a mistake analogous to that which, in singing a fine air with one pervading sentiment, makes a literal variety upon particular words, and, as it were, *acts* their meaning by themselves. Juliet takes no pity on the poor sun ; does not shake her head at its going out of fashion ; thinks nothing at all solemn, or gravely ironical, about the matter. She simply merges it in the idea of the greater sun, her lover, who includes all nature in her eyes, and who must spangle the universal canopy to others as he does to herself. It is the breath of her boundless transport ; a hymn to love and rapture; and she lavishes on it all the fine thoughts she can, just as she would deluge her lover himself with pearls and gold. She would no more finish it with a solemn intimation

and a shaking head, than she would stop to preach him
a bit of sermon, while careering along with him in some
glorious dance.

MACREADY AS VIRGINIUS.

October 19, 1830.

MR. MACREADY reappeared in London last night,[1] for the
first time these two years, and performed the favourite
part of Virginius with so much applause that, besides
repeated approbation throughout, he was called for after
the play. We sat, unfortunately, too far off to see his
face as we should have done ; but his tones reached us,
varied with *their* expression, and trembling sometimes
with the rich and genuine burthen of emotion. It was
said of a famous Italian mimic, that he said fine things
without uttering a word. It may be said of Mr.
Macready, as of Mr. Kean, that he looks fine things
without showing his countenance. You may gather
how he must look by what you hear. We do not mean
to compare him with Kean. We think him as inferior
to that tragedian as we confess we think our other celebrated tragedians inferior to Macready ; or if this be impossible, the difference is in favour of Macready, inasmuch
as his best passages are more allied to the nature of his
superior, than his common ones are to those of the rest.
What we take to be the difference between Kean and
Macready is this—that the former has an instinctive
natural reason for all that he does, and never acts at
random ; is never loud when he might as well be low,
or *vice versâ* ; or if he is, knows it and does it wilfully,
out of some caprice ; in a word, has a finer conception
of the character throughout, and adapts himself to it as

[1] At Drury Lane.

naturally, as gracefully, and with as much self-possession, as the limbs do to the motions required of them. Now we do not hold this to be the case with Macready. He is striking throughout: often fine, sometimes extremely affecting and masterly: but the level of his style is of a more gratuitous order than Kean's. We do not always see the reason for his *fortes* and *pianos:* his grace looks more the effect of study than habit: his personal character does not seem so concerned in what he does. You are not sure what sort of a person he will be when he leaves the stage. From Kean, if you would look for sulkiness or something arbitrary, and not be sure whither his passion might lead him, you would also expect to hear of the most graceful actions, or the development of something good in his worst. Mr. Macready has sensibility, tenderness, passion; he suffers: his passion masters him; he knows how to undergo it with delicacy, to contest with it as though he suppressed it ; but he never does: emotion in some shape or other, positive or negative, controls him. When this is not the case, he is merely acting, though acting to advantage. Kean, on the other hand, though undergoing passion more terribly, still surmounts it with the grace of moral grandeur. He feels the poetry of it more ; that is to say, all the elegance and idealism of which it is capable, compatible with nature. This never fails him ; and this, while it enables him to seize the very best points of familiarity (for those are the perfection of the delicacy) renders his tragedy as superior to Mr. Macready's in general, as poetry is to mixed poetry and prose, or as the mixed poetry and prose of Macready is to the declamatory verse of the purely artificial tragedian.

Mr. Macready was awfully effective in the prison-scene with Appius Claudius, and came beautifully to his senses when the urn was brought him containing the ashes of his daughter. What a manly and sweet-natured play is this of Mr. Knowles's, and how well it moves the heart again after a lapse of years, like music that we have heard at home! We know of no modern production that moves us with greater feelings of regard and respect for the author.

We must not forget that Wallack displayed a genuine burst of passion in the scene before Appius that would have done honour to any actor. It is where he speaks of his betrothed bride, and calls her the life-blood of his heart. His voice, when he dared anybody to ill-treat her, sunk into as real a tone of honest and feeling manhood as we ever remember to have heard. We regret we cannot repeat the passage. It received two distinct rounds of applause.

And the other performers did well. Altogether this is a fine play, finely performed ; and we recommend those who have not seen it, to go and do so next Monday, when it is to be repeated.

MACREADY AS HAMLET.

October 22, 1830.

MR. MACREADY performed the character of Hamlet last night,[1] and exhibited his usual faults and beauties, but not to such advantage as in other characters. Hamlet in the midst of his apparent irrationality, is full of " exquisite reasons." There is, as Polonius says of him, " method in his madness." We think Mr. Macready wanted this method ; that is to say, that he is not so

[1] At Drury Lane.

alive as could be desired to the lights and shades of
Hamlet's feeling, and the deep meaning that pervades
it all. The extreme lowness of his voice in some
passages, and loudness in others, had not their particular
warrant : his familiarities and repulsions were not always
rightly placed : he was now too stationary, and then too
full of impulse. He began his address to the Ghost
capitally well, but when he insisted upon following it,
and threw off his attendants, his sudden vociferations
were quite out of character. Hamlet's respect for his
father's presence, to say nothing of the reverence that
would always be shown a ghost, would never have
allowed him to make such a noise. His most warrant-
able loudness (indeed there it is desirable, because Hamlet
is bullying his own indecision into action) was where he
makes the stab through the arras, crying out " Dead for
a ducat ! " and it was followed by a very fine and effective contrast of tone, in the rapid question—" Is it the
king ? " [1] The scene of the play also was broken up with
great effect. The delivery of the famous soliloquy " To
be or not to be " was too quick and continuous ; not full
of thought enough, nor sufficiently broken with pauses.
On this and on other occasions, Mr. Macready is too
stationary. He should walk the stage more, particularly
as Hamlet is in a restless state of nerves, and would do
so, if we could see him. He is in a condition to pace
his room the whole day. Neither could we admire the
directions to the player. Mr. Macready was not at his
ease enough : he was not enough in his own house, nor
sufficiently free towards his friend the actor ; for he

[1] By what can only be a curious lapse of memory, Leigh Hunt here
writes, " Was it my father ? " and the printer further complicates
matters by printing, " Was is it my father ? "

might have been more so without any derogation from his dignity, nay, with advantage to it; for the link between them is intellectual, and the freedom would have been founded on the prince's very superiority to everything vulgar. We felt as if Mr. Macready ought to have put his hand on the player's shoulder, and led him with him up and down the room, explaining his notions on the subject of playing as he went. Lastly, we must find fault, more or less, with the whole of the supposed mad or flighty scenes between Hamlet and his friends, that with Ophelia included. Mr. Macready was too real in his flightiness; too quick and abrupt; and too gratuitous in his *fortes* and *pianos.* Hamlet is never really mad. He is only a prey to a thousand unhealthy over-refinements of thought and conscience—an excess of the contemplative—which baffles his action, and makes him splenetic with himself and others. Everything he utters, apparently the most absurd, has a delicate link with reason and the occasion, as might be easily shown. He loves to perplex those who come to play upon him, to seem mad in their eyes because they are fools; and at length feels so much relief in venting his spleen, that he must needs indulge it on poor Ophelia, because he is made cruel enough by sorrow to procure himself the pleasure of pitying, and knows that she will bear for love's sake whatsoever he inflicts.

But enough of objection. We must add, for Mr. Macready's comfort (if he cares anything about it) and our own too (for critics as we are, we had much rather praise than find fault) that we never yet saw a Hamlet on the stage, nor do we expect to see one. It is a character, though quite in nature, made up of too many qualities to be represented by any but a Hamlet him-

self. Shakspeare, who invented, should have performed
it ; but it is said that he was but an indifferent actor ;
hindered perhaps of *action* in one way, as Hamlet was
in another, out of the very multiplicity of his thoughts.
We have seen parts of Hamlet's character represented,
but we never saw the whole. Kean himself, if we remember, failed here, as everybody else has failed. Let
us think what Hamlet was. He was a prince, the model
of his father's court,

> " The expectancy and rose of the fair state,
> The glass of fashion and the mould of form ; "

he was accomplished ; he was a wit ; he was in the
highest degree both sensitive and intelligent ; and ill-
health and calamity (for Shakspeare takes care, in his
wisdom, to let us know that ill-health and the common
want of exercise had to do with his melancholy) conspired
to work up his perceptions to a pitch of hypochondriacal
intensity, so that he was in the habit of seeing things in
their anatomy, deprived of the ordinary investments of
custom and natural seeming. Now where is the actor
likely to be found who shall do justice to all this ? Mr.
Kemble had the dignity of Hamlet, but not the grace
and wit, nor the sensibility ; Mr. Charles Kemble had
the chivalrous look, but not the intellect ; Mr. Young
the melancholy but not the profundity ; and so on, of
twenty others : they all had some one or two points, but
none of the rest. Mr. Macready has the sensibility, but
wants the deep thought requisite to vary it properly, and
to shape it. Mr. Kean's Hamlet we doubt whether we
can have seen, as we have no recollection of it ; but we
will venture to say that he would have the moral grace
and the dignity, and more of the other requisites than

most, but fail in the wit and the profundity, and certainly not remind us of " the glass of fashion."

THE SCHOOL FOR SCANDAL.

October 27, 1830.

WE could not help conjecturing, at the *School for Scandal,* last night,[1] what sort of man Charles Surface would have turned out, could we have seen him grown old. Would he not have been like Sheridan? Was not Sheridan like him? We do not say this out of any pedantry of morality. We like a liberal version of life in a young book. But there is something too much of wine and debt in Charles's outset. We should have preferred a little more love, and less post-obit. However, Sheridan drew from what he was acquainted with, and was not bound to be sentimental. We laugh at the notion of such a character as Charles's doing any harm. Sheridan's wit is not of a seductive nature. He makes us dislike a good many things, perhaps more than he looked for. We laugh heartily with his satirical personages all round, at all their butts; and then at the satirists in their turn; but nobody will come away from one or Sheridan's plays, loving anything the better, good or bad. Hypocrites, perhaps, will resolve to take care how they get into scrapes; but we do not love even the heartier side of Charles's character, except in his refusal to sell his uncle's picture. He seems rather to defy economy than to enjoy pleasure. We cannot help thinking that there are marks of an uneasy turn of mind in all Sheridan's productions. There is almost always some real pain going on amongst his characters. They are always perplexing, mortifying, or distressing one another;

[1] At Drury Lane.

snatching their jokes out of some misery, as if they were playing at snap-dragon. They do not revel in wit for its own sake, like those of Congreve ; nor wear a hey-day impudence, for the pleasure of the thing, as in Vanbrugh ; nor cultivate an eternal round of airiness and satisfaction, as in good-natured Farquhar. Sheridan's comedy is all-stinging satire. His bees want honey.

The piece last night was strongly cast, and the house was not disappointed in the performance. It was one of the full houses, which this theatre at present enjoys above its neighbour. The heat in the upper boxes was intense, but nobody seemed to mind it. " The more the merrier" is the word on these occasions ; men come in at the back of the boxes, wondering how they can add so much more cloth and breath to the atmosphere, but they stay and get used to it ; and the deep peals of laughter succeed each other, like the thunder of a merry summer-time.

Dowton was the Sir Oliver, as of old—excellent. We cannot fancy a better Sir Oliver. Farren was the Sir Peter Teazle—admirable. We cannot fancy a better Sir Peter. We saw King [1] once in the character. He was the original, and performed it again on some occasion (we forget what) after having taken leave of the stage. But either he was not the old man he was in his youth (which is likely enough), or he was not to be compared with Farren. He was dry and insipid to him. Farren makes the utmost of every passage without seeming to make any effort. His acting in the French milliner part of that most admirable scene of the screen (one of the

---

[1] Thomas King, the original Sir Peter Teazle, retired in May, 1802, and died in 1805. He unfortunately " lagged superfluous on the stage," and it is quite certain that before Leigh Hunt could have seen him his powers were greatly diminished.

most perfect, if not the most so, in all comedy) was
brought up to a climax of humour, the excess of which
he contrived, wonderfully well, to refer to the imbecility
of age.   He twittered, and shook, and gaped, and giggled,
and was bent double with an absolute rapture of
incapacity.

We do not remember so good a Joseph Surface as
Macready.   We do not see why a tragedian should be
selected for this character ; unless there is something
clerical in tragedy, and Joseph be accounted hardly a lay
character.   Tragedians, from what we recollect, have
generally failed in it ; at least have not done it so well,
as fine comedians could.   We do not remember John
Palmer[1] in the character ; nor can we call to mind any
good comedian we have seen in it.   Mr. Macready was
very good in the love-making scene with Lady Teazle.
We watched his face narrowly, and admired the look of
rising pleasure, mixed with the cunning observance that
watched in his up-turned eyes, as he bent his head
towards her.   In the scene with Sir Peter, where he is
playing a more artificial part—acting the ordinary
hypocrite—we doubt whether his manner was sufficiently
lying.   Hypocrisy, to be sure, is supposed to be least
visible, when it is greatest :—it is said to " lie like truth."
But we doubt whether the *habit* of hypocrisy does not
betray itself more than it did in Mr. Macready ; and
whether the most consummate falsehood ever does, in
reality, " lie like truth."   From all that we have seen of
false faces and manners (and we have encountered a good

---

[1] John Palmer, " Plausible Jack," was the original Joseph Surface.
He was so perfectly suited to the part that Charles Lamb declared that,
so long as John Palmer played it, Joseph Surface was the hero of the
piece.

many in our time) there will be some little betraying
system, some look, some glance, some twist of the mouth,
some little recurrent hem, or cough, or other pretence of
ease, or some exaggeration of unconsciousness and simplicity, which we did not observe in the acting of Mr.
Macready. And recollect, that Joseph in that scene is
not at his ease : he is in momentary danger of discovery ;
and therefore, however he might doubly affect ease, he
could on that very account not attain to it.

We are sorry we cannot speak well of the Charles
Surface of Mr. Wallack, because he evidently took pains
with it, and in one or two passages received a well-
merited applause. But he does not look sufficiently
either the young man, or the man of fashion, and he
wants ease in these parts of gentlemen. He nods or bows
his head too much, in comment upon the text ; and is
not here and there as he ought to be, with a natural
vivacity. He seems afraid of being too lively, like a man,
unused to company, in his new coat at dinner. However,
when he was wrought up to a pitch of pleasurable sarcasm
at the termination of the screen scene, he acquitted himself much better.

And Miss Chester as Lady Teazle ?—What we have
said of this lady on a former occasion applies to the
present one ; with this difference—that she was equally
self-possessed on the present occasion, with less reason to
be so ; for Lady Teazle, in the midst of her lady-like
bearing, is intended to retain something of the simplicity
of her country breeding ; and this simplicity is a different
sort of thing from Miss Chester's look of refined self-
respect and reposing beauty. She is always worth
looking at, however, and a pleasing actress, and will
diminish no house's spectators.

THE MERCHANT OF VENICE.

October 28, 1830.

WE had the pleasure last night of seeing the *Merchant of Venice.*[1] What a transition, from one of Sheridan's plays, with little but sarcasm in it, and the delight of fault-finding and mortification, to one of Shakspeare's—sure to be full of sweetness, however bitter may be its subject! This is one of the points upon which Shakspeare is incomparable. Nobody approaches him in it. Beauty is as much his attribute as force. The sweetness of his nature caresses wherever it can, and forces the most untoward thoughts to show that they can smile. In the piece before us we have a Jew, who is full of revenge, and will be content with nothing but a pound of flesh from his enemy's body ; yet it is out of the very madness of the love of sympathy that this revenge is bred, and he has no sympathy, because it has been denied him. The Jew loves his daughter ; you may see it in the thick of his denunciations of her ; and he was so fond of his wife, that his greatest pang at losing a precious ring is because Leah gave it him. His daughter exchanged it for a monkey : *he* would not have parted with it " for a wilderness of monkeys." The rest of the characters, bating for Christian prejudices, as we allow for Jewish in Shylock, are all made up of love, pleasantness, and friendship. You cannot open a first scene in Shakspeare, but some fragrance of beauty and good-nature is sure to breathe upon you. In the first scene, for instance, of this play, you have not read many lines before you meet with the following passage, in which rocks and shipwrecks are made to produce beauty.

[1] At Covent Garden.

Salario says that if he were a merchant he should be always thinking how his ships were faring at sea : he could not go to church, but the very edifice would remind him

> " Of dangerous rocks
> Which touching but *my gentle vessel's* side,
> Would scatter all her *spices* on the stream—
> *Enrobe* the roaring waters *with my silks.*"

And then what exquisite language, fit for exquisite thoughts! "Let me play the fool," says Gratiano, a little further on—

> " With mirth and laughter let old wrinkles come ;
> And let my liver rather heat with wine,
> Than my heart cool with mortifying groans.
> Why should a man, whose heart is warm within,
> Sit like his grandsire cut in alabaster ?
> Sleep when he wakes ? and *creep* into the jaundice
> By being peevish ? "

The women in this play (another point upon which nobody comes near him) are, like all Shakspeare's women, as charming as nature can make them, though with a difference. What a fine generous test does Portia get up for her lover, in the scene of the caskets ! How delightful is the return home of her and her maid, with the light which they see in the windows at a distance ! And what a pretty perplexity they make with the rings—how prophetic of the sprightliness of their honeymoon !

We like Miss Kemble better in Portia than in any character in which we have seen her yet. The reason is, not that there is more genius in the performance, but that the part does not put her so much upon her declamation, that it allows her to smile and be an ordinary woman, and that she seemed happy in the opportunity of showing that she could be one. Her best passages were decidedly those in which she was arch and affectionate. The speech on *Mercy* was not given better than we have heard it by twenty others ; and all the serious part was open to the usual charge of declamation and monotony, though rendered less violently objectionable by the nature of the play. The applauses were not much, and the houses begin to be very thin ; the third tier of boxes was nearly empty through the whole of the performance.

Why does not Mr. Charles Kemble act Falconbridge, or Don Sebastian, that we may praise him, instead of Shylock, in which he looks more like a sturdy Friar Tuck, than a carking Jew? He seemed as if he ought to have laid about him with his stick at once, instead of waiting for the tedious forms of law. His revenge is too loud and ranting ; he makes the climax of the feeling consist in putting noise upon noise ; though in one instance he uttered the word "revenge" in a very terrible and cordial manner, as if he loved it. The part altogether is one of his least successful efforts.

It appears to us that they put Mr. Blanchard at this theatre in parts too humble for his talents. He made a very good blind old nonentity in this piece, as the father of Launcelot Gobbo ; but he has insight into better things than these, or the characters they put him into in melodramatic afterpieces. Mr. Meadows in Launcelot is too quick, as if he was half-reading his part in character, rather than acting it. We have nothing to say of the other characters, except that Mrs. Keeley is clever, as usual, in the part of Nerissa ; that Miss Forde made a sufficing little Jewess ; and that it does one good to see Mr. Farley as active and sprightly as he used to be many years ago in the character of Gratiano. His voice is music to us, from old associations; though he still speaks, we observe, as if he had a muffin in it.

MISS FANNY KEMBLE AS MRS. HALLER.

November 4, 1830.

YESTERDAY evening [1] Miss Kemble performed the part of Mrs. Haller in the *Stranger*, for the first time. It was a graceful and interesting performance in all the passages for which she found warrant in her own womanhood or domestic fancy; but the moment she thought it her business to be dignified, she made the usual declamatory mistake. We were not present at the scene in which Mrs. Haller describes the happiness of the village children; but an excellent critic, by whose side we had the pleasure of finding ourselves, told us that she did it well—not so effectively or with so touching a self-forgetfulness at the moment as Miss O'Neil—there was more of a lady-like moderation in it—but still interestingly and with nature. One of the touches that we thought excellent, indeed as good as could be, was the tone in which she answered " Oh yes," to the inquiry whether she thought Baron Steinfort handsome. It expressed at once just what it ought to do—good-will, sincerity, a pleasure in saying it, and yet personal indifference. But the moment this young lady has a tragic note to strike up, or thinks she has, then commences the declamation, the drawl, the monotony, the peremptoriness of air, and the dealing forth of stately syllables—in short, the false elevation of manner which she mistakes for exaltation of feeling. There is a sad want of light and shade; and the

---

[1] At Covent Garden.

intervals between the more familiar and lofty passages
have no gradation.   On one sentence, she is pleasing and
has an air of nature ; speaks in simple tones, and promises
to make us at home with her.   In the next, and on the
instant, she resumes the queen-like state of what she
thinks tragedy ; draws up her head ; bridles it back with
a stately remoteness from our poor would-be reciprocity ;
and in a totally different tone, as well as manner, deals
forth her didactics to us, in the style of pride giving an
alms.   It is a cant imitation of Mrs. Siddons, or her
mother, or of both united.   In short, as the poet says—

"What can we reason but from what we know ?" [1]

What can a performer act, but from some little experience for fancy to act by ?   When Miss Kemble
speaks of children, or has a kind welcome to make, or
expresses an opinion of friends' good looks, she has something in her own knowledge to draw upon, and she does
it gracefully.   When she is to be lofty and miserable, she
is but a superior kind of school-girl, drawing herself up,
and reciting her "Enfield's Speaker."

Mrs. Haller is supposed to be a favourable part for
a new actress, because it forcibly interests the feelings on
its own account ; and the conclusion is just, as far as
regards the inexperienced portion of the audience ; but,
in another respect, the advantage is a dangerous one,
because it gives rise in her mind to a false notion of the
cause of her success.   She will probably, and very
naturally, attribute to her performance more than is
due ; her friends will take occasion to confound the
two things, as they did on the present occasion ; and

[1] Pope's *Essay on Man.*

many persons will be led, for the moment, into the same error. Thus a sensation is made which future performance will not keep up. Yesterday evening, a cluster of persons in the pit made a great noise after the play, and renewed the waving of hats, and the call for Mr. Kemble, refusing to hear Mr. Warde give out the pieces of next night. Now his daughter did really perform to more advantage in Mrs. Haller, than in any of her unmixed tragic characters. She has always done the like, and most probably will do it. But the hit was not so excessive as these indiscreet friends would make out; and if a hope has been renewed to the contrary, disappointment will again be felt. During the play, some very indiscreet hands tried to get up claps out of season, and were left in a painful minority. It was just as if they had proclaimed, "This passage ought *not* to be applauded."

We have the most formidable of all words to say for Mr. Charles Kemble's Stranger :—it was respectable. The whisper of his "Yes" was good, when the confession is torn from him that he still loves his wife : but we recollect nothing else that made an impression upon us. Mrs. Gibbs was singularly young in the character of Charlotte, considering her age. Farley is a reasonable Francis ; and Mrs. Chatterley made a very satisfactory Countess Wintersen. She is just the person to act a gentle, soothing part of this kind, her handsomeness being of the genial order, with an open-hearted countenance. Harriett Cawse, in the part of Annette, sang with great taste and feeling the melody composed by the Duchess of Devonshire to Sheridan's words, *I have a silent sorrow here.* And a very sweet melody it is. It makes us inclined to parody the question put to the same

celebrated lady,[1] in Mr. Coleridge's Ode upon her poem
of Mount St. Gothard—

> " Oh lady, nurs'd in pomp and pleasure,
>   Where gat ye that *most pensive* measure ? "

Alas ! from the pomp and pleasure itself : for often, as
the poet tells us,

> " Ev'n in the very temple of delight,
>   Veil'd Melancholy holds her sovereign shrine."

The voice of Harriett Cawse, always good, seems to
improve daily, and her skill with it. We must tell her,
however, that pleasing as her second verse was, and much
less ornamented than most singers who have a voice to
show off with would have made it, the first verse was still
more pleasing ; and she would have seen the house think
so too, if she could have marked their faces. It had no
ornament at all, and was indeed charming and unobjec-
tionable. We were in pain for her as she came to the
conclusion, lest she should spoil it with a shake. She
gave no shake, and the effect was perfect. Why did she
think it necessary to make variations on the second
verse ? A shake may be allowed as a variety, especially
if she did not begin it quite in so deliberate and lesson-
like a manner ; but the more we hear melodies of this
kind as the composer wrote them, the better. The heart
listened to her first verse, and approved it. The ears
began to criticise her second, admired it, and left the
heart comparatively untouched. We could have heard
half a dozen verses with delight, sung with the same
affecting simplicity as the one ; but would have been
content with one or two of the others.

[1] "O Lady, nursed in pomp and pleasure,
    Whence learn'd you that heroic measure ? "

What a curious play this is, and how it triumphs over law and custom, and the actors, and the audience, and the critics, and the writer himself ! For he was but ill suited to the noble task of teaching a humanity above the letter. He has made a young woman quit, for a villain, not only her husband, but her children too ; and the villain bribed her with promises of having more money to spend, and she is persuaded to be unfaithful by the paltry device of a forged letter, which pretends to convict her husband of infidelity. Her husband too, by her own confession, was far superior to the seducer in every respect. In short, it was out of vanity and mortification, that she became faithless ; out of narrowness of heart, and not any overflowing of it ; out of antipathy to the man she had just been loving, and not out of sympathy with him she proposed to love : and yet notwithstanding this most gross of all the cases of infidelity, her penitence restores her in all our eyes ; the hearts of the audience are taken by storm ; the very critics are shaken into tears ; pity, white handkerchiefs, and genuine honest sorrow, prevail all over the house. There are two reasons for this. The house, in the first place, is made up of husbands and wives, and parents : which renders the domesticity of the scenes irresistible. And secondly, the peculiar circumstances of the case are forgotten in the general fact of a wife penitent and a husband pardoning. The world says that a husband must not pardon under any such circumstances ; but the heart of the world, touched by a play, says he shall ; prejudices are fused in the tears of sympathy ; the audience forgive one another all the errors of circumstance and custom, under the shape of that one ; and while they are in the humour, would rather suspect that their notions, outside of the house, may be too rigid, than their humanity, inside of it, ought to be gainsaid. In a word, as Mr. Hazlitt says, in speaking of this and other plays by the author's countrymen, it is felt that " *There is something rotten in the state of Denmark.* Opinion is not truth : appearance is not reality ; power is not beneficence ; rank is not wisdom : nobility is not the only virtue : riches are not happiness ; desert and success are different things : actions do not always speak the character any more than words. We feel this," concludes Mr. Hazlitt, " and do justice to the romantic extravagance of the German Muse."

SHE STOOPS TO CONQUER.

November 6, 1830.

THE plot of the laughable comedy, *She Stoops to Conquer* (which is founded on mistaking a private house for an inn) is said to have been suggested to the author by an adventure which befell himself. And it is easy to believe it. Goldsmith wanted as much address in his person, as he had the reverse with his pen. He was as simple and credulous in one way, as he was knowing in the other ; but above all, like a wise man, he knew his own in-firmities, and like a still wiser, he could draw upon them for profit and entertainment. It is observable that all his productions are full of adventures founded on mistakes and dilemmas ; and we have little doubt that he drew most of them from his own experience. The character of Moses, we believe, in the *Vicar of Wakefield,* is understood to have been drawn from his own. The knavery practised on Moses at the fair, the awkward situation of Young Honeywood with the bailiffs in the

Good-natured Man, the whole character and conduct
of Young Marlowe in the play before us, and even the
Chinese's loss of his watch, in the *Citizen of the World*,
to the beautiful young lady who made his acquaintance
in the streets, and who with so much generosity took
upon herself the trouble of getting it mended for him—
are Goldsmith all over. We fancy Johnson, Garrick,
and others, in the house on the first night of *She Stoops
to Conquer*, recognising the infirmities of their friend,
and admiring the self-knowledge with which he turned
them to such pleasant account.

The play was agreeably performed last night,[1] but not
in the masterly manner we have seen it, when Elliston
was Young Marlowe, and Bannister Tony Lumpkin.
Mr. Farren, too, excellent actor as he is, has neither such
festive nor passionate flesh and blood in him as Dowton,
and therefore does not so well suit the character of Old
Hardcastle. He has not body enough to fill an arm-
chair so well at dinner (where he is supposed to tell his
stories so often) nor to be shaken into so robust a rage at
Marlowe's accumulation of impertinences. Dowton's
face has an oily radiance when he is pleased, and he
tumbles in a passion like a whale. He can afford it.
Farren looks as if a fit of passion might kill him ; which
is a little too tragic. Mrs. Glover, on the other hand, is
something too *cosy* and pleasant-looking for the fidgetty
Mrs. Hardcastle. Mrs. Davenport might have been as
stout, but she looked in less joyous condition ; and then
she dug her words in, as if she was sticking pins. Mrs.
Sparks,[2] perhaps, though inferior in general to either, was
still better in this part, by reason of a certain look she

[1] At Drury Lane.
[2] An actress of whom little is known. She made her first appearance in London in 1797. She was excellent in antiquated ladies.

13

had, at once carking and lavish; precisely the expression for the fond but cheating mother. Mrs. Davison as Miss Hardcastle was far beyond Miss Mordaunt. Miss Mordaunt is a nice delicate girl, of considerable promise, with fine eyes, and a power now and then to be seriously touching. But her voice and manner are both too weak for a part like this; and she has at all times, we observe, an awkward trick of casting down her eyes, probably because they have handsome lids, or she wishes to make the spectators aware of their merits. We do not quarrel with ladies for knowing their merits, personal or otherwise, or for endeavouring to do them justice. On the contrary, we wish them to know them so well, as to be aware that nothing does them entire justice, but an absence of all trick and affectation. By mending this single fault, Miss Mordaunt will go nigh to double the effect of her whole style of acting.

We are loth to say how inferior we think Liston's Tony Lumpkin to what it ought to be. It will not bear a moment's comparison with Bannister's. It may look the character more completely, as far as outside goes—its uncouth lumpishness and round-faced grown childhood; but in all the rest it is a slovenly sketch, compared with the way in which the other used to make every word tell—his fine, round, roaring voice when describing his jollities, and his *frumpish* tone when complaining of not being allowed to come to his "fortun." The mischief, too, about the highwayman, was made as much again of by Bannister. Liston does not even speak half his sentences loud enough. He hardly seems to be aware of the best points; and altogether reposes far too indolently on the character, either from carelessness, or want of tact. We cannot help suspecting, from both.

KING HENRY V.

November 9, 1830.

THE play of *Henry V.* was performed here[1] last night, but to little purpose. It is a *rifacimento* of Shakspeare's play, partly taken out of *Henry IV.*, in order to increase the dramatic effect. But the secret must out. It is not a good acting play—at least not for these times. In every production of Shakspeare's there must be noble passages. There are fine lines in this, " familiar in our mouths" (to quote one of them) "as household words." But the historical plays of our great poet were written, not merely as dramas, but as chronicles. People in ordinary, in his time, were not so well informed as they are now. They went to the theatre, when one of these plays was performed, not merely to see a play as we do, but to receive an historical lesson, to hear about England and France, and take home the legend to their children, as we carry home now a piece of news. Besides, the feeling was not what it is now between the two countries. They affected then (as indeed they did up to a late period) to bully and undervalue one another : Henry V. was a popular prince with our ancestors, purely because he went to France, and read the Dauphin's insolence a terrible lesson. But these times are over now : the French (with illustrious reason) are no longer reckoned boasters : those even who conquered them but a little while since, may not be popular. The English care little for quarrels between kings : audiences at a play want something better than this prince and that stepping out alternately with a flourish of trumpets—then a little

[1] Drury Lane.

huddle of soldiers, which we are to take for an onset—
then the English flag running in, and then the French
flag—with an occasional speech between, about St.
George or St. Denys—and a Welsh captain, who is
proud because the King is a Welshman. In a word, the
play of *Henry V.* was written to please the uninformed
subjects of a despotic government two hundred years ago,
and as it comprises little of the everlasting humanity that
fills most of the plays of Shakspeare, it falls flat on the
ears of an audience in these times of popular spirit ! Of
all the plays that could be selected, it struck us as one of
the least fit to be performed on the eve of our present
Lord Mayor's Day ! and we found it so. Mr. Macready,
though too loud in some parts, made a gallant and a
gallant prince too (we allude to his courtship of
Katharine), and Mr. Webster, in Captain Fluellen,
sustained the reputation he acquired as Sir Hugh
Evans :—but it would not do. The piece was as flat as
the water in Tower Ditch, and about as noisy to no
purpose as the beating to arms there.

MISS TAYLOR AS ROSALIND.

November 19, 1830.

MISS TAYLOR did not do herself justice, when she made
her first appearance in a ranting melodrama. We
thought there was more in her intelligent and sensitive
countenance than she makes out in the *Carnival at
Naples.* The truth is, her forte lies on the side of
enjoyment and comic grace, mixed indeed with as much
of a serious faculty as is necessary to complete it, but still
leaning a good deal more to comedy than to tragedy.

In tragedy she has been brought up in too literal and peremptory a school, thinks it necessary to be too vehement, and is apt to mistake verbal painting for distinctness of passion. We know not what she might have done in serious parts, had her sensibility received better direction. As far as we have hitherto been enabled to judge in that respect, she is a striking melodramatic actress, and nothing more. But we have now to hail her in a new and most desirable light—as one who can act the charming females of Shakspeare, and who has restored Rosalind to the stage. Her performance last night [1] in *As You Like It*, rose in merit as it proceeded, and delighted the house with that rare union of grace, gaiety, and feeling, which the town had almost begun to despair of seeing again.

Miss Taylor in this character is Miss Tree [2] come back, with a greater spirit of enjoyment. In person, as well as everything else, she is a proper complete Rosalind, at least in all the more playful scenes. In the first scene or two, where she is more serious, we confess we did not look for what we found afterwards, though it was all gracefully done. But the moment she put on the youth's attire, she was the genuine female of the poet's drama—arch, graceful, various, full of faith in the goodness and delightfulness of her love, and taking a licence accordingly, in fancy and manner, which nothing but the better sort of love can render perfectly delightful. Her person suited the graceful stripling; her voice has that sort of richness in its ordinary tones, which seems to

[1] At Covent Garden.

[2] Maria Tree (Mrs. Bradshaw) was a singer rather than an actress. She had a very short stage career, making her first London appearance in 1818, and retiring in 1825.

belong to a full heart ; her leg—we are loth to make comparisons between ladies' legs—but if Miss Tree's was perhaps the more perfectly taper and feminine, Miss Taylor's has a light smartness in it, not at all masculine. Her face we hold to be superior to Miss Tree's ; it has more faith, earnestness, and good humour : Miss Tree's was elegant, but there was a look of fastidiousness in the expression of the mouth : her highest grace was in her person and carriage. Miss Taylor's face is of a longer kind, but not too long ; there is something of a southern look in it, both as to the dark eyes and a certain pull forward in the lower part of it—fawn-like, *appetissante*—how shall we describe it ?—in short, more sensitive and *enjouée* than Miss Tree's. When she talked, in the epilogue, of kissing those who had beards to please her, you could take her more at her word ; and it was more decorous on that account. There was more *pertinence* in the speech. We know not whether Miss Taylor's face would be pronounced handsome off the stage. Perhaps it would be thought too pale, or too slender, or the mouth too large ; or there might be some other objection which is none. But it is a very interesting one, to our minds, on the stage. It has the best handsomeness in it—that of a power to be thoughtful with a propensity to pleasure. We have seen Mrs. Jordan in this character, Mrs. Henry Siddons,[1] Miss Tree, Miss Brunton,[2] and twenty others. Mrs. Jordan, with her delightful voice, was cordial in it, and sang the cuckoo-song admirably, but wanted some-

---

[1] Mrs. Henry Siddons was the daughter-in-law of the great actress. She was excellent both in tragedy and comedy, and was for many years manageress in Edinburgh.

[2] Miss Brunton (Countess of Craven) was very beautiful, and was a famous actress of "genteel comedy."

thing of the gentlewoman. Mrs. Henry Siddons, with her fine eyes, was lady-like and romantic ; Miss Tree very graceful and impressive ; Miss Brunton we forget, except that her manner was a good deal like Miss Chester : [1] but we remember no Rosalind altogether, which we like so well as Miss Taylor's. By the way, she sang the cuckoo-song with great good taste and effect, closing the stanzas well, without the loitering of a shake ; and was ardently encored in it. If we were asked out of many passages in the play, to select the one in which her delivery pleased us most, we should say that it was in the part where she asks Orlando if he will come to her cottage, and make love to her.

Rosalind. I would cure you, if you would but call me *Rosalind!*, and come every day to my cot *and woo me.*
Orlando. Now, by the faith of my love, I will : tell me where it is.
Rosalind. Go with me to it, and I will show it you : and by the way, you shall tell me where in the forest you live. *Will ye?*
Orlando. With all my heart, good youth.
Rosalind. Nay, nay, *you must call me Rosalind.*

All these passages marked in Italics were given with that perfect mixture of liveliness and love—the voice melting, as the eyes urged the inquiry—which marks the character of this heroine of Shakspeare's pastoral.

How charming, by the way, are all Shakspeare's loving heroines ! and how perfectly has he hit that perfection of female fascination, which consists in the union of a good heart, a lively fancy, and a pleasurable temperament ! How poor do the women of almost all other dramatic

[1] Miss Chester was an actress of some notoriety, but she owed her fame, such as it was, to her great beauty. She was " Reader of Shakspere " to George IV. !

poets (which they intend to be attractive or seducing) appear by the side of them ! How unlovely their virtues, how vicious and unvoluptuous their love ! What an extremity of remoteness is there between the utmost license or most avowed passion in Shakspeare, and that heartless animal character of Chloe with which Fletcher has embittered his sweet pastoral, the *Faithful Shepherdess !*

Mr. Charles Kemble's Orlando has been long and deservedly admired for its gallant bearing, and complete look of the character. There are parts of it, too, very good on other accounts ; though we think it generally deficient in warmth. Mr. Keeley's Touchstone is the best we have seen since the days of Bannister. Fawcett's was too cut and dry, and had little of the natural fool in it ; for in these characters of Fools there is always implied a mixture of imbecility with their acuteness ; a want of will, in the midst of their pretensions to it. Fawcett carried himself as if he ought not to have married Audrey ; Keeley as if he could not help himself, while he joked her. Mrs. Gibbs's Audrey is an imitation of Miss Pope's. Mr. Wilson seemed disabled from doing justice to his songs by a cold.

The Scenery of this piece is very beautiful. When we did not like any actor who was speaking, *we took a walk in it*; and found ourselves in the midst of glades and woods, "and alleys leading inward far." In one of the intervals between the acts, the orchestra gratified us by playing in a masterly manner, the sweet and apposite air of " Thou soft-flowing Avon." Upon the whole, we have not had such a treat as this play, since we renewed our visits to the theatre. It is repeated on Saturday.

KING HENRY IV.

November 20, 1830.

LAST night the play of *Henry IV.* was performed at this theatre.[1] The historical plays of Shakspeare certainly do not tell, as they used to do—no disparagement to his mighty genius. He could not be expected to render kings, and their quarrels and sophistications, as undiminished in interest for ever as the events common to us all. Part of the interest of these plays arose, as we have before observed, from the paucity of books in his time. We know history better now, and respect the performers in it less. Greater matters engage us : but love is ever interesting, and wit, and domestic pity, and the struggles of the will with the understanding. In Shakspeare's time, audiences were contented with a curtain for a scene, and a few dresses no better than at a booth : they were content to be absorbed in those stories of civil wars and royal successions, with the noise of which their grandfather's ears had hardly ceased ringing. At present, we must dress up the historical play with plumes, and decorations, and real costume, in order to amuse the eye, because the other interest languishes. And we dress it very well, yet it languishes still. Last night, Mr. Cooper's costume as Henry IV. was a real historical picture. We saw the King himself before us, with his draperied head ; and the performer, as he rose from his chair, and remained lecturing his son with his foot planted on the royal stool, displayed the monarch well—his ermined robe, stretched out by his elbow, making a back-ground to the portrait. But the real interest of Henry is gone, when we think so much of

[1] Drury Lane.

this " galanty-show " of him. For our parts, we confess
that we forget all he said, in thinking what sort of a
grand and half-witted wild beast of a man a king was in
those days ; and whether the day were far distant, in
which lions and eagles would be thought fit emblems of
national sovereignty.

There is Falstaff, to be sure, in this play ; and Mr.
Dowton's Falstaff in *Henry IV*. is better than in the
Merry Wives of Windsor. His wit is more exercised
than his enjoyment ; and Mr. Dowton lets no fancy pass
without dwelling upon and recommending it in his
acutest manner. But his Falstaff is at no time the
proper rolling tun of a tavern sensualist ; he is not fat
enough in the throat, nor festive enough in his general
manner : he takes his graver speeches too literally—does
not let us see the vein of invincible self-complacency
running through them : and the other *dramatis
personæ* fall into the same error. Vining makes but
a flimsy Prince of Wales, and Wallack but an ordinary
Hotspur. Wallack's best passage of all was the mode in
which he died. His fall was excellent, and the posture in
which he first clasped the ground, resolute and in good
defiance, without exaggeration. Mrs. C. Jones wants
humour as Mrs. Quickly—we mean a vein of particularity—of quaint exaggeration. She is natural, and
plump, and petulant, and easily placable ; but does not
add that proper garnish to it all, which makes what we
call a character.

"AS YOU LIKE IT" AGAIN.

November 20, 1830.

We regret to observe that in the influential pages of

the *Times* and *Morning Chronicle*, the writers of the theatrical criticisms have pronounced what we cannot but consider a hasty judgment on the performance of Miss Taylor in Rosalind. The former thinks she has "a certain degree of cleverness," is often graceful, and has an expressive face, but that she is very artificial, owes her effect on the audience entirely to a knowledge of the business of the stage, and evaporates that "daring and romantic frankness of Rosalind which, in the poet's happy conception, is the result of a pure mind or want of experience, and of the impulse of a passion of which she knows nothing but the name," in "an attempt to make its expression striking"—turning the "unstudied archness which ought to be its chief characteristic " into an "elaborate knowingness." We are sorry to differ with a writer who so well knows how to express himself. The critic in the *Morning Chronicle* says he thinks Miss Taylor "a clever girl—almost a very clever girl ;" but that he should "think her cleverer, if she did not betray, in the course of her performance, that the effects she produces are the consequence rather of practice and habit than of any acute sensibility or accurate perception of the meaning of the words she utters. In this respect (he continues) she in some degree resembles Madame Vestris, whose acting, when it is good for anything, is good in proportion as it is artificial, and by dint of long experience. Miss Taylor has not had so much experience, and she has more animal spirits, and understands perfectly the use of side-long glances and a white set of teeth. As we have mentioned Madame Vestris, we may add that Miss Taylor's legs are not to be named in the same century, although they are not deficient in symmetry. She was very satisfactorily applauded, and seemed animated by the manner in which her lively efforts were rewarded."

We are sorry that this lively, and, in general, not very exacting critic, to whose good word we owe thanks ourselves, should have diminished the amount of the satisfaction, by leaving himself out of it. The diminution of one young lady's popularity, who was unfortunately overpraised at first, need not make us fearful of seeing too much merit in another, who obtains the enthusiastic applause of the house, without any recommendation but her effect upon them. If that effect had been owing almost entirely, as these gentlemen think, to Miss Taylor's acquaintance with the stage (which, by the way, would in itself be no small evidence of tact and apprehensiveness in one so young), we do not think it could have been so enthusiastic, as it was :—we are certain it would not have touched ourselves as it did. Madame Vestris does not deceive us into a notion that she is artless. We were not deceived by the very different but not less artificial merits of Miss Kemble. How then did we happen to be carried away by the Rosalind of Miss Taylor, and to be content to follow and have faith in it as the very Rosalind of Shakspeare ? We apprehend the secret to be this :—that Shakspeare carried his notions of innocence farther than our brother-critics, and that his Rosalind (as the reader may see plainly, if he consult all she says) did in fact unite a good deal of " knowingness " with her innocence. Young ladies of education (and not the less for having a court education) are very apt to unite it with their innocence ; and the manifestation of it was more allowed in those times than it is at present. Now *Rosalind*, with her heart overflowing with love and candour, not only does not conceal this vivacity of fancy from her lover, but takes a pleasure in keeping from him not a single thought. She is sure of his love ; she is with him in the forest ; she thinks of him night and day ; she is in disguise, which piques her to talk more freely to him ; she has the advantage in birth and fortune, and means to lavish on him all the goods she can—which adds to the general lavishment of her feelings ; she knows the reality of her love ; she doats on the object of it ; she believes (like Juliet) that she can say or do nothing too much to show it ; in fine, she is the beau ideal of one of Shakspeare's mistresses in Shakspeare's time, and talks (we have no doubt) precisely as the poet would have had her talk to himself.

We therefore exhort Miss Taylor to have undiminished faith in the Shaksperian excellence of her portrait, and to present it again to the public in precisely the same style she did on Thursday night ; in which case, and no other, she will do herself and the character full justice, and we will warrant her obtaining the same joyous and heart-felt applause as before. Let her have no mis-givings. Rosalind's good heart had none : neither must she.

MISS HUDDART AS BELVIDERA.

November 23, 1830.

LAST night Miss Huddart (from Dublin, we believe) made her first appearance in London[1] in the character of Belvidera. We took care to get nearer the stage this time, in order that we might fall into no more errors than we could help ; and armed ourselves besides with one of those magical powers which, according to the Arabs of the Desert, make the mountain come to a man, without

[1] At Drury Lane.

his being a Mahomet, to wit, an opera-glass. We are
sorry we have no such report to make of what we saw,
as ladies must desire who make their first appearance,
and critics too, if they are not ill-natured. But the
truth is, the whole performance is in a style not suited
to this temperate region of England, nor, we think, to
nature. Miss Huddart has a fine person, with a face
whose age it is not easy to decide amidst the lights of a
theatre. We should take it not to be very young. The
eyes have force, but want depth, being too much on the
stare. But the worst of the countenance is, that it wants
softness and expression. Belvidera is a part in which
actresses are fond of making their *début*, for an obvious
reason—because it has many striking points that " come
home (as the philosopher says) to men's business and
bosoms ; " it tends to a confusion of the actress and the
character in the minds of the audience, and engages
them, as it were, personally in her interest. But for the
same reason there are two perils in it ; first, that the
performer, if she succeed, may attribute too much to herself, and too little to the " boat that has helped her
over ; " and second, that if she do not, the audience may
instinctively resent the advantage taken of so favourite
a part, and be the more angry at the failure because of
the imposition it seems to have attempted. This is
hardly fair on their side ; but on the other hand, the
character (so to speak) is hardly a fair one for first
appearance, especially if the lady be young and handsome. We know not what was thought of Miss Huddart
in the latter respect : but she was taken by some about
us for not more than seven-and-twenty, and was pronounced to be " a fine woman." Accordingly, she was
applauded beyond measure in her first scenes : by

degrees, towards the middle of the play, the applauses began to lessen; (indeed there were symptoms of laughing at the passage where she reminds Jaffier "to remember twelve"); her vehemence occasionally revived them, nay took them by storm; which was doubtless resented by many, for on the falling of the curtain, the thunder of approbation was mixed with hisses and cries of "No, no," and so was the announcement of the piece for repetition on Wednesday.

The truth is, there was great vehemence and little passion in Miss Huddart's performance. She is used to the stage, and delivered several traditionary points with effect. She now and then ventured upon a little domestic touch of familiarity, and succeeded. But this was dangerous ground, and trod with unsteady footing. There was a sort of random, uncouth, unhinged floundering in her style which, unless held up by vehemence, left her voice without modulation, and her hits without object; and she had almost the same unvaried expression in face throughout the play, something between stare and sedateness, amounting to the stony. In short, it is painful to us to say any more on the subject. The whole performance of the play was disagreeable, to our taste; and as we dislike, with all its genius, the play itself, we had a pretty time of it. Mr. Macready at all times is apt to contrast his delicacies with too great a vehemence. Mr. Wallack's melodramas render him prone to the same fault: the bullying character of much of the play tends to excite the actors to make a noise; and certainly a most prodigious noise those two gentlemen made. They forget (or must we rather say they are instinctively aware?) that the secret of this excessive vehemence is the escape from expression

—a wish to avoid details—a merging of nice passion and intellectual difficulty into one sweeping and stormy seizure of the vulgar ear.

MACREADY AS KING JOHN.

November, 29, 1830.

King John was performed here [1] last night—the King by Macready, Constance by Miss Huddart. We found no reason to alter the opinion we expressed of this lady on her first appearance. Her manner, if one could take but a general and dim view of it, such as may be supposed to be taken by the galleries, is not without something forcible and imposing : but it is deficient throughout in weight and balance. There is an unsteadiness in it, a giving way both in tone and look when you least expect it ; something faltering, stumbling, and slip-shod : the eye wanders, the very mouth wanders too, the words suddenly fall into disjointed weakness, as if with premature old age ; and there is an indistinctness of articulation on the letter *s*, which aggravates the infirmity of the sound. But we have implied all this before. Miss Huddart has a fine person, and is hand-some, we understand, off the stage. We agree with the *Chronicle*, that she might become a very useful actress in second-rate parts, and that it is a great pity clever performers of her class will not condescend into their proper place. In any part, however, we fear it would be not unlikely that, if she went out of a certain tragic style, and at all ventured into the familiar, the fault above-mentioned would hazard an effect now and then bordering on the ludicrous. Her best points last night were those of the sarcastic order. She had also in some

[1] Drury Lane.

measure controlled the vehemence she gave way to in Belvidera.

Mr. Macready's King John is made up of his usual mixture of fine and indifferent points. He is best where he approaches domestic passion, and has to give way to soft or overwhelming emotions. His greatest deficiency is shown in passages where the ideal is required ; where nature puts on the robe of art, and speaks her truths, as it were, in state. Nothing could be finer than his loud whisper to Hubert in the words " A grave ; " or put in a better tone of affected ease than the following passage,[1] in which he says he could be merry now, and will not tell Hubert what he intends for him. As a whole, too, we must say that we think his King John the best that we have seen ; not that it was so kingly as John Kemble's (or what he thought kingly, for he was a King John of his own, in his way) but because his was more like the real historical King John, the vacillating, weak, wilful monarch, less poetical than petulant and a bully. On the other hand, as an instance of the want of the ideal, we may adduce the delivery of the commencement of John's dying speech, and the fine passage where he speaks of the winter. We conceive the vacillating style of the king, between royalty and meanness, to be so well maintained in the first part of this scene, that we will quote it, to show more distinctly what we mean. The three ruling passions of the king are " strong in death " —his sense of royalty—his fear, amounting to self-degradation—and his spirit of exaction.

(*Re-enter Bigot and attendants, who bring in King John in a chair.*)

    K. John. Ay, marry, now my soul hath elbow-room ;
      It would not out at windows, nor at doors.

---

[1] Act iv., sc. 3.

In these two lines, which are evidently spoken during a suspension of his pangs, the natural levity of the king resumes its royal airs : he is acting his Majesty again, and swelling into comparison with the universe about him. In the lines immediately succeeding, the agony returns, and he is bent, as it were, *doubly* double, with pain and natural meanness : he uses the poorest and most worthless image he can think of to describe himself by :—

> There is so hot a summer in my bosom,
> That all my bowels crumble up to dust :
> I am a scribbled form, drawn with a pen
> Upon a parchment ; and against this fire
> Do I shrink up.

P. Henry. How fares your majesty?
K. John. Poison'd,—ill-fare ;—dead, forsook, cast off—

Here he is again using the meanest terms he can think of to describe his wretchedness. The sense of royalty and habitual power then comes again over him, and he talks in the following splendid strain, in all the amplitude of imperial will :—

> And none of you will bid the winter come,
> To thrust his icy fingers in my maw ;
> Nor let my kingdom's rivers take their course
> Through my burn'd bosom, &c.

How fine, by the way, is the homely word *maw* here ! How expressive of boundless desire and infinite voracity ! How poor the word *mouth* would have been to it !—Now Mr. Macready died extremely well as a poisoned and agonised man, and his departure was quiet and without fear—suddenly worn out—as it seems to be implied in Shakspeare : but we think he would have perfected the speech as that of the dying John, had he given a more ideal and even theatrical force to these *royal* parts of it. We would have had him resume his old imperious airs, when the pain (as it were) might be supposed to give him leave—first in the lines, where he speaks of having elbow-room again, as if he once more bade his courtiers keep their distance, and secondly, in this noble passage about winter, where, half-royal and half-delirious, he talks in a kind of poetico-imperial madness, and gives such a magnificent idea of the extent of what he has just been suffering, in saying that his courtiers will not send for Winter himself to heap his fiery craving with ice, nor send the rivers of his kingdom to flow through his bosom. What a world of will and misery does he make that bosom expand into! We would have had Mr. Macready sit up at this passage, and madly seem to collect about him all the regalia of his thoughts.[1]

MACREADY AS THE STRANGER.

December 14, 1830.

WE saw the latter scenes of the *Stranger* here[2] last night,

[1] In the *Tatler* for December 10, 1830, appears the following letter:—"Sir,—In your notice of *King John*, you do not remark upon one failure or mistake in Macready's personation:—in conferring knighthood upon the roysterer Faulconbridge, he goes through the ceremony as if it were a grave matter of state rather than following up a sort of joke. His manner, though earnest, ought to have had some jocularity about it. One other particularity makes his John inferior to the late Mr. Kemble's, who managed to throw an indescribable something into his performance, that at once accounted for the frank partizanship and even attachment of the Bastard: whereas Mr. Macready makes him such an assassin sort of personage, that the gallant Sir Richard's adherence to him is inexplicable. Macready played the Hubert scene wonderfully well. Didn't he?—Yours, A. Z."

[2] Drury Lane.

and the greater part of *No Song No Supper*. We have noticed the performance of these pieces at other theatres, and have little to say upon them at this. The Stranger is not a difficult character to represent; and there is no tragic one at present performed in England, in passages of which Mr. Macready does not surpass all other actors. In the expression of a trembling tenderness nobody equals him. But easy as we think the part of the Stranger, it appears to us that it has been rendered *too* easy, too passive and stationary, by its having originally been in the hands of John Kemble, something of whose formal manner became identified with the character, so that it has ever since been coined in his mould. Now John Kemble could not act a man to love, or to be loving. To be sure, he could act one to run away from. He was handsome, but not after a loving fashion. He had just that severe formal cut both of aspect and manner, which you could suppose might frighten away a young bride into the arms of a fellow who could look more sympathetic. Charles Kemble has quite another appearance; but in the Stranger he endeavours to be as cold and motionless as his brother. Macready has been in some measure seduced into this mode of performing the part, if seduction it can be called; and does not enough give himself up to his own genius. It appears to us, that if we were in his situation, and had his powers, we would contrive to unite the habit of grief with greater freedom of action, and a less formal restriction to one place and manner. Heavy sorrow meets the faces of common things with as common a face as it can wear; because it is heavy, and would fain become familiar with its load. It even endeavours to encounter uncommon ones in the same manner; because it has still greater reason for it. However, Macready's is the best Stranger we have seen. John Kemble was the best man to run away *from* ; Charles Kemble was the man to run away *with* ; Macready is the one to come back to. He has most sensibility.

WERNER.

December 15, 1830.

LORD BYRON's tragedy of *Werner*, as adapted to the stage by Mr. Macready, was produced here [1] last night with success, to an overflowing audience. It dragged in parts, but excited much attention in others, particularly as it drew to a close, and was given out for repetition on Friday, Monday, and Wednesday next, amidst enthusiastic applause. It is not, however, a tragedy of a high order. Lord Byron's real genius is to be found in *Don Juan*. He is fine in passages only of his graver writings, chiefly those in which sarcasm is to be found, and a reference to his personal experience. His spirit was self-revolving and satirical : he could not go out of himself sufficiently to sympathise with varieties of men, and therefore he wanted the very stuff of which the drama is made ; and for the same reason, as well as for a want of faith in moral beauty, he could not enrich, and adorn, and reconcile its darker hues with poetry. Pure will and childish passion occupy the place of the noble infirmities, the abundant thoughts, and the sustaining, winged fancies of the great tragedians. In them, the action is always on the rebound. Human nature tends to rise again, while it falls. Hope is kept up, even by the beauty of the despair. In the tragic criminals of

---

[1] Drury Lane.

Lord Byron, there is always an offensive selfishness—something that renders poetical beauty foreign to it, and the interest of which must be maintained by excess and turbulence. The plot of *Werner* is founded on a nobleman's stealing a purse! And this sorry patch he attempts to fix upon the mighty pall of time and destiny. It is as if he should attempt to make a comet of a scarecrow. The audience, by the help of the adaptation and the actors, are interested : but it is on no higher grounds than when they are interested by the common and cheap excitement of melodramas in ordinary, and their Newgate stories. They pay the same attention as to a criminal or mysterious case in the newspapers. There is interest, but nobody is the better for it ; the actors, we suspect, are the worse. They are led to confound an easy excitement with their power to raise it ; and Mr. Wallack, an able melodramatic performer, fairly divides the applause with Macready, a fine tragedian !

Lord Byron was a wit, a man of genius, an extraordinary individual, and the finest satirist since the days of Pope ; but when he came to touch the ark containing the spirit of a diviner poetry, his hand withered ; for he approached it in presumption, and not in reverence.

EDMUND KEAN AS RICHARD III.

February 1, 1831.

THE manager of this theatre [1] says he has prevailed on Mr. Kean to reappear for a few nights in some of his best characters ; and Mr. Kean accordingly presented us last night with that of Richard III. He was welcomed, if not with the thunder of a whole house, yet with the

[1] Drury Lane.

acclamations and waving hats of an enthusiastic pit ; nor was a good deal of applause wanting from some other parts of the house. It was not the deafening crash of his most favoured times ; but considering the formal dislike of some persons to any kind of broken word,[1] the jealousy of others, and the grudges of various sorts which may be supposed to beset the return of such a man to the stage, it was a handsome reception. For our parts, we think the broken promises of a man of genius much more excusable than those of lovers ; and, in our critical capacity, we felt thankful to Mr. Kean for letting us again behold him. He is unquestionably the finest actor we ever saw. Nobody comes near him except Macready ; and he, we think, even surpasses him in one point—the expression of domestic tenderness. Kean's tenderness is a voluntary grace ; Macready's, a real emotion. In everything else, though more approached by that fine actor than any other, he reigns lord paramount.

We say reigns, for he still does so, having resumed his dominion ; but we are sorry to add that he does not grasp his sceptre with the same physical force, nor can he issue his commands so loudly. In plain words, his voice, which was never of the strongest, painfully fails at times ; nor does he distribute over his evening's performance the same amount of vigour as formerly. But we look upon the falling off as entirely physical ; at least there was nothing in the performance of last night to indicate that it had anything to do with mental decay. All the fine points appeared to us as well conceived as ever, and only impeded (when they were so) by manifest bodily weakness. In the tent scene for instance, where

---

[1] Kean had taken leave of the public in the previous July, in view of a visit to America, which never took place.

he starts up from his horrid dream, he made such a feeble
business of the rush forward (or coming rather) that the
house seemed inclined to be angry with it : yet he
began it, on first awaking, with as fine a dismal and
natural groan as tragic spectator could desire ; and it was
clear to us that his bodily strength suddenly failed him.
So in "A horse ! a horse ! my kingdom for a horse !"
he could hardly get the words out ; and a similar want
of power was observable throughout the play generally.
It was thought at first that he was husbanding his
strength ; but it did not turn out so. We could not help
persuading ourselves that Mr. Kean might recover all
that he wanted. There is nothing in his time of life to
hinder it, if the excitements of his style of acting and
the consequences but too natural to them do not hinder
it. We have always wondered how actors of sensibility
could bear up as they have done ; and we have had a
profane notion in consequence, that Garrick could not
have been quite so fine as he was described. Kemble had
no more wear and tear than a statue. We fancied Mr.
Kean looked a little larger than he used in the cheeks.

While speaking of deficiencies, we will notice the only
fault we observed in this great actor last night—which
we take to be a common one with him, and hardly to
have been expected in a man of his extreme sense of the
natural. We do not mean to applaud the homely
natural at the expense of the proper tragic mixture of
natural and ideal, which no man exhibits better than he,
even in the passages in which he seems most familiar ;
for the ideal is only the imaginative added to the extreme
of feeling, or rather the extreme in the most imaginative
state of which it is capable ; and there is always a certain
grace as well as force of truth in what appear to be the

homeliest of Mr. Kean's ebullitions.   But in the instances
we allude to, which are those of the more tranquil kind,
he appears to us to abandon his usual relish of the truth,
for a strange kind of acquiescent commonplace, little to
be expected of him.   Thus, last evening, in speaking the
fine lines descriptive of the noises of either army the
night before the engagement,[1] he did not pause, and
hearken (as it were) over them—he did not lay forth his
ear to catch the sounds, or look as if he was particularly
sensible of them.   He did little but repeat the verses
with an undulating tranquillity of recital, like some mild
gentleman with an "Enfield's Speaker," reading them out
of the book.

But how fine he is, when he *is* fine ! how true ! how
full of gusto ! how intense ! what a perfect amalgamation
there is of the most thorough feeling and the most
graceful idealism ! The first four lines which Richard
utters on coming on—

> " Now is the winter of our discontent," &c.

were as beautifully delivered as they ever could have
been, especially the last—

> " And all the clouds that lower'd upon our house,
> *In the deep bosom of the ocean buried.*"

Kean, in speaking this last line, held forth his arm, and
in a beautiful style of deliberate triumph, uttering his
words with inward majesty, pointed his finger down-
wards ; as if he saw the very ocean beneath him from
some promontory, and beheld it closed over the past.

Several of his favourite passages were given with their
old effect, notwithstanding what has been said above.

[1] Interpolated by Cibber from *Henry V.*

Among them was the question about Stanley's friends, "What do they in the North?" &c.,[1] and particularly the order for Buckingham's execution.[2] We think we never heard the latter given even so finely. There was a contemptuous levity on the word " *Buckingham* "—a sort of fondness and *forsoothness* of sarcasm (if the expression be allowed us) which seemed to set the poor Duke and his pretensions at a distance ludicrously immeasurable. The points in the wooing scene with Lady Ann were also much applauded—the only unnatural scene (for we cannot help thinking it so) in Shakspeare.

But the crowning point was the look he gave Richmond, after receiving the mortal blow. This has been always admired ; but last night it appeared to us that he made it longer and therefore more ghastly. He stood looking the other in the face, as if he was already a disembodied spirit, searching him with the eyes of another world ; or, as if he silently cursed him with some new scorn, to which death and its dreadful knowledge had given him a right. We thought he overdid the subsequent length of the *talk of him*,[3] while lying on the ground : but his look was still very terrible.

MISS FANNY KEMBLE AS BEATRICE.

February 18, 1831.

Much Ado about Nothing was performed here[4] last night to a full house, and given out for repetition with the

---

[1] Shakspeare, act iv., sc. 4.

[2] Cibber's celebrated clap-trap.

[3] Cibber's added speech for Richard after he has fallen, part of which is taken from *King Henry IV.* (Part II.).

[4] Covent Garden.

greatest applause. The effect was rather languid in parts, the plot, in truth, being thin enough, and taking pains to make itself seen through : and in almost all Shakspeare's plays, wonderful as they are, there are some scenes which argue either occasional failure of stage tact, or indifference to the level part of the story, or a singular compliment to the understandings of his audience ; whom we are to suppose interested in delicate points of language and character, such as have excited little attention with audiences of later times. We must observe at the same time, that we think there is a very visible improvement in the critical faculties of the humblest playgoers of the present day, owing, we have no doubt, to the sharpening of the public wits in other matters, and to the diffusion of that " Two-penny Trash " which has turned out to be so formidable to actors on a greater stage. The interest of *Much Ado about Nothing* chiefly arises from the scenes in which Benedick and Beatrice are concerned ; and not only did these obtain as great a share of attention as we ever knew them, but all the little points of wit and subtlety produced a general acknowledgment, to a degree we do not remember to have witnessed before, and in which the participation of the galleries was as plain as that of the pit.

Miss Kemble appeared in the character of Beatrice, for the first time. We always feel loth to criticise this young lady, because we have never recovered the disappointment occasioned us by the immoderate praises bestowed on her in the first instance, and which led us to rate her, in imagination, by a very high standard. Perhaps the standard we judge all performers by is in general higher than their modesty or a sense of their interest would desire ; but this is what we cannot help, nor can we con-

sider it a fault ; because the standard is such as Shakspeare and the other geniuses of the stage suggest to us ;
and we are not to blame, if in having our enthusiasm
strongly excited by the nature and beauty of the portraits
they set before us, we expect the best possible similitude
to them in those who claim to be their representatives.
What notion of sweetness can be too great for such a
character as Imogen ?　What perfect love and ingenu-
ousness ought we not to look for in a Desdemona?
What an union of cordiality with court shrewdness in
Rosalind ?　What a retreating inward of the soul in
Viola, watching nevertheless through the eye, when the
beloved object was present and could not see it ?　What
a round-cheeked, perpetual, laughing mixture of grace
and malice in Beatrice, arising from health, and indulgence, and a good sovereign opinion of a wit for which
she had evidently been praised from her childhood ?　We
see she has ruled the nursery, and her father, and her
gentle cousin, Hero, and has only escaped being disagreeable because of the sweetness of her blood.　When
Shakspeare has made all these charming women talk in
the most intellectual style, run riot at will in the most
graceful fancies, in short, utter the best things in the best
manner, and challenge our very imaginations to come up
to them, how is the critic to be wondered at, who thinks
he cannot estimate them at too high a rate, and feels
himself compelled to judge the actress accordingly ?　If
their " nature " is to be judged of, undoubtedly it must
be the highest and most charming kind of nature.　If
their " grace," it ought to be the most graceful thing in
the world.　It becomes, above all, totally impossible to
admit a *theatrical* manner, even the most perfect of its
kind, as the style and habit of these delightful creatures.

Miss Kemble's Beatrice is very clever. We look upon it as one of the very best of her characters—certainly the one in which we should see her again with the most pleasure. It wants, we think, the flowing and perpetual giddy grace of Beatrice, who is like a girl at the top of her school, and whose movements ought to run on like her tongue. Mrs. Jordan gave more of this than Miss Kemble—a great deal more ; and her laugh and heartiness were always inimitable : but she wanted the air of good breeding. When Beatrice is sent to ask Benedick to come in to dinner, we do not think Miss Kemble ought to make so regular and ordinary a scene of it. She should hang at the side scene, as if she had just run thither, ask him carelessly to come, reply to his answer in the same quick indifferent manner, and telling him that he has "no stomach," or in other words, that she sees he does not want to come, be off again on the wing. Hero describes her on one occasion, as coming along, running "close by the ground, like a lapwing." She was coming, it is true, to overhear her cousin talk ; but this is a specimen of the extreme to which she ran in general. She did everything in the liveliest manner, and the fittest for the occasion. Miss Kemble's sarcasm, as usual, was good ; and she received great and deserved applause in the speech where she half good-humouredly, half peevishly, says and unsays her confession of love to Benedick, ending it abruptly with the tearful words, "I'm sorry for my cousin." This ebullition of the chief thought which she has at her heart at the moment, was excellently, admirably given ; and made a great sensation. For the most part, Miss Kemble's performance told in occasional hits, rather than as a whole. There was a balance in it, as usual, between the artificial and the natural manner ; but the latter had a more than ordinary ascendency : and with a few less peacock-like movements of the head and gait, and a little more abandonment of herself to Beatrice's animal spirits, the character, in her hands, would come very nearly in merit to that of her father's Benedick, which we have only left ourselves room to say is one of his most effective performances. His utterance of his grand final reason for marrying—"The world must be peopled,"—with his hands linked behind him, a general elevation of his aspect, and a sort of look at the whole universe before him, as if he saw all the future generations that might depend on his verdict, was a bit of the right masterly gusto—the true perception and relish of the thing, any discrepancy from which would have been a false reading.

EDMUND KEAN AS OTHELLO.

February 21, 1831.

WE saw Mr. Kean last night in Othello,[1] and regret to say that we saw a difference from old times, which we had not discovered in his Richard. The reason is, we suppose, that Othello is a much finer character than Richard, and demands a greater amount of thought and feeling ; and Mr. Kean, whether from exhaustion, or immediate languor, or whatever other cause, may have been content to give it no greater attention. But certain it is, that it was not the Othello of old. There was more of that undulating, careless style of delivery, which we used to observe in his performance of characters that did not excite him ; a speech, begun finely, would end poorly (which looks as if physical weakness was more concerned

[1] At Drury Lane.

in it, than any other falling off) ; but what we missed
more than all was the famous passage—

> "Had it pleased heav'n
> To try me with affliction," &c.

which in Mr. Kean's mouth used to be the finest passage
in the finest performance on the stage. We remember
his standing apart, when he delivered it, alone, absorbed,
as if he was left desolate, and then his voice rose with
calm misery as though he had the tears in his eyes, and
so he continued for several lines. Last night he neither
commenced in this style, nor resumed it. It was a speech
that others might have made. We thought of the
exquisite delivery of old, and felt grateful, and sorry.
We wish to speak on this occasion with every respect of
Mr. Kean, both on account of the genius and sensibility
which must have produced such performances as his, and
because we understand he bears himself among his brother
actors with a generosity and companionship worthy of
his genius. No man after all could give us such an
Othello as his is still. The delivery of another famous
speech—

> "O now for ever
> Farewell the tranquil mind,"

was as beautiful as ever ; perhaps had a still more touching
melancholy. His repeated fare-wells, with the division
of the syllables strongly marked,—

> "Fare-well the tranquil mind ! fare-well content !
> Fare-well the plumed troop," &c.

were spoken in long, lingering tones, like the sound of a
parting knell. The whole passage would have formed an

admirable study for a young actor, in showing him the beauty of sacrificing verbal painting to a pervading sentiment. It was right to give emphasis to the word Farewell, because the speaker is taking leave of all his felicities, and has the strongest sense of doing so : but Mr. Kean gave no vulgar importance to "the plumed troop" and the "big wars," as commonplace actors do ; because the melancholy overcomes all : it merges the particular images into one mass of regret.

Miss Phillips's style of acting and personal manner have more of *womanhood* in them than those of any other of our tragic actresses : nor do we think that any other Desdemona, on that account, would equal hers. She obtained great applause last night, when she fell on her knees, and protested that she had never been unfaithful. The point was well given : yet we preferred her gentler passages, and the natural way in which she wept her astonishment, and tried to laugh it away and to reassure herself, when she first becomes sensible of a change in her husband.

This character of Desdemona is one of the loveliest ever conceived. She has the heart of a child with all the feelings of a woman. She is generous, painstaking, patient, pleasurable, unwitting of ill. Her ruin comes of her goodness. Some gross commentators have delighted, by Iago's help, to discover that she was more sensitive than she need be, or at least not less so than the liveliest of her sex. Why should she be, if she was good and warm-hearted ? She fell in love with Othello for his mind and soul first, and for all which he had gone through. True sympathy was the ground of her passion. If upon this, all the rest of her being followed, and we are to suppose that her love was a world of pleasure as well as pride to her, it only shows that she was in every respect the woman she ought to have been—as perfect in body as in heart. Grossness is when there is no heart at all, and no just passion.

MACREADY AS MACBETH.

March 15, 1831.

Macbeth was performed here[1] last night—the principal character by Mr. Macready ; Lady Macbeth by Miss Huddart. We are loth to find fault with one who gives us so much pleasure as Mr. Macready ; but his Macbeth is not one of his most effective performances. It wants the poetry of the original ; that is to say, it wants in its general style and aspect that grace and exaltation which is to the character what the poetry is to the language ; which, in fact *is* the poetry of the tragedy ; and which, without depriving it of its nature, enables the tragic criminal to move fitly in the supernatural sphere of his error. In other words, the passion of Mr. Macready's Macbeth wants imagination. There is the same defect in it, but in a greater degree, as was observable in his King John. It wants the Royal warrant. We do not mean the mouthing and strut of the ordinary stage King ; which are things that Mr. Macready is above ; but that habitual consciousness of ascendency, and disposition to throw an ideal grace over its reflections, whether pleasurable or painful, which enables the character to present itself to us as an object of intellectual and moral contemplation, with whatsoever infirmities it may be accompanied. Now the Macbeth of Mr. Macready, before he commits the murder, is (so to speak) *nothing* but a mis-

[1] Drury Lane.

15

giving anticipator of crime ; and after it, nothing but the misgiving or despairing perpetrator. He has no golden thoughts in him, before or after ; no morning hopes, nor sad beams of evening :—not a leaf is gilded by a ray. Whereas, however weak and unhappy a character Macbeth is, he cannot talk as he does, and vent the poetical images with which his mind is graced, without showing that there is a divinity within him, though an enfeebled one, and though at once ashamed, and angered, and over-awed by the intrusion of some monstrous stranger.   The very first words Macbeth utters, when he comes on the stage, show the natural vivacity of his character, and its tendency to be divided in its feelings ; and the way in which these were spoken by Mr. Macready did not augur well for his performance.

> " So foul and fair a day I have not seen,"

says the good-humoured conquering general, looking cheerily up at the sky, and playing, as it were, with the harmless struggle of the elements.   Mr. Macready delivered the words like a mere commonplace.   So when he says, in the third act (in that beautiful picturesque passage)

> " Light thickens; and the crow
> Makes wing to the rooky wood,"

he spoke these words, as merely intimating a fact—a note of time—pointing with his hand as he did it, and as he might have pointed to a clock, to convince his witness of the truth of what he was saying.   And again, in what follows,

> " Good things of day begin to droop and drowse,
> While night's black agents to their prey do rouse."

This was spoken with too much rapidity and indifference, as a fact, and not with the solemnity required by the reflection of a man in a melancholy state of mind, at once aggravating and exalting his melancholy by it. Mr. Macready seems afraid of the poetry of some of his greatest parts, as if it would hurt the effect of his naturalness and his more familiar passages : but such a fear is not a help towards nature ; it is only an impulse towards avoiding a difficulty. The highest union of the imaginative with the passive is the highest triumph of acting, as it is of writing. It is this which has made Mr. Kean so surpassing an actor. He always gives you the grace and the nature too—the ideal with the common—the charm of the thought with the energy of the passion. Mr. Macready, who is a fine actor when he is at his best, is most graceful and ideal when he is moved by domestic tenderness. He is best in the pain which seems to have a right to take pity on itself ; which may complain justly, and shed honourable tears, and has a right to combine manliness and softness. He cannot so well fetch out " the soul of goodness in things evil." Violent or criminal pains he makes simply violent and criminal. Nothing remains to him, if his self-respect, in the ordinary sense of the word, is lost. In the rest, he is often admirable.

Miss Huddart's Lady Macbeth is liable to the same charge of a want of the poetical. This lady has force, and often a lively conception of the natural ; which is apt to be spoilt by a singular want of command over her tones ; so that a passage which begins as if it would charm you, shall sometimes become awkward and almost ridiculous before it concludes. But in acting the highest parts of the drama, she is at a great disadvantage with those who recollect Mrs. Siddons. Imperiousness appears to be substituted for dignity ; a loud demand, for the secure triumph of natural elevation. Miss Huddart's Lady Macbeth wants the *brighter* part of the blood—that which makes it able to bear the darker, and to carry us along with it by dint of something joyous in its very enormity. She is too much like an ordinary instigator and abettor ; not like one carried away by the thrilling idea of a crown about her temples. A single instance will suffice. When Lady Macbeth, in her anticipations of royalty, apostrophises her absent husband, and tells him she wishes she had him with her on the spot, in order that she might set aside, in his thoughts,

" All that impedes him from the golden round,"

Miss Huddart says this in an ordinary, wishful manner, not without fervour, but with no particular marking of the extreme sanguineness of the desire, and all which it implies. Mrs. Siddons used to elevate her stature, to smile with a lofty and uncontrollable expectation, and, with an arm raised beautifully in the air, *to draw the very circle she was speaking of*, in the *air about her head*, as if she ran her finger round the gold.

MISS FANNY KEMBLE AS CONSTANCE.

March 25, 1831.

MISS FANNY KEMBLE repeated last night [1] the part of Constance in *King John*, which she played for her benefit on Monday. It is not one of her best performances, especially in the eyes of those who recollect her aunt in

[1] At Covent Garden.

the character. It wants movement and effect. It wants passion. We do not mean vehemence, of which it has rather too much, but suffering and impulse. Finally, it wants dignity. There is now and then, in this as in other performances of Miss Kemble, a passing shade of family likeness to Mrs. Siddons. Her head dress last night assisted it. But to institute a direct comparison with her is surely unfortunate. The Constance of Mrs. Siddons was one of the most natural, passionate, yet dignified of her performances. The passage in which Constance wildly seats herself upon the ground, and exclaims,

"Here I and sorrow sit : let kings come bow to me," [1]

produced no effect last night. All who remember Mrs. Siddons must remember its electrical effect, and how marvellously she reconciled the mad impulse of it, with habitual dignity. Miss Kemble was almost always stationary in her grief. Mrs. Siddons used to pace up and down, as the eddying gust of her impatience drove her, and all her despairing and bitter words came with double force from her in the career. And then what a person she had ! and how regal she used to look ! hardly more so as Queen Constance than as Mrs. Siddons herself ! lofty tones and conscious modulations seemed natural in her mouth, as expressing the beauty of all that was ideal both in her theatrical and personal character. In Miss Kemble (without meaning to imply that she is not otherwise quite as estimable a person in every respect) they always carry with them an air of elaboration and assumption—

[1] "Here I and sorrow sit ;
Here is my throne : bid kings come bow to it."
ACT III., Sc. I.

we mean assumption in the literal sense — something taken up for the purpose of the moment, and foreign to her in the abstract. Her best passage last night was the quiet and exhausted manner, the momentary patience, into which she fell from her general vehemence, just before she resumed it and tore off her diadem. But the performance upon the whole was flat, and thought to be so. Miss Kemble never does anything without showing great occasional cleverness : in some characters, as in the *Fair Penitent*, she does more : but Constance is certainly not one in which any of her powers is elicited to advantage, not even in the sarcasms directed against Austria, which seemed rather the effusions of quiet spite than of uncontrollable contempt. We doubt whether she will be tempted to repeat the character often.

To mention Mr. Charles Kemble's Faulconbridge is to praise it : for everybody knows how excellent it is.

THE DEATH OF ELLISTON.

July 10, 1831.

WE have to lament, with all the lovers of genuine comedy and fervid animal spirits, the death of our old favourite Elliston, who was carried off last Friday by apoplexy—a death not peculiar, as many suppose, to the sluggish and over-fed, but too common to those who have lived a life of excitement, and drawn much upon sanguine heads. Elliston was of no spare class of men either : he seems to have eaten and drunk stoutly enough, perhaps too much for one who had so much to do, and whose faculties were half made up of sanguineness. We believe the wonder is that he lasted so long, especially as he had had severe attacks of illness on and off for a good

many years, some of them of a mortal aspect. We remember hearing a long time back that his hands had
become useless with palsy ; he recovered that shock,
gesticulated as much as ever, and not long since had
another attack. He recovered again, appeared on the
stage as if nothing had happened, and was meditating,
we believe, new characters, when he was taken off. A
man of a less vital order would have been killed long ago.
But the mystery of life, in some people, seems to carry
itself on in spite of obstacles. They have more of the
life of life in them than others. This is what is understood by the familiar but no less mysterious term, animal
spirits. We have a theory respecting the cause of it, with
which we will not trouble the reader. All we shall say
is, that we take a man's parentage to have a great deal
more to do with it than his education.

The death of a comic actor is felt more than that of a
tragedian. He has sympathised more with us in our
every-day feelings, and has given us more amusement.
Death with a tragedian seems all in the way of business.
Tragedians have been dying all their lives. They are a
" grave " people. But it seems a hard thing upon the
comic actor to quench his airiness and vivacity—to stop
him in his happy career—to make us think of him, on
the sudden, with solemnity—and to miss him for ever.
We could have " better spared a better man." It is
something like losing a merry child. We have not got
used to the gravity. Mrs. Siddons, the other day, was
missed far less than Elliston will be. She had withdrawn, it is true, for some time ; but her life was, in a
manner, always withdrawn. She lived with the tragic
pall round her. Kemble was missed by those who had
been used to him ; but he was missed rather as a picture

than a man. There is something of this in the popularity of Charles Kemble ; but as the picture is of a more
gallant and agreeable kind, none of the family will have
been so cordially lamented as he will be when he dies—
next century : for we suppose he does not mean even to
grow old for these forty years.[1]

Mr. Elliston was the best comedian, in the highest
sense of the word, that we have seen. Others equalled
him in some particular points ; Lewis surpassed him in
airiness ; but there was no gentleman comedian who
comprised so many qualities of his art as he did, or who
could diverge so well into those parts of tragedy which
find a connecting link with the graver powers of the
comedian in their gracefulness and humanity. He was
the best Wildair, the best Archer,[2] the best Aranza[3] ;
and carrying the seriousness of Aranza a little further,
or making him a *tragic gentleman* instead of a comic, he
became the best Mortimer, and even the best Macbeth,
of any performer who excelled in comedy. When Charles
Kemble acts comedy, he gives you the idea of an actor
who has come out of the chivalrous part of tragedy. It
is grace and show that are most natural to him—the
ideal of mediocrity. Elliston being naturally a comedian,
and comedy of the highest class demanding a greater
sympathy with actual flesh and blood, his tragedy,
though less graceful than Charles Kemble's, was more
natural and cordial. He suffered and was shaken more.
The other, in his greatest grief, is but like the statue of
some Apollo Belvedere vivified, frowning in beauty, and

[1] Here follows some biographical gossip, which we omit as being of
no great authority or importance.

[2] In *The Beaux Stratagem*, by Farquhar.

[3] In *The Honeymoon*, by Tobin.

making a grace of his sorrow. The god remains impassive to ordinary suffering. Elliston's features were nothing nearly so handsome or so finely cut as the other's, but they were more sensitive and intelligent. He had nothing of the poetry of tragedy; the other has the form of it; but Elliston, in Macbeth, could give you something of the weak and sanguine and misgiving usurper; and in Mortimer, in the *Iron Chest*,[1] he has moved the audience to tears. It ought not to be forgotten that he restored that character to the stage when John Kemble had killed it with his frigidity.

The tragedy of this accomplished actor was, however, only an elongation, or drawing out, of the graver and more sensitive part of his comedy. It was in comedy that he was the master. When Kean appeared and extinguished Kemble, Elliston seems prudently to have put out his tragic lamp. In comedy, after the death of Lewis, he remained without a rival. He had three distinguished excellencies — dry humour, gentlemanly mirth, and fervid gallantry. His features were a little too round, and his person latterly became a great deal too much so. But we speak of him in his best days. His face, in one respect, was of that rare order which is peculiarly fitted for the expression of enjoyment: it laughed with the eyes as well as mouth. His eyes, which were not large, grew smaller when he was merry, and twinkled with glee and archness; his smile was full of enjoyment, and yet the moment he shook his head with a satirical deprecation, or dropped the expression of his face into an inuendo, nothing could be drier or more angular than his mouth. There was a generosity in his style, both in its greater and smaller points. He under-

[1] By George Colman, junior.

stood all the little pretended or avowed arts of a gentleman, when he was conversing or complimenting, or
making love—everything which implied the necessity
of attention to the other person, and a just, and as it
were, mutual consciousness of the graces of life. His
manners had the true *minuet dance* spirit of gentility
—the knowledge how to give and take, with a certain
recognition of the merits on either side, even in the
midst of raillery. And then his voice was remarkable
for its union of the manly with the melodious ; and as a
lover nobody approached him. Certainly nobody approached a woman as he did. It was the reverse of that
preposterous style of *touch and avoid*—that embracing
at arm's length, and hinting of a mutual touch on the
shoulders—by which the ladies and gentlemen of the
stage think fit to distinguish themselves from the characters they perform, and even the Pollys and Macheaths[1]
propitiate our good opinion. Elliston made out that it
was no shame to love a woman, and no shame in her to
return his passion. He took her hand, he cherished it
against his bosom, he watched the moving of her countenance, he made the space less and less between them,
and as he at length burst out into some exclamation of
"Charming!" or "Lovely!" his voice trembled, not with
the weakness, but with the strength and fervour of its
emotion. All the love on the stage, since this, (with the
exception of Macready's domestic tenderness) is not
worth two pence, and fit only to beget waiters.

July 14, 1831.

In calling to mind the pleasant hours that had been
given us by the talents of the late Mr. Elliston, we forgot

[1] In Gay's *Beggar's Opera.*

to mention his defects. In tragedy, for want of a strong sympathy with the serious, he sometimes got into a commonplace turbulence, and at others put on an affected solemnity, and he was in the habit of *hawing* between his words. The longer he was a manager, the worse this habit became. He was not naturally inclined to the authoritative ; but having once commenced it in order to give weight to his levity, he seems to have carried about the habit with him, to maintain his importance. Unfortunately, he fancied that he was never more natural than on these occasions. He said once, at the table of a friend of ours, clapping himself on the knee, and breathing with his usual fervour, "Nature-*aw*, sir, is everything-*aw* : I-*aw* am always-*aw* natural-*aw*."

Theodore Hook had a ludicrous story of his calling upon Elliston at the Surrey Theatre, and having some conversation with him in the midst of his managerial occupations. In the course of their dialogue, Elliston would start in a grand manner from the subject, and give some direction to his underlings. He called for two of them successively in the following manner :

ELLISTON (turning suddenly to the right, and breathing with all his fervour). "Night watchman !" (Enter night watchman, and has a word or two spoken to him by the manager).

ELLISTON (scarcely having resumed the discourse, and turning suddenly as before). "*Other* night watchman ! " (Enter other night watchman, and is spoken to in like manner. The histrionic sovereign then resumes his discourse with Mr. Hook, with tranquil dignity).

We had an hour's conversation with him once at Drury Lane, during which, in answer to some observation we made respecting the quantity of business he had to get through, he told us that he had formed himself "on the model of the Grand Pensionary De Witt." Coming with him out of the theatre, we noticed the present portico in Brydges Street, which had just been added to the front, and said that it seemed to have started up like magic. "Yes, sir," said he, "energy is the thing. I no sooner said it than it was done—it was a *Bonaparte blow.*"

There was real energy, however, in all this, and the right animal spirits, as well as an innocent pedantry: nor did it hinder him from being the delightful comedian we have described. He could not have been it had he not been pleased with himself, and a little superfluous self-complacency off the stage was to be pardoned him. A successful actor would be a phenomenon of modesty if he were not one of the vainest of men. Nobody gets such applause as he does, and in such an intoxicating way, except a conqueror entering a city.

We must not forget to mention that Elliston's *homely* tragedy was excellent. He has rivalled Bannister in the performance of the Brazier in *John Bull;* and his Sheva in the comedy of the *Jew* was admired to the last for its pathetic delicacy. Upon the whole, as the gallant of genuine comedy, and an accomplished actor of all work, he has left nobody to compare with him. He was as far superior to the gentlemen comedians now going, as Kean was superior to him in tragedy.

KEMBLE AND KEAN.

July 25, 1831.

THE *Athenæum*, in its Saturday's number, after paying us a compliment, of which we are sensible, upon our remarks on the late Mr. Elliston, protests in strong terms against something we said incidentally respecting Kean and John Kemble. It was observed in *The Tatler* that "when Kean appeared and extinguished Kemble, Elliston seems prudently to have put out his tragic lamp." Upon this the *Athenæum* has the following passage :—" Surely the critic's own lamp must have gone out suddenly, and left him in the dark as to what he was writing. What, Kean extinguish Kemble ! As well might a rocket, brilliant and dazzling as for the moment it is, be expected to extinguish the steady and enduring light of the moon in whose face it is discharged. Kean extinguish Kemble ! Why, Garrick himself, whom, by all accounts, it would have taken two Keans to make, could not have done it. Again, to carry the simile still further, what now remains of our theatrical rocket and our theatrical moon ? In some one of the surrounding minor theatres, upon the stage of which it has fallen, may, perhaps, be found the stick and the half-consumed case of the one ; whereas the memory of the other is still cherished with respect as well as admiration by all who were fortunate enough to behold its beams ; while its pure and classical light still hangs reflected upon the very walls of the theatre where it last and longest lingered. We have no wish to detract from the well-earned fame of Mr. Kean, but we cannot consent that any part of it should be built upon even the imaginary ruins of Mr. Kemble's. The one was a man of genius and a clever actor—the other was both these, and besides, a consummate artist and an accomplished gentleman. We might go on to draw a comparison between the farewell performances of the two, both of which took place under circumstances of great bodily infirmity ; but we forbear, because our object is, not to attack the one, but to do justice to the other."

Now, whether the comparison of the "stick and the half-consumed case" is not a greater attack than anything we said of Mr. Kemble, we shall not stop to inquire, because we feel nothing but friendliness towards the *Athenæum*. We shall only say, with regard to that matter, that we should as soon think of attacking the coronation man in armour, as the memory of John Kemble. We do not *attack* players, dead or alive; we only criticise, and express an opinion. We believe it was the opinion of a great many besides ourselves that Kean did extinguish Kemble : at all events, we hold it for certain that Kean hastened his going out ; and we are greatly mistaken if Kemble did not intimate as much to his friends, putting the case as Quin did on a like occasion respecting Garrick,—that new notions had come up in acting, and that if those were true, it was time for the teachers of the old ones to be gone. Garrick's nature displaced Quin's formalism : and in precisely the same way did Kean displace Kemble. The opinion is no new one on our parts, nor on those of many others. We expressed it at the time. We always said that John Kemble's acting was not the true thing ; and the moment we heard what sort of an actor Kean was (for circumstances prevented our seeing him at the moment) we said that he would carry all before him. It was as sure a thing as Nature against Art, or tears against cheeks of stone.

We do not deny a certain merit of taste and what is called "classicality" to John Kemble. He had one idea about tragedy, and it was a good one ; namely, that a certain elevation of treatment was due to it, that there was a dignity, and a perception of something superior to common life, which should justly be regarded as one of its constituent portions; and furthermore, that in exhibiting the heroes of the Roman world, it was not amiss to invest them with the additional dignity they had received from the length of their renown and the enthusiasm of scholarship. These ideas were good : and as he had a fine person, a Roman cast of countenance, and equal faith in the dignity of his originals and his own, he obtained, in the absence of any greater and more natural actor, a whole generation for his admirers, many of whom could not bear to give him up when the greater came. This is the whole secret of the fondness entertained for his memory. It is a mere habit and a prejudice, though a respectable one ; and we should be the last to quarrel with it were nature let alone. It is observable that Mr. Kemble's admirers never enter into any details of criticism or comparison. They content themselves with a fine assumption or two, like his own—a stately or sovereign metaphor—and a reference to his *gentility*. Now Mr. Kemble had a solemnity of manner off the stage, analogous to what he had on it, and we believe he kept "good company," in the ordinary sense of that phrase ; but that he was more of a gentleman than Mr. Kean, either in his strongest or weakest moments, we have yet to learn. Allusions are frequently made to a habit in Mr. Kean, which his predecessor certainly shared with him, though with comparative harmlessness to his less sensitive temperament. On the other hand (for we never saw him in private) Mr. Kean, we believe, is as much of a gentleman in ordinary as Kemble was ; and we have heard accounts of his behaviour to his brother actors and inferiors, which argue an inner gentility—a breeding of the heart—which at all events we never *did* hear of the other. In the *power* of appreciating moral and intellectual refinement, we should say that there could be no sort of comparison between the man who can act Othello as Kean does, and the dry, tearless, systematical, despotical style of all Mr. Kemble's personations. Everything with Kemble was literally a *personation* —it was a mask and a sounding-pipe. It was all external and artificial. There was elegance, majesty, preparation: it was Gracchus with his pitch-pipe, going to begin—but nothing came of it. It was not the man, but his mask; a trophy, a consul's robe, a statue; or if you please, a rhetorician. It was Addison's " Cato," or an actor's schoolmaster, which you will; but neither Shakspeare nor genuine acting.

The distinction between Kean and Kemble may be briefly stated to be this: that Kemble knew there was a difference between tragedy and common life, but did not know in what it consisted, except in *manner*, which he consequently carried to excess, losing sight of the passion. Kean knows the real thing, which is the height of the *passion*, manner following it as a matter of course, *and grace being developed from it in proportion to the truth of the sensation*, as the flower issues from the entireness of the plant, or from all that is necessary to produce it. Kemble began with the flower, and he made it accordingly. He had no notion of so inelegant a thing as a root, or as the common earth, or of all the precious elements that make a heart and a life in the plant, and crown their success with beauty. Grace exalts the person of Kean. In Kemble's handsomer figure it came to nothing, because it found nothing inside to welcome it. It received but " cold comfort." Kean's face is full of light and shade, his tones vary, his voice trembles, his eye glistens,

sometimes with withering scorn, sometimes with a tear :
at least he can speak as if there were tears in his eyes,
and he brings tears into those of other people. We will
not affirm that Kemble never did so, for it would be hard
to say what Shakspeare might not have done in spite of
him ; but as far as our own experience goes we never
recollect him to have moved us except in one solitary
instance, and that was in *King Lear*, where there is the
fine passage about children's ingratitude and the tooth of
a serpent. Now Kean we never see without being
moved, and moved too in fifty ways—by his sarcasm, his
sweetness, his pathos, his exceeding grace, his gallant
levity, his measureless dignity : for his little person absolutely becomes tall, and rises to the height of moral
grandeur, in such characters as that of Othello. We have
seen him with three or four persons round him, all taller
than he, but himself so graceful, so tranquil, so superior,
so nobly self-possessed, in the midst, that the mind of the
spectator rose above them by his means, and so gave him
a moral stature that confounded itself with the personal.

As to Garrick, whom we are told it would have taken
two Keans to make, he was no doubt what Kean never
was, an admirable comedian as well as tragic actor ; but
on the latter score we have very great doubts whether he
could have been equal to Kean ; and they are founded on
the stories told of him, on his character, on his writings,
and on his portrait by Sir Joshua. From all these it
would appear that his serious faculty must have been
pretty nearly confined to the stage. He had a fine eye
and an expressive face, but the latter wanted the grace
and melancholy of Kean's. His writings argue little
inclination to anything serious. He had the reputation
of being narrow in money-matters, which at least is a

drawback upon the "great style" in art! And in his personal intercourse, in the midst of much that was admirable as a companion and a man of sense, he was vain and fidgety. We do not wish, as our *Athenæum* friend says, to detract from his merits, but we owe gratitude to Kean for being the finest tragic actor we ever beheld, and for doing justice to the poetry of Shakspeare; and if Kean, as a comedian, would leave one half of Garrick unrivalled, we cannot but conjecture, till we have more grounds to form a judgment upon, that as a tragedian he must have surpassed him. We do not forget, at the same time, that Garrick probably restored *Nature* to the stage. This was his great triumph, as it was Mr. Kean's; and probably his contemporaries always judged him in reference to Quin and the others, whom he displaced.

MR. KEAN AS RICHARD III.

August 30, 1831.

MR. KEAN made his appearance last night,[1] as Richard III., in a house of the proper dimensions for exhibiting a fine tragedian, and filled with an audience at least too much alive to his merits to interrupt him with unseasonable noise. The *Tatler* has already given its opinion respecting the way in which he performs this character of late years. Its faults are those of too level, or rather too undulating and languid, a style in the more indifferent parts of the dialogue, and occasionally a colloquial contrast pushed to too sudden and violent an extent; but its beauties are still also those of an order far surpassing the character in the hands of any other living performer.

[1] At the Haymarket Theatre.

Nobody at all approaches, or even professes to approach, (for nobody else acts Richard) the majesty of its will, the wonderful and killing relish of its sarcasm, its mixture of intellectual grace with moral deformity, or even the buoyancy of its animal spirits—that gallant self-reconcilement arising from the mixed sense of its valour and its deformity, and delivering the spectator from the most painful part of its guilt. The applause was great with certain portions of the audience, sometimes excessive, particularly at some of the favourite old points ; those, for instance, of the dreadful death, where he continues fighting in so ghastly a manner with his dying arm—and of the famous sarcastic speech, "So much for Buckingham." The latter we never heard better delivered in Kean's most triumphant days, and it was received with rapture. Some of the other points fell comparatively flat, and it is not to be denied that years and sickness have made a difference in him, fine as he still is beyond all other fineness. But we have an observation to make which struck us forcibly last night, and which we would fain impress on all the admirers of this great actor who intend to see him again. Mr. Kean has obtained and deserved in his time the most rapturous applause ; he has been accustomed to have it twenty-fold where he gets it now ; and yet we are not only sure that he deserves it almost as warmly in every instance, but it should be recollected that the spirits of actors are nourished by applause, and that he would probably be still more like what he was in his best days, if encouraged in something like the same manner. At present, he fairly compels the house to applaud him. Their shouts do not leap forth, as they used to do, at every turn and bidding of his genius ; and we could not help thinking last night that

some of his very finest passages met with a very ill and a
very *ungrateful* reception, and that he felt it, and was the
worse for it.   We shall not do him so poor a turn as to
sue for a more considerate treatment of his wonderful
acting *in formâ pauperis.*   That would be disgracing his
rights.   But we say to the audiences who go to see him :
Do at least justice to your own discernment, be at the
trouble of applauding what you think worth going to
see, and let not the town-talk with which a man of
genius has been mixed up, and with which his genius
has nothing to do, induce you to sit as if you were afraid
to applaud him, and had no business where you are.
Pray let the generous reader think of this, and if he go
to the Haymarket, do his best to hinder some of the
finest points of acting in the world from being blunted
against the dull doubts of the boxes.   If people are,
ashamed to express their pleasure, they ought to be
ashamed to be pleased.

KEAN'S PERFORMANCE OF DYING SCENES.

TO 'THE TATLER.'

September 23, 1831.

" Sir,—Amid the many admirable criticisms that have
appeared upon Mr. Kean's acting, I cannot recall one that
has done justice to the beauty and fidelity of his dying
scenes.   I do not write with the vain view of *attempting*
what you can do so admirably, but to awaken your
attention to the subject.   To enjoy Mr. Kean's acting,
the auditor should be as near him as possible, and I have
had most favourable opportunities of observation, having
had the pleasure of performing with that gentleman in

different parts of the United Kingdom. As I am not aware that any member of Mr. K.'s profession has yet recorded his opinion of his acting, may I intrude a few observations upon your readers?

" In playing Macduff, Richmond, Laertes or Horatio, Cassio, &c., to Mr. Kean, it is evident much that escapes the audience may become visible to the actor. Kean always discriminates between the manner of death with reference to its cause. Richard, for instance, has fought five combats, and has traversed the field in a frenzy ; when he meets Richmond, he is in a state of the highest excitement, smarting with wounds. How finely does Kean depict this as the contest concludes !—he is reduced to a state resembling the stupor of intoxication — he falls from exhaustion—and as loss of blood may be presumed to cool his frame and restore his sanity, so does he grow calmer and calmer through the dying speech, till his mighty heart is hushed for ever.

" In Othello, death is occasioned by piercing himself to the heart with a poignard : can you not mark the frozen shudder, as the steel enters his frame, and the choking expression, with distended eyes and open mouth, the natural attendants of such an agony? Death by a *heart* wound is *instantaneous*. Thus does he pourtray it ; he literally dies standing ; it is the dead body only of Othello that falls, heavily and at once ; there is no *rebound*, which speaks of vitality and of living muscles. It is the dull weight of clay seeking its kindred earth.

" But the scene that actors admire most (perhaps, auditors from the remoteness least) is his death in Hamlet. The Prince does not die of a sword-wound, but from the poison impregnated in that wound : of course, from its rapidity in doing the work of death, it must have been a powerful mineral. What are the effects of such a poison? Intense internal pain, wandering vision, swelling veins in the temple. All this Kean details with awful reality : his eye dilates and then loses lustre ; he gnaws his hand in the vain effort to repress emotion ; the veins thicken in his forehead ; his limbs shudder and quiver, and as life grows fainter, and his hand drops from between his stiffening lips, he utters a cry of expiring nature, so exquisite that I can only compare it to the stifled sob of a fainting woman, or the little wail of a suffering child.

" Trusting that you will favour your readers with some remarks on this subject, I remain,

" Yours most truly,

" An Actor."

to ' the tatler.'

" *Monday, November* 7.

" Sir,—As the various claims on your renovated strength prevented you from noticing the representation of *Macbeth* last Monday at Drury Lane, and as the performance is to be repeated this evening, I take leave to send you a few remarks upon it, which you may use if you should find further rest necessary, or cast aside if you should be able to gratify us with a criticism of your own. The recollection of this play, as I have repeatedly seen it performed, supplies the highest idea I have of acted tragedy. The tremendous interest of the two first acts— combining in a degree wholly unapproached, even in Shakspeare, the strongest melodramatic effects from the force of incident, with the finest and most rapid development of character, and the richest embroidery of poetic thought—the witchcraft, the music, the movement, the awful contrasts of royal festivity and murder in the third and fourth acts, and, in the last, the quiet terrors of the sleep of the mighty murderess, and (better far than this), the fine abstractions of Macbeth, which, embodying the profoundest suggestions of our own hopes and fears, which we know, but want strength of imagination to shape, are more real to us than his atrocities, which we have only *seen*, and win our sympathies for him in despite of all—were wrought into present being, under the auspices of Kemble, and by his acting, and that of his sister, with more entire satisfaction to the senses, and with less injury to the image within us, than any play of Shakspeare's which was ever subjected to acting.[1] Mrs. Siddons filled, nay, expanded the idea of the lady, by the appropriate grandeur of her person and the regality of her movements ; and though the part was by no means one in which her greatest powers were put forth—for, as it is entirely simple and self-sustained, there is no ebb and flow of passion, and the points are too bold and too palpable to be missed, except by the mere want of power to grasp them—still the looks, the tones, the action, were majestic and fearful, as might befit the Clytemnestra of Æschylus. But more wonderful, if not so complete, was Kemble's performance of the far more difficult part of Macbeth—of Macbeth, the imaginative, the weak, the wayward soldier, assassin, and poet—open to all 'skiey influences,' mingling thoughts of quiet beauty with images of death, and meditating on life and man in the extremity of his own fortune, touching in crime, and noble in infamy. With what an abstracted air he passed through the first act, as if his eye saw strange sights unseen of others! With what a trembling hand, confessing irresolution of purpose, did he grasp his contemptuous

[1] This sentence defies emendation.

wife, and decline to proceed 'further in this business,' while his eye yet seemed to gloat and glisten at the visionary crown which was leading him to Duncan's chamber ! His murder scene was not superior to that of some others ; in that which follows it he looked a poor craven beside his heroic sister; and in the following scenes he was only tame, and kingly, and superbly attired ; but the last act was his great intellectual triumph. The force of voice and gesture never approached nearer to an adequate expression of the most affecting and beautiful thoughts suggested by the force of terrible exigences. While the thrilling suddenness of his agony in the utterance of the words 'Liar and slave,' and the terror of his eye cowering over the messenger who had half dispelled his charm, yet haunt me, I remember with equal vividness how his voice trembled and fluttered among the fond images of decay, and clung with melancholy grace to the blessings 'which should accompany old age,' and touched on the emptiness of human hope with 'the still sad music of humanity!' But I have been led far astray from my purpose, and must reserve for some other occasion the full confession of my dissent from the comparative estimate you have often hinted of this tragedian and the most popular of his successors.

"Mr. Macready's Macbeth will scarcely bear to be thought of after Mr. Kemble's, in the scenes where Mr. Kemble's was not merely languid, yet it is by far the best we have. Mr. Young's is mere butchery—his countenance remains unmoved, like an iron mask—and his mind does not seem to accompany the words, even when he speaks them correctly.[1] Mr. Kean's—except some fine

---

[1] Mr. Young is habitually incorrect in the text, to a degree which is inexcusable when that text is Shakspeare's, excepting in Hamlet,

touches in the scene after the murder, which belong to
the situation merely, and not to the character, and his
death—is nothing at all. When first presented, in the
freshness of the enthusiasm he created, it was only
redeemed from failure by the touching remorse of the
scene in the second act, and by the heroic fighting in the
last ; for the rest was merely dull, level speaking, relieved
by very poor trickery; and the weakness, the poetry,
the abstraction of the part, were wholly wanting. Mr.
Macready is admirable in the scenes just before and
after the murder, in the banquet scene, and in the death
—but these are not the scenes which distinguish the
character from all others—and the great difficulty is in
the characteristic marking, in which he succeeds to a
degree that provokes instead of satisfying us. We see
that he has studied the part deeply, we feel assured that
he understands it thoroughly, yet he often fails to hit on
the right tone to communicate the feeling—and we fancy
we can see how. He pitches his design too high, o'erleaps
the sense, and 'falls on the other.' In trying to show an
entire absorption in the spirit of the scene, he becomes
careless of the expression of particular words, and in
such a part as Macbeth, where a life of thought and
action is curdled into hours, 'words are things,' and the
lightest of grave import. In such a play, above all
others, it is necessary for an artist to remember that he is
not acting a long history of the hero's life and death, but
a work of art, in which every line should contribute

which he plays with decent accuracy. He covers his misreadings,
which often break the harmony of the verse, by a sort of melodious
chanting ; but, in spite of the tune, they grate on the ear of all who feel
with Mr. Hazlitt, that it is scarcely ever possible to substitute one word
for another in Shakspeare without injury.

as far as possible to the general effect, and in which he must often endeavour to substitute appropriate symbols of passion for its exact representation. Thus Mr. Macready speaks the first line after he has reached the blasted heath, 'So fair and foul a day I have not seen,' as a mere casual remark on the weather ; so probably Macbeth himself would have uttered it ; but the purpose and the space of the poet require that, in these words, the audience should feel a strange contention of the elements, fit for the supernatural appearances which are at hand, and a mood in the mind of the speaker which makes him fit subject for their 'supernatural soliciting.' Thus he lets the words, 'If chance will have me King, why chance may crown me Without my stir,' slide from his lips without emphasis, as if he were dismissing the thought from his mind ; whereas he is yet busy with the dream of ambition ; and that 'Chance' to which he inclines to leave his elevation, is only the mightest power in his mind, because it seems to supersede the necessity for criminal action. The hurried and unemphatic tone adopted in these and other passages in the early part of the play, gives great dissatisfaction to old play-goers, which we cannot help partaking, although convinced that these are the results, not, as they suppose, of carelessness or affectation, but of an over-anxiety to avoid bombast and mouthing. In the murder scene, Mr. Macready, at least, equals any one we have ever seen —his whispered intimation that he has done the deed is fearful—in the banquet scene, he far excels Kemble and every one else, and his last scene is a succession of terrible pictures. He could play all the last act finely, if he would play it more slowly ; and perhaps the effect would be greater if he would assume the appearance of incipient old age—for years *must* have passed since the murder of Duncan, when he was in the bloom of life— though in this stupendous tragedy (in which, as Schlegel observes, 'the drags are taken off the wheels of time'), we date by events and passions, not by years!

"Miss Phillips played Lady Macbeth for the first time, in a style far surpassing our expectations; for, though tall, slender, and fair, she did not look the character, she pitched her voice in so low and awful a tone, and dis- played so much sense and vigour throughout, as to make amends for the faults of youth and loveliness. Her sleep- walking scene was very spectral, and in one respect had the advantage over that of her greatest predecessor, who (with reverence be it spoken) made too much parade of lifting up an imaginary water-jug and pouring its con- tents on her hands, while Miss Phillips merely rubbed hers as in fevered agony.

"Mr. Wallack played Macduff with sufficient energy and judgment, but he follows the multitude in the erroneous reading of one of the most touching little speeches in the part: '*He* has no children.' This he gives with an outbreak of fury as applicable to the absent Macbeth, on whom he cannot have just revenge because he has no children to be immolated; whereas we apprehend it applies to the last speaker, Malcolm, who has been proposing to Macduff comfort in vengeance, and from whom, as unable to understand a father's feelings, he turns to Rosse for sympathy. There is no reason to suppose that Shakspeare intended to represent Macbeth as childless (though the piece is too busy for a family introduction), for Lady Macbeth speaks of having given suck, and the fears of Macbeth lest Banquo's issue should reign after him, 'no son of his succeeding,' imply that he has sons on whom the sceptre might descend. When Mr. Serle played this part to Mr. Kean's Macbeth at the Coburg, he gave this passage in the way we have suggested, and its deep and true effect was far beyond that which can be produced by any denunciation of impotent vengeance.

"We must not conclude without noticing Mr. Farren's performance of one of the Witches, too often made ludicrous—it was absolutely awful. Probably from the time of Shakspeare so much justice has never been done to one of his most terrible conceptions. Mr. Farren deserves the thanks of every one who can bear to see Shakspeare acted at all, for accepting a part in so small compass, and for filling it with such an image of grotesque horror.

"With heartiest congratulations on your recovery,

"I am, as ever,

"Your daily devourer,

"*⁎ ⁎* "

INDEX.

[It has been thought convenient to place in the Index, rather than in the body of the book, brief biographical notes as to the actors who form the leading subjects of Leigh Hunt's essays.]

THE WALTER SCOTT PRESS, NEWCASTLE-ON-TYNE.